I0549759

THE RC ACT

"GRIPPING, INTENSE - TAPLIN'S THRILLER HITS A HOME RUN."

~ Susan Wingate (Award-Winning Author & #1 Amazon Best Seller)

"PHENOMENAL! SEXY! I COULDN'T PUT IT DOWN! THE SHOCKING STORYLINE KEPT ME WONDERING - WHAT'S GOING TO HAPPEN NEXT!?"

~ Samm Adams (Morning Show Radio Host – KROC)

"THE RC ACT, A NOVEL BY VINCE TAPLIN, IS A CRIME DRAMA/THRILLER THAT WILL UNDOUBTEDLY RISE TO THE TOP OF READING LISTS."

~ Editing, TLC highly recommends The RC Act by Vince Taplin

THE RC ACT

A NOVEL

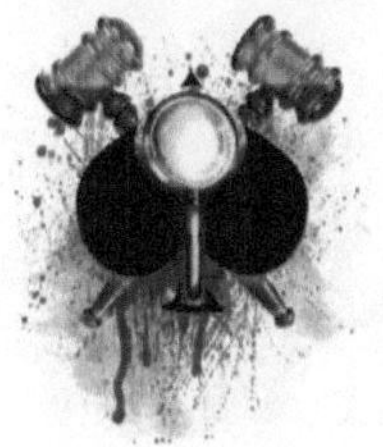

VINCE TAPLIN

Heroine Press
Addicting Books. Period.

Visit our Website:
www.HeroinePress.com or www.TheRcAct.com
ISBN: ISBN 978-1-7348138-7-6 (2021 Reprint)
First Electronic Copy 2011

ISBN: 978-0-9859519-9-3 (softcover)
ISBN: 978-0-9859519-8-6 (audiobook)
ISBN: 978-0-9859519-8-6 (electronic copy)

LCCN: Library of Congress Control Number: 2012913929

*To my oldest nephew Rocco,
whose first breath gave me a second chance.*

Matthew 10:34

King James Version (KJV)

"Think not that I am come to send peace on earth: I came not to send peace, but a sword."

THE RC ACT

A NOVEL

VINCE TAPLIN

PROLOGUE

Outside of Los Angeles, California

"Respond to a two-eleven-Adam in progress at 7313 East Worthington."

The volume of the police radio startled Deputy Caudillo. His aged cruiser shifted cleanly from fourth to second as he simultaneously mashed the accelerator, flicked on the overhead lights, and set down his black cup of coffee.

The bank was nearby, situated only a few blocks from his car. He slowed for traffic lights, scanning the upcoming intersections like a school kid during a driver's test.

He closed quickly on the bank, eyeing every pedestrian as he slowed. He parked half a block away, angling his car awkwardly in the center of the street to block traffic.

His door opened with a cautious creak as he stepped from his cruiser. "Three-forty, station, I'll be ten-ninety-seven, on scene at the bank alarm."

“Ten-four, three-forty,” the dispatcher replied abruptly.

Barren parking lots surrounded the bank. Caudillo shook his head. *Another bank alarm? What a fuckin’ waste of time.*

Traffic slowed to a stop behind his car. A purple-haired retiree stepped from her oversized sedan. She hobbled in the deputy’s direction.

“Get outta the road! I have a hair appointment!” she yelled.

“Ma’am, please go back to your car. This will be over soon.”

“My hair appointment is in eight minutes! Jesus, how long will this take?”

“Ma’am, please! Just get back in your...”

Deputy Caudillo flew backward with the force of a hurricane. His ears were a deaf tone as a ball of rolling fire mushroomed from the bank. Glass and rubble rained violently, covering the streets with the tattered remains of the Luxemburg Bank.

In shock, Deputy Caudillo sat up from the pavement. His broken sunglasses slid easily from his face as the hushed sounds of car alarms, screams, fire, and devastation crept into his ringing ears. He reached for his radio, sluggishly missing the dusty button on the first attempt.

“Three-forty, station, send me fire and medics now; code three!”

CHAPTER 1

Hotel Circle: San Diego, California
32°45'30.8504"N 117°10'59.5247"W

Bleach.

Dominick Craig wiped the steam from the mirror with a circular smear.

Why do hotel bathrooms always stink like bleach? Craig thought as he pulled his towel tightly around his waist.

His watch slid onto his wrist with ease. While quickly checking the time, he ran a comb through his hair. He admired his looks, while noticing the clumps of sporadic grey hair sprouting from his scalp.

He readied quickly, leaving a cloud of body spray, hair gel, and cologne as he walked from the hotel bathroom. He checked his watch again as his arm slid into the white oxford shirt, then pulled his glossy belt into place as he peered to the glowing TV on the dresser. A sexy, twenty-something reporter nodded her head wildly as she spoke into the camera: "The Luxemburg Bank released the following footage of the moments before the explosion."

Craig paused to watch the footage. The video showed the bank lobby from a high angle. People walked casually below the camera, checking bank receipts and stuffing envelopes into their pockets. Moments into the news clip, the shape of a small, automated vehicle pulled into view. It bore a resemblance to a miniature tank, no larger than a child's wagon. The top of the tank was stacked with flickering electronics and a glowing monitor.

Curious patrons stopped, peered at the screen, and bolted from sight. The camera angle changed, showing a nervous banker sitting behind his desk. The device parked itself beside his oak desk and displayed a message on the monitor. The sharply dressed banker visibly began to tremble as he reached for his vault keys.

The camera switched views several times as the small vehicle followed the quivering banker to the safe. As the man opened the heavy door, a security guard appeared, eyeing the small tank. In a quick, unplanned movement, the guard picked up the front of the tank and flipped it violently onto its side. The wheels moved freely in the air as the tank spun without control. The security guard's eyes grew in surprise as he read the screen. A flash of light and debris filled the lens as the news footage faded to black.

Craig pushed the power button on the side of the TV, peeked at himself in the mirror, and scanned his watch for a final review. He slid the hotel room key into his wallet and left his room. The Luxemburg Bank video was devastating and violent; precisely what he'd hoped for. His smile faded as he walked past the palm tree laden pool area. Again, the smell of bleach and chlorine filled his senses. He held his finely pressed shirt over his nose until he was clear of the pools and bikinis.

The air was warm, but tolerable. He disarmed the alarm on his government-issued sedan and hopped inside. The leather was hot against his back, a luxury Craig never quite understood. He much preferred a plush, cloth interior versus the acid-burn feeling involved with leather in Southern California. As he navigated through the parking lot, he removed a piece of perfectly folded paper from his right breast pocket. He unfolded it, looked over the names, and stuffed it back into his pocket. It contained three names that had been pulled from the military intelligence database, all of whom scored in the 98th percentile. All three were local college graduates as well as accomplished military intelligence personnel.

Craig slid onto Freeway 8 and headed east. He silently rehearsed their personal information as he drove. Under his breath, he recited their names, ranks, previous accomplishments, relationship and family status, as well as intelligence statistics.

He pulled off the freeway in an unfortunate part of East County San Diego. The streets were unkempt and littered with liquor stores and discount grocers. After a mile or so, he drove into the parking lot of Little Larry's Gentlemen's Club.

The club was located under two seemingly innocent overpasses. What Craig knew, and only a few other local members of military intelligence knew, was that these overpasses were built with reinforced iron containing compressed coal. This combination of iron and coal scattered GPS signals and didn't allow for voice tracking or recording. The overpasses also made it impossible for a direct satellite line of sight. There were 18 bridges and overpasses in San Diego built to this specification, however, Craig liked the Gentlemen's Club more than the others for obvious reasons.

Little Larry's Gentlemen's Club

La Mesa, CA | 32°44'47.3554"N 117°1'7.499"W

A thin, tattooed girl rolled along the stage, draping her panties along the floor by her heels. She winked at the wrinkled men who circled the stage, gleefully collecting her tips as she passed. The club was dark, loud, and smelled of body lotion and old carpet. An energetic announcer spoke loudly into the microphone, introducing the next song and dancer.

Adam Luster, an accomplished computer programmer, sat near the rear of the club. His eyes wandered from the stage as tan legs passed his table.

"This is no place for a married man," Agent Craig said loudly as he sat down. Adam nearly spilled his drink due to the surprise introduction. "Adam Luster, GS12, the software engineer, I presume?" Craig extended his hand.

Luster was quietly nervous. He firmly shook Craig's hand. "Yes, Sir. Are you Intelligence Officer Craig?"

"Intelligence *Agent* Craig. Yes, I am." Craig had a dominating presence as he spoke.

A skinny Asian interrupted Craig by parking her pink satin panties on his shoulder. "Do you want a drink? A private dance? What do you want?" She dipped her head close to Craig, nearly touching her lips to his cheek.

“Excuse me, Luster.” Craig turned to the sultry, half-naked girl and looked only at her eyes. “I’ll have a seven and seven.” Craig didn’t hesitate, or allow himself even the slightest distraction by her excessive breasts as they pressed against him. She trailed her hand along his chest as she walked away, flashing snippets of her upper thighs at Luster as she walked.

“As I was about to say, Luster, I don’t like to repeat myself. So, I would prefer to wait for the others.” Agent Craig checked his watch and looked around the room. His eye caught an overweight man sitting at the front of the flashing stage. He was sharply dressed but sloppy in the details. Craig mentally looped the three descriptions and personal information and realized he had a match.

Nathan Briggs sat uncomfortably in a chair at the front of the dance floor. His thick forearms rested on the rim of the stage, while he gazed in a stupor. A blonde dancer spun slowly on the pole, gazing down at Nathan. He flicked a five-dollar bill on the stage, where it landed near a few of the others he had tossed. The dancer grinned and slithered down the pole toward him.

Craig sat down next to Briggs and tossed a twenty-dollar bill to the stripper. Craig spoke loudly to combat the thumping music. “I’m going to borrow him; I hope you don’t mind.”

Briggs snapped out of the trance quickly, getting up to properly introduce himself. “I am sorry, Sir, are you Officer Craig from Intelligence?”

Craig gripped his hand firmly. “*Agent* Craig. That’s the second time today someone has accused me of being an officer. Please, sit with us." Craig pointed to the other end of the club.

"Yes, Sir; absolutely. It is nice to finally meet you." Briggs walked clumsily as they passed between the labyrinth of men and chairs.

Craig sat down. He took a few gentle sips of his drink as he watched Briggs and Luster. The two men sat snugly on the opposing side of the table, waiting for a word from Craig.

"We are waiting on one more person," Craig said, turning slightly to watch the door.

As the last word left his mouth, the curtain opened revealing Kim Nguyen, the Vietnamese prodigy. She was a double major in software engineering and mechanical design and a flight officer in the Marine Corps. She was as sharp as a tack and as rough around the edges as a bottlecap. She was perfect.

Craig motioned for her to come to the table. Nguyen looked curiously at a few gossiping strippers as she passed through the front hallway toward the group.

She introduced herself to Craig, seating herself uncomfortably beside the others.

"You all may be wondering why I called last week, however, I am going to make it very clear in the next few minutes. If you have any questions, please, don't ask. Does everyone understand me so far?"

The group muttered and nodded as Craig continued. "Good." He took another sip and checked his watch. "You all are being reassigned, effective immediately. You are being transferred into my division. Your commanding officers have been notified and your office material has been moved to an offsite location."

Nguyen lifted her hand off the table, stopping Craig. "Sir, with all due respect, I am in the middle of research. If my progress is slowed for even one week, the program may not meet the deadline."

Craig irritatingly moved his neck to one side, popping the knot from his spine. "Yes, you are correct. Your progress will not only slow, it will stop. You are under my supervision now." Craig pulled three envelopes from his pocket. He carefully handed the envelopes to each of the three. "Inside these envelopes, you will find your official release forms, signed by your commanding officer, as well as a U.S. Treasury check for one hundred thousand dollars..." A passing dancer heard the number and flocked to Briggs' shoulders and began to whisper into his ear. He pushed her head away and nodded for Craig to continue. "This is your nonrevocable bonus for the year. You will each receive your salary as usual; however, this is an advance on the end-of-assignment bonus."

Agent Dominick Craig had their complete attention.

"You will also notice the map and address for your new office. Starting Monday, you will report to that address at 0800. You will wear civilian clothing and leave your cell phone and other identifying information at home."

The group shifted in their seats as their curiosity grew.

"If you have any questions, again, don't ask." Agent Craig stood up, smiled, checked his watch, and said, "Thank you for your time. I will see you at 0800." Craig walked out of the club without another word.

Los Angeles International Airport — LAX
Los Angeles, CA | 33°56'33"N 118°24'29"W

The drive to L.A. was short. Agent Craig flicked the stub of his cigar out the window as he navigated through the airport parking structures. He parked in lot R-46, which was a lengthy walk from the entrance to the airport. As he walked through the endless rows of shiny cars, travelers on cell phones hurried by, loudly dragging their rolling suitcases along the concrete. Tourists were an endless source of entertainment for Craig. In his spare time, he often found himself sitting in airport lounges, simply to watch the bizarre array of people packed into one building.

Craig checked his watch and smiled. Early, he thought. As he approached airport security, he slowed his pace. The security personnel were standing lifelessly behind their x-ray machines and magic wands. Occasionally, he would see a spark of life in their eyes as they waved people through.

"Excuse me, Officer," Agent Craig said to one of the TSA drones. He knew they loved to be called officer, yet he couldn't understand why.

"Hi, what do you need, man?" The guard was young, maybe mid-twenties and sported an oddly shaped piercing below his lip.

"I have a Class 7 meeting in Terminal 2. I have a government security clearance." Craig pulled an ID card from his wallet and presented it to the guard.

"Uhhh, I am not sure how to handle this. Let me get my supervisor." The TSA guard leaned close to his radio and called for a manager. After a few moments passed, a man with a cheap brown suit appeared from a side office.

"Good afternoon, Sir. I am Airport Security Manager Nixon. Not related to the president." He stretched a hand to Craig. "What can I do you for?"

Craig shook his hand with little vigor. "I have a meeting in Terminal 2 and I am an agent of the U.S. Government. Here is my Level C credential. Please let me through; I am in a hurry." Again, Craig showed his card.

"Ahhh, okay." The manager looked over his card. He bent it slightly, angling it to check the holograms on the face. He leaned over one of the security workstations and scanned the barcode on the rear of the card. Nixon read the screen for a few moments and returned. "Okay, Officer Craig, follow me."

Craig thanked him as he passed through the last maze of ropes to the finish line. He didn't mind the hassle of security checks. The government clearance gave him instant access to security-free travel. It also allowed him to carry his pistol past the restricted zone.

The airport was packed. Suits ran frantically with leather bags in one direction while Hawaiian shirts dragged their duct-taped luggage in the opposite. The crowds nearly drowned out the echoing security announcements. Craig sauntered into the Gordon Beer Bar on the far end of the walkway. He straightened his shirt and sat in a booth near the back of the bar. He scanned the room, looking for anything out of the ordinary. Spotting a tail or an eavesdropper was easy for anyone; his intelligence training taught him to spot hidden cameras, concealed weapons, handcuffs, and microphones. The steps of evaluating a room were simple. Agent Craig dubbed it "The Noun Check."

People — Step one. The room was full of them: some young, some old, all of varying sobrieties. No one stood out. Too often, surveillance teams wore an overcoat or a thick jacket to mask their concealed guns, restraints, and cameras. No one was facing away from him, looking at his reflection in a mirror or pane of glass. His mind raced through the checklist of precautions, mentally tallying an "X" over each completed task.

Places — Step two on the noun check. He pulled a folded photo from his pocket. He'd taken the picture a month prior, from the same seat, looking in the same direction. Other than the position of the bar glasses, the room remained unchanged. This safely assured that cameras hidden in clocks, frames, or plants hadn't been stashed.

Things — The last step. Things were a dead giveaway. If a room has too few things or too many things, they all were a clue, potentially pointing to a red flag. He checked the other customers for things too. He scanned purses, packs, bags, and containers, anything that could hold something sharp or go boom.

His eye caught a man leaning on the bar, who was in his forties and slightly overweight. Craig knew instantly who he was and what he did. The man was a cop, but not from L.A. or any other big city, because those cops know that they look like cops and try desperately to lose the cop walk, the cop talk, and the cop style. This guy, this mustached, tucked-in, beer-bellied Nebraska cop with a fanny pack didn't have any idea he reeked of pork. His fanny pack was weighted awkwardly to the right side. This odd bump sang songs of a heavy pistol that sat in the belly of the fanny pack. Craig knew instantly that he wasn't there for any actual law enforcement duties. He was simply traveling.

Craig relaxed a bit. The lounge was safe from prying eyes. He ordered a drink, sipping it slowly. Out of habit, he checked his watch again, realizing that his guest was to arrive at any second. The meeting had been planned for months. The preparations had been made. The customs documents were signed. He'd studied the details day and night.

CHAPTER 2

Los Angeles International Airport — LAX
Los Angeles, CA | 33°56'33"N 118°24'29"W

Jürg Becker walked into the bar and ordered a light beer. Becker nervously looked around the room, trembling unreasonably. He was the international operations manager for Lufthansa, a German airline. He was a square guy, but clearly had a weak spot. He was taking a huge risk, anticipating an enormous reward. The bartender slid a frothy beer to his waiting, nervous fingertips.

"Thanks, keep the change," Becker spouted as the bartender took his bill. His German accent was light, but noticeable. He waved uneasily to Craig and walked across the small bar to the booth where Craig was sitting.

"Tell me again why we always meet in the airport?" Becker asked, looking apprehensively behind him as he spoke.

"Relax, Jürg. No one in an airport cares who we are, what we're doing, or why you ordered such a wimpy drink." Craig smiled and pushed a legal-sized envelope across the table.

"Skipping the formalities...aren't you, Dom?" Becker had known Agent Craig for fifteen years. He knew he disliked it when people called him Dom instead of Dominick.

"I am running late, Jürg. Do you want to sign or not?" Craig dismissed his playful slander. He simply wanted to finish the deal and move along to the next meeting. Becker pulled open the envelope and sipped his beer while he perused the fine print. Craig watched his eyes flow back and forth as they scanned the pages.

After ten minutes of silent reading, Becker finished his beer and document review. He scribbled a wide-lettered signature on the bottom of the last page. "There. Done. You happy?"

"Happy?" Craig picked up the pen, signing below Becker's signature. "Am I happy? You're the only man I know who would be upset with millions of dollars." Craig slid the contract back into the envelope.

Becker grabbed his pen from Craig's hand in a flash of aggression. "Dom, do you know what kind of trouble I could get into? Do you have any idea? These are federal charges! No, no! International charges! I could go to prison in three different countries for this shit. You tell me why I should be calm."

Craig leaned across the table gently and whispered, "Because you will be the third wealthiest person in Europe if you don't get caught." Craig abruptly stood up and extended his hand to Becker. "Always a pleasure, Jürg."

"The pleasure is all mine," Becker said sarcastically as they shook hands. Becker quickly left the bar, shaking his head as he walked. Craig walked to the entrance of the bar to make sure Becker was out of sight. Once he knew he was far enough along in the terminal, he sat back down and took another swig of beer.

He checked his watch and pulled out his cell phone. It was a bit beat up, but the government never issued shiny new smartphones.

He sent a text message to Eric Price: Meet me at the Gordon Beer Bar on level one.

Eric Price was a big shot at BlackRiver. He controlled the contracts, finance, and the operations of the company. BlackRiver was the heaviest of hitters in the global soldier-of-fortune trade. Agents of BlackRiver found Osama Bin Laden. They gave credit to the Navy SEALs, as promised. BlackRiver made a cool twenty million for the discovery, courtesy of the U.S. Government.

Price was a thick man, gained solely from time in the trenches. His swagger could be seen from a quarter mile away. The glisten from his shaved head was as shiny as a newly waxed show car.

He was late, as usual. He skipped the beer and headed straight for Craig's table. The booth shook as he sat down without a hint of grace. "Dominick! How are ya?" The men shook hands and traded smiles.

"Price, I am surprised you made it back from the sandbox." Craig enjoyed talking with Price. He seemed to have an edge to his personality that clicked with his own.

"I made it back, safe and sound. I don't get to do much of the fun stuff anymore. We've got ex-Army Delta lining up for that job."

"Delta? You guys aren't messing around."

"Nah, we've got operations all over the globe. Uncle Sam doesn't want to get his hands dirty, so we do it for 'em."

"Out of the kindness of your heart, I'm sure," Craig smirked.

"Indeed. And the cash they drop into our offshore accounts."

Craig pulled another envelope from his pocket and slid it across the table for a signature. "Let's finish what we started."

Price didn't read the fine print, nor did he spend any time reviewing the details. He simply signed the forms and flipped the pages back to Craig.

"When did you get into airline sales, Dominick? I mean, I know your hand stretches far, but this is reaching. Even for you!" Price arched an eyebrow, smiling at his new purchase.

"It is all part of the game, Price. I'll tell you about it when we're all in the Bahamas, sipping piña coladas." Agent Craig slid the signed forms into the envelope.

Farewells were exchanged as they shook hands. Price walked toward his private gate while Craig walked innocently toward the exit. Craig instantly gained a fifteen million dollar deposit, while Price and Becker gained a small fleet of clean, gently used airliners.

Seaport Village

San Diego, CA | 32°42'32"N 117°10'15"W

Seaport Village was an odd collection of tourist traps and restaurants. Sadie Shae stood on the dock, enjoying the smells of the ocean. She was tall, thin, and possessed a peculiar sexiness. She smiled with a nickel gap in her front teeth, yet somehow, it was a most admired feature.

She operated her business like a bulldog; she made a lot of noise, regardless of the situation and moved like a tank through anything that stood in her way. With one exception. Craig. They shared a checkered personal past.

Craig admired her satin dress that blew in the wind. She turned, looking daringly to Craig. He stopped.

"Fifteen 747s!" She crossed her arms unhappily. "*Fifteen*? I thought we were sticking with five! Ten max!"

Craig laughed and continued toward her. "Fifteen little planes? You're the best exporter in Southern California, Sadie. This is a cakewalk for you."

She knew he was flattering her simply to shut her up.

"I know I am the best. I am the best because I rarely do anything stupid. I calculate every risk and fifteen is too great. You're just being greedy, Dominick."

"Did you get my check?" Craig asked, avoiding any further discussion about risk.

Her weight shifted, hinting a brisk sign of change in her attitude. "I did."

"How much was on that check? Was it enough for you to start thinking about all fifteen?" He knew it was plenty.

"Okay, the money was right, but Mexico, Dominick? We're flying them into Mexico? Why not Canada or Hawaii? Anywhere else!" She feared Mexico. The drug kingpins had taken over everything, from local cops to the federal police. Not a peso was moved in that country without the drug lords being involved.

"Sadie, I've cleared it with the military. Everyone is on the payroll." He paused for effect. "I mean everyone! Besides, I only need you to sign the export paperwork. You won't even need to be there."

She paced the dock, noticeably apprehensive about the job. Craig put his hand on her shoulder. He comforted her softly by explaining the weighted risk. It was practically nonexistent. The question was not if they were going to get caught, the question was: Why didn't they think of this earlier?

Willow Creek Apartment Complex

Lakeside, CA | 32°49'37.8057"N 116°54'15.7692"W

Monday Morning 0730 hours

Nathan Briggs was already waiting. His car idled near the rear of the parking lot. Scents of fast food wafted stoutly from his car, only overpowered by the smell of cigarette smoke. His fat fingers held his cigarette out the partially open window. Craig pulled into a poorly painted parking stall a few spots away from Briggs. Craig's door opened smoothly as he surveyed the lot. Both buildings were three stories, clustered with balconies and screen porches. The structures were aging poorly in the California sun. The elevator reeked of seventies wood paneling and expired safety checks. The pool however, looked clean, usable, and completely overrun with bleach-like chemicals. Craig hastily passed the pool, rounding the corner to apartment number two.

Craig slid the key into the door and entered their new apartment and temporary office. Chairs, desks, couches, and a few amenities were aligned in a pseudo-office formation in the living room. The room held the slight scent of mildew, mixed with an occasional waft of fresh paint. Craig placed his laptop on the desk in the dining room. He opened the screen and waited for them to arrive.

Nguyen was the third to park. She pulled her small car to the side of the building, scoffed at the quality of the architecture, and began to scout apartment numbers. She scanned doors as she walked. Some numbers were not in order, others were painted, and others were upside down. Clearly, she had stepped into some kind of white trash suburbia the military dubbed a "temporary field office."

When she reached door number two, she stopped and pulled a lint roller from the depths of her stockpiled purse. Her hair was tightly pulled back into a bun. Her collared shirt was clean, pressed, and contained less than a freckle of lint. Her face was chillingly clean and sharp. She took a breath, paused, and entered the room with confidence.

"Good Morning, Nguyen; 0753 hours. You're early."

"I am always early and always the last to leave," she announced with poise.

Craig nodded, slightly impressed. "Good. Take a seat. You can take any desk you would like." He caught himself being kind, an oddity in his reserved personality. "You understand that you will be the team leader for this operation. You answer to no one except me."

"Yes, Sir. Understood."

As she arranged her equipment on her desk, Nathan Briggs made his way past the front windows to the door. He knocked and entered. He was a bit less gracious. He too unpacked his bag of computers and keyboards. Briggs placed a twelve-pack of soda on the edge of his desk. In a well-practiced maneuver, he ripped open the box and split open his first can. He set the cold drink on a coaster he either made, or purchased from a thrift store. Nguyen had a different method of arrangement. Her desk was orderly and clean, reeking of anal aptitude.

Agent Craig greeted Adam Luster at the door. "You are one minute late."

"Yes, Sir, I am. I couldn't find the apartment." He handed Craig a cup of coffee. "My apologies, Agent Craig."

The coffee revised Craig's annoyance of tardiness. "Take a seat."

Luster unpacked an array of four monitors, two laptops, and a broad selection of other blinking devices. It took a few minutes for the room to become wired, buzzing with warm electronics.

"I am looking forward to the next few months. Right now, the light at the end of the tunnel is dim and no larger than a peephole. If we do this right, we will be swimming in operational success before you know it." Craig sat on Nathan's desk, nearly toppling his beverage. "I would like for you to get to know one another. We will be family for the next few months and I would like for everyone to be treated as such. Please, stand and introduce yourself." Craig motioned for Nathan Briggs to go first.

Nathan got up in a heavy huff. His Hawaiian shirt screamed something obnoxious as the colors danced along the seams. "Good morning! I am Officer Briggs, of the sixteenth battalion."

Agent Craig interrupted him. "Please, keep your original placement confidential. Continue."

"Okay. Well, I am an officer. I graduated with a degree in engineering. Ummm. Well, after school I went into the military and have been building flight models for the past five years. I'm single. I have a few dogs. Other than that, I'm a pretty normal guy." He swayed nervously. Craig watched his hands twist as he spoke. Clearly, he was a topnotch engineer but his public speaking skills were far below par. Craig thanked Briggs and motioned for Nguyen to stand.

"Hello, my name is Officer Kim Lea Nguyen. Before I joined the military, I graduated from USD with a double major in software and mechanical engineering. I worked as a consultant for Lockheed Martin for two years until I was snatched up by the military. For the last few years I have been working in grey ops." She paused and looked around the room. She stood firmly as she spoke. Craig watched her perfect balance, paying close attention to her plush, eastern-toned lips as she spoke. He listened intently as she finished. "As for my personal life, I too am single. Married once to a Marine, but, we all know how that story goes! Lastly, my pets. Back on base, I have a spoiled cat and a goldfish."

"Thank you, Nguyen. Luster? Tell us a little about yourself."

Luster wasn't shy. He reeked of programming brilliance, giving off the distinct cologne of "I am smarter than you," which was a fragrance that few could wear appropriately. Luster, was one of those few.

"Good morning." He waited for everyone to reply. "My name is Officer Adam Luster. You can call me Adam. I didn't go to college and quite frankly, I think it was the best thing I could have done. I started my career writing spyware after high school. I realized that selling private information to penile enlargement companies wasn't the way to go when I was picked up by San Diego's Finest. Instead of locking me up, they offered me a position in the cyber crime task force. They called it community service, but in reality, I was just a publicly funded hacker. I made more money for them than most cops make in a lifetime of speeding tickets. Soon after I was released, NSA picked me up. I've been working in security programming for five years now." He paused, took a drink of his green tea, and continued, "I am one of the few people that can say I am happily married. I have a few dogs, one of which belongs on a hotdog bun. I don't talk much when I work, so please don't take it personally. That is all I need to say." He looked at Agent Craig, smiled, and sat down.

"Thank you, Luster." Craig nodded at him in professional appreciation. "You all may be wondering why I've assembled such an odd collection of military personnel. Well, I'll give you your answers." Craig swung his laptop around so that all could see his screen. "We are building one of these." The screen showed a rotating image of a miniature tank. The dimensions showed a wheelbase of three feet two inches, a length of five feet, and a height of just less than three feet. It held a computer screen on the top of the unit and several camera domes on the surface, jutting out like bumps on a pickle. "We, as a team, will build the smallest, most advanced remotely operated vehicle of its kind."

Nguyen leaned in her chair, focusing on the image. "A radio-controlled car? We're building a radio-controlled car?" Her words were immune from emotion, lacking the sarcasm it desperately deserved.

"Not just a radio-controlled car, Nguyen." Craig casually walked in between the desks. "Think bigger. Where would we be today if it weren't for the Predator unmanned flight plane? They too built a radio-controlled plane, but with an added bonus: payload." The light bulbs appeared above their heads as they nodded and began to understand the simplicity of the idea. "We will build a radio-controlled car, capable of driving 50 miles without a recharge." Craig unveiled a briefcase, exposing its contents. The inside of the case was lined with foam, hugging several plastic boxes. As Craig pulled each of the boxes from the case, an octopus of wires flopped from the container. "This small tank will operate on exactly the same GPS navigation and flight control as the Predator, except, on the ground *and* below ground." He emphasized the below ground capability.

The puzzled murmurs were noisy in the small room. "Below ground? What application requires a below ground, unmanned vehicle?" Luster asked.

Agent Craig replied simply, "This application."

For the next hour, Craig began to delegate intricate tasks to each of his underlings. Nguyen, the project manager, was to handle testing and design management of the project. Luster was given the task of developing the operating system for the unit, as well as the control software for driving the machine. Lastly, Briggs was to design and build the structure of the RC. Their desks were quickly filled with schematics, forms, spec sheets, and parts as their project began to tumble forward.

One can of soda turned to eight as Briggs sketched designs on his laptop. Luster drank his tea in silence as the glow of his four computer monitors tanned his face. Nguyen also worked diligently. She tapped her fingers rhythmically on her desk as music drummed into her headphones.

The first day drew to a close. Their eyes adjusted to the setting sun as they walked from the apartment. Craig followed the group outside. As he pulled the door closed, his cell phone rang. "Senator…" He quickly held the phone to his chest and excused the group. "Tomorrow. Same time. Same place." He walked away, talking quietly into the phone. Nguyen, Luster, and Briggs exchanged niceties and headed in separate directions. Nguyen was the last to leave the parking lot. As promised.

The Capitol Building — Private Senate Chambers

Washington, DC | 38.889°N 77.0072°W

Senator Royce was hard, smooth, and a bit quirky. He once attended a meeting sporting a pinstriped suit, a five o'clock shadow, and flip flops; ever since, he was known as the California King.

Agent Craig sat across from him in his private chamber. Senator Royce swirled a glass of fine scotch as he watched Craig pull a few items from his laptop case. Craig opened his laptop, presenting Royce with a clear shot of his screen. "Senator, the operation is entering phase two." Craig opened images of spreadsheets and floor plans. Royce paced around the room, holding the empty glass. He nodded as Craig told the story of their progress carried on endlessly with numbers, risk, and a barrage of other topics of which Royce could care less.

Mid-sentence, Craig was interrupted by Royce's firm hand closing the laptop. He then pulled a small baggie from his coat pocket and flicked it with a few fingers. He dumped a small cluster of cocaine on Craig's laptop. "Your plans? Your vision? Your progress?" Royce leaned down, snorting a cloud of coke from the lid with a loud sniffle. "Means nothing to me. I don't care where we stand or how we got there. I want results. Period. I didn't work on this with you so that we could have meetings about it. For fuck's sake, I have fifty meetings a day! Make this happen and make it happen right." He rubbed his nose lightly and raised his brow as the intensity of the cocaine kicked in.

"Why did you call me all the way to Washington if you don't want to hear an update?" Craig was a bit taken aback by Royce's shortness. Clearly the stresses of leadership had changed him. "We've been working on the RC Act for years. Don't think because I got you into the Senate, you get to boss me around."

They had a lot of history, both business and personal. The RC Act was the biggest and most profitable operation they'd designed. Their previous schemes were playschool comparatively.

"Will you have the project done on time?"

"Of course. Relax. There is no need for a pissing contest. It will be over soon."

Senator Royce calmed slightly, either because of the coke or because it wore off. As he relaxed, he wanted more details about their progress. Craig knew the stresses of politics were daunting, but also knew that Royce was a strong, smart, and easily corrupted adversary.

Royce paid particular attention to the airport and casino operation. He knew the feds would be watching. The feds were no Barney Fife. They were highly skilled in finding their man. The goal, of course, was to lead them astray, or at least baffle them for a few centuries.

Royce signed the articles of incorporation. His signature was swirly and short, appearing much fancier than required. "Patriot Barrier Corporation? Interesting name." Royce handed the papers back to Craig.

Craig responded quaintly, "It's catchy."

CHAPTER 3

Willow Creek Apartment Complex

Lakeside, CA | 32°49'37.8057"N 116°54'15.7692"W

The remote-controlled tank had become simply the "RC" when it was discussed. Stacks of soda cans spewed from Brigg's trashcan as the days withered by. Luster, as he had done for weeks, sat in total silence. He occasionally murmured a few numbers or rattled off an equation. Nguyen lay on the floor in a back bedroom. The RC was constantly being dismantled and reassembled. Nguyen measured a shock absorber just above the wheelbase. The small flashlight sat snugly between her lips as she examined the integrity of the machine. Her petite fingers gripped the screwdriver as she attached small struts and connectors at the base of the RC. Craig stood in the doorway, quietly admiring her craftsmanship.

"Finally! Done with the suspension!" She was a girl for a moment, not a driven overachiever. She smiled, glinting a spark of young bubble as she focused on Craig. She looked away shyly and regained her composure. She heard an earful from Craig when they fell behind, but today, they were weeks ahead of schedule. Her excitement was difficult to contain. She'd developed a faster, cheaper, and more efficient way to steer the vehicle, saving hundreds of hours in construction. For a moment, she lost herself in Craig's gaze. She'd silently admired him as an attractive man, but something changed. Admiration turned to a blend of cold dominance and Stockholm lust. She slowly slipped the metal wrenches into their sockets. She sweated slightly. Her eyes bounced from man to machine. Her khaki pants were pulled tightly around her legs and upper thighs, which she allowed to be prominent as she looked at him from under the RC. She reached under the wheelbase once more, allowing her shirt to rise just above her bellybutton. Her tan skin kissed her red panties as they peeked out from above her waistline. The warm tingle struck again as he spoke.

"Looks good. What next?" Craig asked curiously. He couldn't help but gape. Her body oozed sensuality as she worked.

Her heart pounded as he entered the room. He set his laptop gently on the desk, avoiding the miscellaneous hoard of parts that lay strewn on its surface. He leaned down, peering under the RC. He smelled of cologne. Not sweet and not rich. A combination of luxury and sport; something James Bond would wear as he nonchalantly played golf in the middle of a firefight. Craig's eyes were light and radiated in a color not normally seen on white men.

He touched her leg innocently as he kneeled, staring into the abyss of wiring and mechanics. "What next, Nguyen?" He repeated himself without annoyance.

Nguyen stared. His eyes were fixed on her. His blend of confidence and assurance beamed. "What's next? That's a complicated question." She paused, meeting his eyes with quiet flirtation. "We need the receiver, cameras, an upper monitor, and guidance chips for the RC." Succinct and sexy were the only words to describe her response. She smiled calmly and leaned back to the open belly of the RC. Before he left the room, she caught one more look as he rounded the corner.

Luster sat in his chair, facing the array of computers he'd set up like a cockpit. His hand flicked the mouse between screens, opening and closing windows as the cursor passed. Craig sat behind him for a few minutes, watching the madness that Luster called organization. On the screen to his left, a zombie movie played. Text, frames, and tech websites littered the other three screens. Luster typed faster than a courtroom stenographer with a meth problem. Craig rarely intervened with his work. He always completed his work on time and remarkably, error free. It was obvious that Luster wasn't working at full capacity, but he made the rest of the room look like it was standing still. Craig never mentioned the movies or frequent breaks. Luster produced; that is all Craig cared about.

Briggs, on the other hand, was a bit more lenient in every aspect of his work. He rarely made mistakes, however, he was a chronic social media junky, who took every opportunity to cook, eat, munch, chow, nibble, and chomp anything and everything that he brought with him. Briggs sat in one of the far rooms. He set up the command center, which was the control room for the RC that required two people to operate it: one to move the machine and one to watch everything around it. A third person would be required if missiles, projectiles, radar, automatic assault rifles, or jammers were installed, but this model wasn't designed with an arsenal in mind.

"Briggs! Tell me something good," Craig announced as he walked into the room.

"We're nearly operational. The GPS units are functional and the RC is mobile. We're just working out the kinks with the guidance." He was breathing heavily as he worked on wiring from beneath one of the desks. The back of his extra-large shirt was drenched in sweat.

Craig sat with him for an hour or so, reviewing the structural issues that had occurred in prior weeks. All in all, Briggs was a competent, good man. But slow.

Craig left without notice, which was not uncommon. Nguyen peeked through the blinds to watch him leave.

Two weeks passed before any word from Craig surfaced. He sent an email in his absence.

> *Nguyen,*
> *Meet me at the San Onofre testing field, coordinates 33°22'59.5964"N 117°31'19.3419W". Be there on Tuesday at 0900 hours. Bring the RC. Leave Luster and Briggs at the apartment to drive and operate the unit.*
> *Thank you,*
> *Agent D. Craig*

Monday morning, the group was scrambling to achieve a perfect operation. Briggs was glued to the command center. His caffeine buzz and anxiousness promoted a nervous shake when he operated the joystick. Luster too, was a bit nervous. He showed it in focus, not fear. He learned every jiggle in the controls as he drove the RC up and down the hallway of the apartment. Nguyen watched nervously. She was feeling the pressure of the deadline. She'd taken to sleeping at the apartment. Her sleep pattern had been redefined into a pattern of short, restless naps. She usually lay awake in the glow of her laptop, reviewing specs and RC diagnostics.

The RC was fully operational. Six, knotted tires operated independently, allowing the vehicle to swivel like a tank, yet remain quick and stealthy. Its chassis was strong, supporting a suspension system that rivaled most off-road trucks. The internal electronics, chips, and four computer boards were housed in a bullet-resistant steel compartment. Several sets of cameras were slotted on the front, top, sides, and rear of the unit, allowing a complete range of vision for the driver. Lastly, a standard computer monitor was placed on the top of the unit. It angled like a windshield off the trim and was protected by thick plastic.

As the sun began to dip past the desert mountains, Nguyen left the apartment. She quickly returned, sporting a six-pack of beer and a smile. She popped open the bottles and passed them out to her subordinates. A toast was made to the RC, Craig, the team, and of course, the money at the end of the mission.

San Onofre Military Training Grounds
San Diego, CA | 33°22'59.5964"N 117°31'19.3419"W

Just west of the SONGS Facility (San Onofre Nuclear Generation Station), lies the military training field dubbed *The Playground.* Acres of hills, craters, and demolished plant life were a second home to Agent Craig. He'd acquired sixteen hundred hours of documented field exercises, as well as six scars from this lovingly dreadful space. Craig knew every nook and every blind spot. It was a perfect environment for the RC.

He parked his car near the end of the gravel road. The Five Freeway was a distant rumble to the west. His chest expanded as he smelled the familiar odors. He closed his eyes and picked apart the scents — gunpowder, ocean salt, campfire, and warm desert sand.

He opened his eyes to the familiar rumble of tires on distant gravel. Nguyen's car could not be seen yet, but the plume of trailing dust made her easy to spot. Craig leaned against his car, carefully pulling a cigar from the case in his breast pocket. He clipped the tip and struck the flint of his chrome lighter. The sweet musk filled his mouth as he inhaled the smoke.

Nguyen drove cautiously up the path, cringing at every bump. The RC was nestled carefully in the backseat of her car, bouncing wildly on every divot. Craig came into view as she turned down the last stretch of gravel. The creases on his khaki pants protruded like a knife's edge. His white oxford dress shirt was pressed and perfectly tailored. His expression was blank as he stared from behind his dark glasses. He flicked the cigar to the ground and stepped on it lightly. She parked a few paces behind his car.

"Good morning, Sir." The coffee had not quite woken her from the sleep she finally deserved. She clouded the dark circles with makeup and sunglasses.

"Good morning, Nguyen. Punctual as usual." He walked toward her, calculating every step.

Nguyen opened the rear door and began lightly tugging the monster from her backseat. Craig pushed her aside gently and yanked on the frame of the RC. It weighed well over a hundred pounds, hitting the ground with a heavy thud. The sound of the RC smashing to the ground sent a chill up Nguyen's spine. She nervously watched as he manhandled the machine off its side onto the rocky road. "It's tougher than you think, Nguyen." The RC was built to withstand enormous pressures and extreme conditions.

Briggs and Luster sat on the edge of their seats at the apartment. They watched anxiously through the RC's cameras. Their view was tilted as it lay on its side. Briggs held his hand over his mouth in worry as Luster ran through the diagnostics. "It's fine, Nguyen," Luster said over the radio. "Diagnostics aren't showing any damage."

Nguyen unclipped the satellite radio from her belt and responded politely, "Thank you."

Craig pulled the radio gently from Nguyen's hands. With the radio raised to his lips, he spoke clearly, "Okay, gentlemen, let's move to Checkpoint Bravo."

Luster acknowledged the radio call from Craig. He lifted his tea to his lips, took a gulp, and grabbed the joysticks with damp palms. His monitors showed multiple camera angles around the RC. Luster's cockpit held twelve screens, nearly surrounding his full range of vision. Briggs, too, sat in a cluster of monitors. He sweated heavily as he adjusted the navigation systems. Luster carefully pressed the control stick forward, moving less rapidly than he'd practiced. The knobby wheels began to push against the gravel. Nguyen smiled as the unit crept forward. The gravel crunched and popped as the RC moved. Craig's expression didn't change, regardless of how proud he was to see it in action. Nguyen walked behind the RC, checking the wheelbase as she walked. Craig, Nguyen, and the RC crept toward the testing site. Thankfully, the machine rode smoothly, running over holes and bumps with heavy balance. Nguyen paced behind Craig, wondering what conversation to make while she worried helplessly about the RC. She envisioned a furious Agent Craig as he stood over a broken-down machine. Her troubled thoughts stirred with tire pressure, axle strength, wiring clusters, energy usage; everything that could go wrong.

CHAPTER 4

San Onofre Military Training Grounds
San Diego, CA | 33°22'59.5964"N 117°31'19.3419W

Craig and Nguyen watched from the viewing platform. Hesitantly, the RC approached the training building. The two- story building was large and appeared to be viciously abused. At the apartment, Luster watched the monitors as the sidewalk curved toward the front door. The cameras could see Craig and Nguyen standing high above, watching intently as Luster drove the RC from 40 miles away.

The RC moved smoothly along the sidewalk, pushing the front door open with its reinforced bumper. Briggs switched three of the cameras to heat vision to ensure they spotted any intruders during the training. Luster maneuvered the unit through the entry, toward what appeared to be a mock-kitchen. The tires rolled cleanly on the battered carpet. Little by little, it turned the corner, making its way under the counter of the kitchen bar. Luster got on the radio. “Craig, where do you want us to take her?”

Craig watched as the drone rolled through the kitchen, avoiding obstacles with jerky grace. “Can you drive the RC a little more smoothly, Luster?” Craig avoided Luster’s question.

“I can try, Sir. Where shall we go next?” Luster asked again.

Craig gripped the radio tightly, holding it a few inches from his mouth. “Luster, get the unit through the house to the rear entrance. Can you handle that without asking any more questions?”

Luster could hear the irritation in Craig’s voice. “Yes, Sir.” His response was militant.

Luster looked at Briggs through a crack in between the monitors. “Find me a way out, Briggs.”

Briggs moved the cameras, scanning the house for clear paths. The exit at the other end of the house was only a few rooms away. Briggs could only see the heat from the crack at the bottom of the door. “Head due north. The door is that way.” Briggs pointed, even though Luster couldn’t see his hand from behind the monitors.

Craig and Nguyen watched as the RC moved from room to room, steadily making progress toward the back door of the house. Craig smiled as the RC entered the next room. He turned to Nguyen. “Surprise.”

He pushed a button from a remote control hidden in his khaki pocket. A spinning red light on the side of the building flashed while an obnoxiously loud alarm chirped.

Luster flew to the front of his chair as the lights flickered in the room. Three holes in the wall emitted a cloud of smoke thicker than frozen molasses. The dense fog flickered from the strobe lights. Luster and Briggs began to sweat, flipping through camera angles to acquire a line of sight.

"There is a map of the house taped to the back of your desk," Craig said calmly through the radio.

Luster leapt to the floor. His hands ran between the wall and his desk until he felt the map at his fingertips. He tore the map from the wall and hopped into his chair.

"You have three minutes to get out of the house," Craig chirped over the radio.

"Where are we?" Briggs yelled, peeking his head through a layer of monitors.

"I think we are here, by the hallway!" Luster set the map on the desk and began to maneuver the vehicle toward the west wall of the hallway.

THUMP! The cameras flickered as the RC slammed into a wall.

"Two minutes, forty-five seconds," Craig said over the squelching radio.

Luster quickly reversed, slamming into the other side of the hallway. He eased the stick in the direction of the next room. The RC found new speed as it ripped down the hallway. "Okay, okay, we are right here; tell me where to go." Luster flipped the map to Briggs. He grabbed the map and pulled it closer to his eyes. "Uhhh, okay, make a right into the next room." Briggs' voice was nervous.

"What next room? I can't see anything!" Luster's calm demeanor was slighted by the surprise.

Briggs flipped on the thermal camera and changed the heat settings. The black monitors turned into a rainbow of red and orange as the walls appeared as distant shapes on the screen. "There! There! That's it!" Briggs yelled. The walls absorbed heat throughout the day, making them a flat blob of warm color on the screens. Luster moved cleanly through the next room.

"Two minutes!" Craig yelled through the radio.

Luster looked through the cameras for the warm opening to the outside door. They were completely turned around in the darkness. He pressed the throttles through an opening. He recognized the pattern of the room. "We're back in the kitchen!" Luster told Briggs. "Read the map! NOW!"

"Head down the hallway and make a left into the first doorway."

Luster tooled through the kitchen, turning sharply as he made his way down the familiar hallway.

"Good, turn there!" Briggs said, pointing on the monitors.

Luster pitched the joysticks toward the opening. The RC smashed against the edge of the doorway. Nguyen and Craig watched the RC on monitors set up around the evaluation platform. Nguyen cringed every time the unit careened into a wall.

"One minute, fifteen seconds," Craig announced on the radio.

Luster and Briggs hollered to each other like a drunken married couple. Luster finally saw what appeared to be the back door. His hands jammed the joysticks to a 45-degree angle, pushing the motors to their max acceleration. The RC jumped to speed, ramming the back door at nearly thirty miles an hour.

Craig smiled as the RC shattered the door. The unit slammed to the ground with a loud rattle. Briggs quickly adjusted the cameras for normal viewing. Luster relaxed. They'd proudly escaped the training house.

"Thirty seconds left on the clock," Craig announced. "You should have made it out in one minute or less." The scowl in his voice was evident. Luster's contentment quickly turned somber as he realized that their escapade through the smoke was simply not good enough.

"Bring the unit up to the cars and put yourself on screen. It's time for a meeting." Craig slapped the radio into Nguyen's chest and huffed away.

"We'll just keep trying until he's happy," she whispered into the radio.

Briggs was drenched in sweat. His brow was a wasteland of beaded water. They flipped on their webcam and moved their faces onto the screen of the RC. They parked a few feet away from Craig and Nguyen. Briggs and Luster could see their faces clearly on the monitors, just as Agent Craig and Nguyen could see theirs. The meeting began.

"Nearly three minutes. *Three* minutes? What have you guys been doing all this time?" Briggs and Luster sat in silence as Craig's disappointed words echoed through the speakers. "Officer Briggs. You should have had the thermals calibrated for this. And you, Luster! You should be driving this thing like an old Cadillac, not like a retarded golf cart! I am starting to think I picked the wrong crew." He paced on the gravel as he pulled another cigar from the other side of his case. "Nguyen, get this unit squared away. I will meet you here next week. Same time, same place."

Craig clipped a cigar, replaced his sunglasses, and drove away. Gravel pelted the RC as he sped from the training area.

A few minutes of silence wafted through the airwaves until Nguyen clicked the receiver. "Briggs? Luster? I need you down here to load the RC into my car."

Hotel Circle

Agent Dominick Craig's Hotel Room

San Diego, CA | 32°45'30.8504"N 117°10'59.5247"W

Craig's keys slid to a halt on the TV stand as he closed the door to his hotel room. He removed his watch, his ID, and his wallet. They sat neatly in a pile along the small round table in the corner of the room. He sighed and flopped onto the bed. After five minutes, despite the pungent odor from the overly chlorinated pool, his eyelids fluttered closed.

He sat up in a flash. His cell phone rang, spinning gently from the vibration. "Agent Craig," he answered.

"Vee have a problem." The heavy Hispanic accent made his voice immediately recognizable.

"Lieutenant Lopez, what is the problem?"

"Feefteen planes ees too moch. My men can land maybe fife, or seecks, but feefteen? You are outta jor focking mind."

A brief pause lingered on the line. "It's fifteen or nothing." Craig ended the call with a flick of his thumb. He missed the good old days where a guy could slam the phone down to make a point. Cell phones made the hang-up process much meeker.

The phone rang again. Craig pushed the talk button and listened.

"I veel land all feefteen, but I want a beeger cut. Transfer fife meelion. For feefteen planes. That ees my final offer."

"Done." Craig hung up. Numbers circled in his head. His mind was a synchronized trap of information. He knew every penny, every offer, and every person involved. Lines of account numbers, bribes, and currencies swirled into a ball of tired mush as his eyes closed.

The sound of a knock at his hotel room door woke him. He sat up, wiping the sleep from his face.

"Who's there?" His pistol slid from the holster. He peered through the peephole only to find the empty, bubbled view of the pool and elongated porch. He pulled back, a bit confused. He pushed his eyebrow to the door once more to see a blur in the peephole.

The splintered wood from the doorframe flipped violently into the room. The locks blew easily as the man kicked the door. Craig's head was a ringing concussion as the door slammed against his skull. He fell, only to meet up with a large hand and a pistol to his cheek.

"Get the fuck up!" the voice trailed and echoed oddly.

Craig squinted and attempted to focus on his attacker. His sight blurred. The man's hand gripped his shirt, dragging him to the porch. The sun appeared as a haze on frosted glass. Craig pushed against the terrace, trying to stand. His hand pressed against his knee, only to be met with a blunt kick in the ribs. Craig flipped to the ground, holding his chest, gasping for air. The man kicked again, directing the force to his back and kidneys. Craig coughed, sending a red blob of liquid to the cement.

Craig choked. "What do you want?" As the last sound trailed from his lips, the deafening sound of the pistol swept into his ears. The crisp burn of the bullet ripped through Craig's chest. He coughed again, moaning with a whistle from his collapsed lung. He reached for anything. The man. His gun. Something to help him fight. His vision sharpened. The gun barrel was warm against his forehead. Craig clenched his jaw. Time was slow as fire from the barrel burned his skin. The sensation of the bullet entering his left temple felt more like a pinprick than a gunshot. As the slug breached his skull, the whip-crack of the firing shell reached his eardrums.

Craig sat up sweating. He glanced around the untouched hotel room. His clock ticked. The door wasn't broken. He was dreaming.

Willow Creek Apartment Complex
Lakeside, CA | 32°49'37.8057"N 116°54'15.7692"W

Luster yawned. It was nearly midnight. The RC drove slowly through the field behind the apartment. Nguyen was ruthless, pushing Luster and Briggs well past their bedtime. She stood outside the apartment building, watching the RC in the deserted field just below the freeway onramp.

Impatience echoed through the radio as she pushed for Luster to drive through the makeshift obstacle course. He acknowledged, moving the RC through the track for the third time. Briggs crushed a soda can and tossed it into an overflowing garbage bin as the RC pushed through the finish line.

Two evil words poured through the speaker on the radio: "Again. Faster!"

Briggs and Luster were military officers and knew how to sigh respectfully. They gave each other a bloodshot eye roll and moved the RC back to the beginning. Briggs leaned heavily on his right arm, adjusting the brightness of the infrared lights on the front of the unit. The green outlines of buildings, dirt, and track were brilliant blurs on the screen.

Three and a half hours passed. Luster was typing on his keyboard as he drove the unit through the course for one last time. Briggs was nearly drooling as he moved the cameras slowly around the course.

The radio squawked: "Good job, boys, bring it in. Make sure you take it slow through the parking lot. We don't want anyone to see it."

Delta's Tavern Casino

Alpine, CA | 32°50'37.3893"N 116°47'2.6418"W

Lights flashed brightly as Craig pulled up to the casino. Rolling strings of blinking lights welcomed him as he threw the keys to a young valet. "Keep it under eighty, son." Craig grinned playfully, despite the indifference of the valet. As Craig walked to the door, an armed guard greeted him. He nodded and scanned the guard's gun belt. Craig's mind cataloged the contents of his gear:

> Ruger pistol, unpolished hammer.
> Mini-Maglight.
> Late model radio with earpiece.
> Two magazines, not sagging along the beltline.
> Handcuff case, pristine condition.
> Large ring of keys, unprotected.

Craig knew that the guard was unprepared and poorly trained. The Ruger pistol was unpolished. The lack of care clearly stated: "I don't care about my equipment." The clean strap meant he did not practice with it, therefore was a bad shot. The mini-maglight was a sad excuse for a light source. In the late 90s, cops started carrying brighter, well-designed lights that gave off more light than the surface of the sun. His radio was solid, but was clearly issued through his security department. The magazine case looked unused, another indicator of bad training. The lack of sag on his belt was a clear indicator that the magazines were empty, leaving the possibility of only eleven shots in his pistol. The handcuffs looked new and unscratched. Lastly, the cluster fuck of keys showed that the guard didn't care if people heard him coming: a rookie mistake. Not only was the guard unprepared and poorly trained, it appeared that his uniform had been passed down from a guy twice his size. His pants sagged in all the wrong places. His shirt looked like he'd slept in it. The guard was a soup sandwich. A weakling. Easily conquerable.

Another voice greeted him. A young, red-haired, thin-waisted beauty smiled showing her white teeth. "Welcome to Delta's Tavern Casino!" she said kindly, hinting at a southern drawl. Her uniform was similar to a cocktail waitress at a sleazy club, but somehow, with the glitz and glam of the casino, it looked natural.

As she opened the second set of doors, Craig stepped into the casino. The deafening buzz of the slot machines was more distracting than the wall of cigarette smoke. Grannies and punks sat side by side, plugging bills into the flashing screens. The simulated sound of coins hitting metal buckets was excessively loud as people cashed out their slots. Craig strolled up the poorly designed carpet, toward an area with a spinning car. His cell phone buzzed in his pocket, signaling the first of several stages. Craig ducked into a bathroom, passing a gaggle of blonde bombshells and their tattooed companions. The door swung open, revealing an exquisite layout of marble and tile. He sniffed, winced, and closed his eyes in frustration and thought, overused chemicals, as always. He slid into the farthest stall and closed the door.

The text he'd received was simple, stating only: "Ready when you are."

His fingers moved slowly along the small letters on his phone keyboard as he responded: "STAND BY."

Craig walked from the stall, washed his hands in the lavish sinks, and calmly exited the restroom. The blackjack tables were filled with drunken businessmen and wisecracking youngsters while the pai gow tables were brimming with Vietnamese, all of which appeared to be either eighteen or in their late seventies. The main entrance was in view, just beyond a few tables. Craig walked through the doors and again was greeted by a beauty and a beast. The beauty was another young greeter, more slender than the previous gem. The beast was much more equipped than the last. The security guard at the front door was stocky and looked as square as a Marine. His shirt was fitted and pressed. His boots were shined and his belt was stocked. The leather around his gear was worn, but well kept. His hands were placed strategically along his hips, safely protecting his gun and weapons. He was a solid adversary.

Craig walked through the cluster of people outside the door. Buses littered the sidewalk with elderly travelers and minorities. He reached into his pocket, pulling his cigar case. With a flip, he pulled, clipped, and lit his stogie. He slid his phone from his pocket, savored a deep plume of smoke and typed: "BEGIN PHASE ONE."

CHAPTER 5

Delta's Tavern Casino

Alpine, CA | 32°50'37.3893"N 116°47'2.6418"W

Nguyen eagerly picked up her phone at the apartment and read Craig's text message. She paced behind Briggs and Luster as she went through the checklist.

"Luster, are you in position?"

"Yes, Ma'am."

"Good. Briggs, are the cameras clear?"

"Yep, we're good to go, Nguyen."

"Good. Move the RC to the front door and begin the operation as rehearsed."

Craig's hand nestled deeply into his right trouser pocket, pushing the button on the remote. In his car, a line of eight Motorola security radios lay bolted in succession. As he pushed the button, a small motor smashed each of the "talk" buttons on the radios. As an added bonus, the mechanism also pressed play on his music player. He streamed opera music into the radio microphones, rendering any wireless security or police communication useless. Craig pulled a rugged drag from the cigar, watching with great anticipation.

At night, the casino administration building was only used by the reservation police to eat sub sandwiches and chatter uselessly. No one watched the large drain tunnel behind the building. The opening was six feet in diameter and crossed under the adjacent freeway. Luster drove the RC down the pipe while Briggs watched for headlights in the night vision cameras. The drainage pipe was wet and littered with brush and garbage. The cameras bounced and jostled as they moved through the isolated wasteland of the tunnel. Distant flashes of the casino lighting blurred the RC's view, a factor not accounted for during their initial assessments. Briggs adjusted the lighting levels and continued down the tunnel.

The RC touched dirt and hummed quietly as it passed the building. Luster took a hard right onto Oak Tree Road. Briggs smacked Luster's arm. "Wrong way! Turn around."

Luster ignored the ignorant pat he'd received on his shoulder and turned the RC in the correct direction. The ditches were perfect cover. The RC climbed in and out of the deep ruts on the side of the road. The main drive to the casino was in view. "Here we go, Luster! Let's make it count!"

A voluptuous black woman stood, danced, and cheered wildly as her ace was drawn. "Twenty-one!" the dealer called, pulling a few chips from his case. The elderly Asian man sitting on the adjacent seat moved quickly as the woman's ballooned butt swung wildly in his direction. "What the fu--?" A crowd gathered as the RC unit pulled past the buses into the main entrance. The rugged RC looked solid and intimidating. The officer from the front door approached the RC in guarded curiosity.

The screen was black, with the exception of a blinking cursor. People gathered around the unit, waiting for something to happen. Slowly, words trickled across the screen: "I AM A BOMB."

Briggs watched on the small monitors as the tall guard grabbed his radio, clicking the button without success. Instead of a transmission, it belted soothing opera music through the tiny speaker.

"SECURITY OFFICER, TAKE ME TO THE MAIN BANK OR I WILL EXPLODE. DO NOT FRIGHTEN THE GUESTS, OR I WILL EXPLODE. NOD IF YOU UNDERSTAND."

The guard nodded and tried again to call into his radio. His head spun wildly, contemplating his options. "NOW!" The RC printed the word in all capital letters, emphasizing the tone. The RC moved through the entrance onto the plush carpet. Sweat pooled along the collar of the guard's uniform as he waved the crowd aside. Briggs smiled from his chair as he watched the crowd panic and wiggle from view. They moved the unit through mazes of the blackjack tables toward the bank.

A guard carrying a clear box of poker chips stopped, scratched his head, and tried to radio the walking guard. Briggs zoomed the cameras to watch the stray guard. In a flash, the guard moved the box of chips to a cashier's cage and was on a wall phone, assumedly calling dispatch.

"Ten minutes on the clock." Nguyen pointed to Briggs, who started the countdown timer. He clicked start, revealing a large red digital counter. Seconds began to count down.

A swarm of armed officers surrounded the unit. Luster stopped and flashed the message again: "ESCORT ME TO MAIN BANK, OR I WILL BLOW UP THE BUILDING. I AM PACKED WITH ENOUGH C-4 TO LEVEL THE CASINO."

The officers developed their plan as they walked through the crowd. ID badges pressed harshly against magnetic locks, opening doors with a subtle swing.

The small hallway behind the bank of machines was thin and bland. Sterile white walls blanketed the hidden passage. As the doors swung open, two men in suits slipped through, pacing a few steps behind the pack of guards, cell phones pressed tightly against their worried faces. Their arms flailed as they reported the incident. The clock was ticking.

The hall wound through the heart of the casino. Three officers, two suits, and a sergeant walked carefully behind the unit as they opened the door to the soft count room. The aged, freckle-faced banker didn't seem to notice that they'd entered the room. She continued running stacks of bills through the counters. Briggs sent another message and opened the bay at the rear of the RC.

"PLACE BRICKS OF 100-DOLLAR BILLS INTO THE OPEN BAY."

The guards quickly grabbed stacks of bills from the clear counters. The shrill sound of a buzzer echoed from the RC.

"DO NOT PLACE TRACKED BILLS IN THE BAY. IF DYE PACKS, GPS, RF TRACKING, OR SERIAL TRACES ARE IN THE BATCH, I WILL DETONATE. IF WE DISCOVER THESE TRACKING DEVICES AFTER WE'RE OFF THE PROPERTY, WE WILL RETURN WHEN YOU ARE LEAST EXPECTING IT."

The officers shared a look of dismay. Slowly, a guard pulled the two stacks from the bay and returned them to the counter.

Piles of hundreds filled the RC. Nguyen watched carefully, keeping a close eye on the vehicle weight. As the last stack of bricked hundreds was loaded into the carrier, the bay closed.

"EVERYONE, REMOVE YOUR WALLETS AND PULL OUT YOUR DRIVER'S LICENCE."

Glares passed between guards as they read the intensity of the statement.

"THIS IS NOT THE TIME TO BE A HERO. DO YOU WANT TO BE RESPONSIBLE FOR THE DEATH OF 2,000 INNOCENT CIVILIANS? DO IT NOW, PULL YOUR ID'S AND SHOW IT TO ME."

One by one, the guards pulled their California driver's licenses from their wallets. They held them closely to the tinted camera bubbles.

A tall, militaristic-looking officer shook his head. "I'm not doing it, no fuckin' way. I am not..."

Briggs snickered and turned up the microphone volume. The man's stand was notable, respectable, and stupid. Without hesitation, Luster typed commands wildly, opening a small compartment in the RC. Luster snickered: "Time to ride the lightning!" The guard stopped and stared at the open hatch. Prongs from an embedded TASER popped in his direction. The prongs hit the officer in the neck. With a thud, he fell to the floor, moaning wildly. Luster smiled wickedly as he watched the monitor. Five seconds of surging voltage passed through his body. The banker in the vault shrieked loudly, causing Briggs to readjust the volume. The voltage stopped, allowing the frantic officer to jerk his wallet from his pocket and wave the ID in front of the camera.

"Better," Luster said under his breath, releasing the electrified wires from the unit.

"THANK YOU FOR YOUR COOPERATION, ESPECIALLY YOU, TOM SMITTY. NOW, LEAD ME THROUGH THE CROWD TO THE MAIN ENTRANCE." Luster enjoyed naming the brave officer.

The group walked cautiously out of the vault. The RC was guarded heavily in the hallway, surrounded by the armed men who swore to protect the very money the RC was taking. The doors to the casino floor opened, exposing the flashing lights and sounds of gaming. The crowds who had not seen the original message on the RC were completely oblivious. The circle of guards walked wearily through the tables, across the floor to the main entrance. Briggs focused on the red and blue lights that waited down the road and Briggs produced the last message as he pushed past the main entrance doors.

"FOLLOW ME AND I WILL DETONATE. ATTEMPT TO STOP ME AND I WILL DRIVE TO YOUR HOUSE AND BLOW UP YOUR FAMILY. GO BACK INSIDE THE CASINO AND TURN AWAY FROM THE DOORS."

Each officer was thinking only of his family and the addresses that now lie in the hands of the thieves. One by one, the officers turned away and walked inside the casino.

"Go!" Nguyen poked Luster. The RC moved from a steady walk, to rolling thunder as it sped down the street. Briggs worked wildly to keep the cameras steady as the RC whizzed across the intersections. The reservation police knew nothing of the threat of explosion, as the radios were completely contaminated with opera music. One of the officers must have called dispatch, learned of the robbery, and phoned the other units. It was another obstacle they'd not foreseen.

The police were quick to react, flooring their cruisers toward the RC. Luster watched as the red and blue lights closed on the unit. The throttle twisted, angling the RC back up the driveway to the administration building. Two police trucks screeched behind as they followed the unit up the drive. The rugged driveway popped and jostled the RC as it flew forward. Briggs yelled, "Ughhh, they're getting closer. Luster, *go faster!*"

Briggs watched as the grille of the police truck pulled closer to the RC. Luster gunned the accelerator, much faster than he'd practiced. The cameras shook wildly as he swayed to maintain control. The cops slowed as the RC blew past the administration building, through the brush, and safely into the tunnel.

Nguyen let out a sigh and released her tightly balled fists. Briggs fell back into his chair, grabbing a new can of soda with sweaty palms. Luster, however, maintained his demeanor. He drove the unit through the labyrinth of tunnels to another opening a few miles down the road. Briggs turned on the headlights as they maneuvered through the litter-infested underworld of tunnels.

Nguyen's pocket buzzed.

"STATUS?"

Nguyen poked at her cell phone keyboard with woodpecker speed.

"Operation was a success, see you in a bit."

Craig sighed, smiled, and took another puff of his nearly finished cigar. Everyone at the poker table noticed his smug expression. He laid down a set of kings, pulling the pot to his corner of the table. Discouragement raged across the faces of the other players. No one at the table knew he had pocket kings...and no one knew he'd just robbed the very casino where they sat gambling.

Willow Creek Apartment Complex

Lakeside, CA | 32°49'37.8057"N 116°54'15.7692"W

Craig's car scraped the pavement as he pulled up the steep hill of the apartment parking lot. He parked in a stall close to the front of the building, looking cautiously at the balconies above. With a grunt, he pulled the RC from the rear door of his sedan. It crashed to the ground with a heavy thud. Craig mumbled, "0215 hours," as he eyed his wrist. He swung open the door, exposing Nguyen's cross expression.

"With all due respect, Sir, what the hell was that? It seemed more like a robbery than a mission!" Nguyen was visibly upset.

Craig opened his duffel bag, exposing a bottle of fine champagne, a cube of cigars, and stacks of hundred-dollar bills.

He waited to answer. He enjoyed the humanity in her voice.

Briggs, too, chimed in: "Craig, who authorized this mission? Are we returning the stolen money?"

Craig sat, leaned back in his chair, and popped the champagne. Briggs and Nguyen stood in front of his desk, wide-eyed, awaiting his response. Nguyen grabbed his champagne bottle and slammed it to the desk. Frothy bubbles spewed from the neck. Craig grabbed the bottle and slid it back to his end of the desk, brandishing disapproval across his brow.

"This operation was a success, not a robbery."

"It sure felt like a robbery."

Craig poured a tall, golden flute of champagne. "Nguyen..." he paused, sipping the foam head off of the top of the glass. "How do you think SWAT teams were started?"

Nguyen shifted her weight. "No idea. Was it a robbery?"

Craig smirked and again sipped the champagne. "SWAT teams began because the criminals were getting smarter, faster, and more daring."

"Great. Thanks for the info. But, please tell us what that has to do with robbing a casino!"

"In the 1920s and 1930s, mobsters overpowered the police. They had truckloads of Thompson automatic machine guns, while the local cops held their puny revolvers and rusty pump action shotguns. Bank robberies, speakeasies, and prostitution ran rampant, only because the bad guys had better firepower."

Nguyen cocked her head. "Again, what does that have to do with us robbing a casino? I don't want to play this game."

Craig motioned for her to hush. "The government needed to fight back. They needed a solution." Craig lifted his glass of champagne and took another satisfying sip. He pointed to the bottle. "Anyone want a glass? This is very good champagne."

"No, thank you. Please continue," Nguyen spouted.

" J. Edgar Hoover designed a program that eventually funded the opening of the FBI. He designed a SWAT team. The acronym, SWAT was later dubbed 'Special Weapons and Training,' however, that's only because the true acronym has been classified. SWAT originally stood for *Steal, Win, Attack, Triumph.*" He paused, not for dramatic effect, but to simply enjoy another sip. "Hoover had a vision. A winning, triumphant vision. He held a meeting with the sheriffs and police chiefs of every major city. He ordered every official to instate a SWAT team. These four-man teams were directed to look, act, dress, and duplicate the mobsters' actions. Their prime directive was to rob banks and make it look like the undesirables were responsible for the crime."

Nguyen and Briggs were leaning forward, taking in every word. Luster sat in the background, completely carefree. He didn't care if he robbed a bank, or nuked a village. He simply wanted his check.

Craig continued, "The SWAT teams collected thousands of dollars in the first few months, creating two major points. One: bank robberies were on the rise and police needed more support. Two: police departments were secretly acquiring better firepower and a better budget for their officers." Craig pulled three champagne flutes from the kitchen, filling them as he spoke. "In 1932, Hoover gained enough funding and support from law enforcement officials to open the FBI. When he was placed as the director of the FBI, he authorized police departments to purchase and use high-powered rifles, Tommy guns, and higher caliber 1911 pistols. Finally, law enforcement had an edge."

Craig passed out the champagne. Nguyen sipped from her glass while Briggs gulped. Luster ignored the bubbling flute.

"Slowly, the mafia enterprises were minimized, beaten by their own game." Craig swiveled his laptop monitor to the group, showing gruesome, classified pictures of high-ranking mafia personnel from the 1930s and 1940s. "Hoover ordered the records sealed and kept them classified. He stole. He won. He attacked and he triumphed against opposing forces."

"Is this operation part of SWAT?" Nguyen asked.

Craig chuckled, "No, Operation SWAT has been closed since the 1940s. This is simply a new take on an old program. The economy is in the tank. The government is using new ways to develop war technology." Craig pointed to the RC that lay lifeless in the center of the living room. It was much more in-depth than they'd imagined, however, it answered their questions.

"Enough! This is a night of celebration." Craig called Luster from his desk and raised his glass. "To Hoover!"

Nguyen regained her alluring composure as she clinked Craig's glass. Briggs chugged the champagne and strolled to the kitchen to pull out the pizza that had been cooking far too long. "Want a slice?" Briggs asked Craig.

"No, thank you, Briggs, you go ahead." Craig was disgusted by the greasy food that Briggs shoveled into his body, but it wasn't his place to mock his diet.

"Get some sleep tonight, team. We start a new project in the morning." Craig sat on the corner of Nguyen's desk, watching her lips touch the glass as she drank the last drops of champagne. She smiled at him and patted his leg. "My apologies, Sir, for not trusting you."

"You were concerned for the wellbeing of your team; I respect that." Craig was silently mesmerized. Behind the innocence of his words and posture, he scanned her face and body. Her thin curves were accentuated from below her tank top.

"Have a good night, team. Good work." Craig walked around the RC, past the desks to the front door. "Almost forgot." He pulled three envelopes from the black duffel bag around his shoulder. He tossed them onto Briggs' desk. "There is one here for each of you."

CHAPTER 6

Willow Creek Apartment Complex
Lakeside, CA | 32°49'37.8057"N 116°54'15.7692"W
72 hours later

The tall, plastic garbage can echoed a hollow thud as Agent Craig dropped it on the floor between their desks. Adam Luster turned from his work to peer at the ruckus.

"Looks like a garbage can, Agent Craig," Luster said sarcastically.

"Very observant, Luster. That's why I hired you," Craig retorted.

"Right, but what are you doing with it?" Nguyen asked.

Craig looked her up and down, eyeing the summer dress she wore with sensual grace. "I need 15, flat, disc-shaped

RCs to fit in here." Craig pointed to the interior of the trashcan. "Additionally, I need the trashcan itself to be remotely operated."

Luster, Briggs, and Nguyen were speechless.

"How? What do the smaller RCs need to carry?" Briggs was confused with the concept.

"All fifteen units need to be able to drive, via remote control, and deliver an on-screen message, exactly like our original RC."

"Do you have a model?" Nguyen asked, sliding on a pair of reading glasses.

"Nope. I have you," Craig announced, motioning to the group. "You have four weeks."

The gasp was audible from space. The group muttered amongst themselves. "Four weeks?" Nguyen asked. "*Four*?"

"Of course, Nguyen. You didn't expect to breeze through this, did you? I like to challenge you. You will succeed."

Agent Craig pulled a file folder from his duffel bag. The group surrounded him as crude drawings poured from the manila cardboard. Luster picked up a few unsophisticated drawings, puzzling over the design. "Nothing is impossible, Craig," Luster piped. "This is just another SAT-controlled device, just smaller. What do we need? A few motors? Control chips and a few screens? Easy peezee."

Briggs and Nguyen looked at Luster like he was on fire, but appreciated his enthusiasm.

"I'll give you 24 hours to devise a list of parts." Craig looked at his watch. "I'll be back here tomorrow at 0900 hours."

As expected, Craig left in a hurry. They looked at one another with curious expressions. "Can we do this?" Nguyen was frantic. She tore through the sketchy drawings that should have been on bar napkins, not schematics. Briggs scratched his head and shrugged. Luster again announced that they could do it and that it would be a walk in the park. Luster also reminded them of the monetary benefits of completing said task.

"We can do this," Nguyen said, lacking the surety that it deserved.

San Diego International Airport — Lindbergh Field

San Diego, CA | 32°43'56.7066"N 117°12'31.8356"W

The airplane hangar was larger than he'd imagined. Craig walked up the swaying, iron steps to the door of the cargo plane. He ducked his head as he walked into the spacious hull. The stale musk of the interior was barely tolerable. Scattered wooden boxes and debris clouded the walkway as he made his way to the rear of the plane. His eyes perked up as he saw Sadie Shae sitting in the captain's chair.

"She's a beauty, isn't she, Dominick?" Sadie echoed in the empty plane. She stood, strutting flirtatiously toward Craig.

"Not bad for a used plane, Sadie." Craig turned and focused on her as she walked. She knew he was watching. Subtle sways emphasized her hips and chest. Craig watched carefully from behind his sunglasses. Her features were smooth, drawing his attention to the silk that hugged her skin.

"What do you want this piece of shit for anyway? It's been in here for 10 years; hell, the airport doesn't even know it's here anymore!"

"That is exactly why I want it."

She eyed him as she walked in a gentle circle around him. "Why exactly does that make it more appealing?" She ran her hand along his shoulder. She slowed behind him, wrapping her arms around his shoulders, pressing her lips to his ear. "It's all yours, Dominick."

Agent Craig turned, sliding his lips through hers. He smiled and pressed his lips to her ear, whispering, "It's just business." He pulled his arm from her embrace, gently pushing her away. "I need all the paperwork you have on it."

She backed up, frustrated, and quietly aching. "There is no paperwork, Dominick. No one even knows this thing is still in one piece...and it's not just business with you. It's always been personal."

"It's always been personal because you let your emotions get in the way. Does the plane have identifiers? Serial numbers?" He knew it didn't. He planned the operation with this plane in mind and knew the story long before he knew she would sell it.

"The serial numbers never existed on this plane; I bought it without paperwork. I let my emotions get in the way, because we never finished what we started, Dominick." She longed for Craig's touch. He'd slid passionately in and out of her life without warning, without hesitation for many years.

"When is the last time anyone has been in here?"

"Cut the shit, Dominick! I can't keep doing this!" He interrupted her with a brute hand pulling her lips to his. Her hands wrapped his cheeks, pulling forcefully as he kissed her. He pulled the warmth of her body closer. Bliss pulsed through her heart as they stood in a sudden embrace.

He released her after a few moments, lessening his grip on her waist. She opened her eyes in total innocence, staring at Dominick. Waiting. Anticipating. For a moment, utterly fragile.

"When was the last time anyone was in here, Sade? I've gotta know." Craig hoped the kiss would be enough to keep her talking and ultimately cooperative. He rarely had time for passion.

She wiped her lips and blushed a pink bliss along her cheeks. "No one has been in here for years. I keep it locked."

"Good. No matter what happens, you can't claim this plane or tell anyone that you sold it to us."

Sadie Shae nodded, still clutching the sleeves on his crisp shirt.

"I'll need the keys, Sade."

She opened her hand, revealing a small key ring. "I need to leave now, but I'm not trying to disappear, I simply am mid-mission. I'll call you later." He loosened his grip and kissed her brow.

"Always on a mission, Dominick. Always." She looked up at him, kissing his lips one final time. "Please, don't disappear again."

Willow Creek Apartment Complex

Lakeside, CA | 32°49'37.8057"N 116°54'15.7692"W

Crude sketches lay neatly on the desk. Nguyen, Briggs, and Luster hovered over the drawings. Each of the large, coin-shaped RCs were to be two-inches thick, with a diameter of almost exactly the same as the trashcan. The wheels popped out from the bottom like landing gear, allowing the units to be stacked like a roll of coins. Each of the RCs contained a computer screen that was on an angled tilt, allowing it to pop up when activated. Nguyen was weary of the design, but knew it was the only possibility of loading the RCs into the garbage can. Unexpectedly, Craig's keys jingled on the other side of the front door. Nguyen's heart skipped a nervous beat.

"Good morning. Do you have the parts list ready?" Agent Craig didn't waste any time getting to the point.

Nguyen picked up a printed, three-page list of parts. "Done," she said as she handed him the list.

"Incredible," Craig said as he looked at Nguyen. "Luster." Craig moved his attention to the opposing side of the room.

"Yes, Sir." Luster turned from the screen and attentively stood.

"Do you know how to play poker?"

"Yes. Yes, Sir, I do." The question was curious, however, Luster was intent on figuring out where the conversation was headed.

"Do you have your ID?"

"Yes, Sir."

"Come with me. We have work to do."

Luster trailed behind Agent Craig as they headed toward the exit of the apartment.

"Wait, what are we supposed to do?" Nguyen too stood, awaiting her orders.

"Begin building the RCs, of course. Did you think you could just sit around in a circlejerk? Get moving." Agent Craig walked out the door. Nguyen was speechless. She was a bit taken aback by his comment. He was oddly cynical at times, but she quietly admired the abruptness of his attitude.

Agent Craig motioned for Luster to get into the car. Craig moved a newspaper and a few folders from the passenger side as Luster waited. Craig appreciated Adam Luster. He held a quiet dignity that allowed for little room or judgment. Luster cared little if people liked him, including

Craig, but he was respectful and appreciated people that treated him with the same respect. Agent Craig pulled from the driveway and headed west on Freeway 8. A deep-voiced talk radio host murmured as they sped along. After ten minutes, the silence was cut.

"Do you like poker, Luster?" Craig asked.

"Sir, I've played many times." Luster knew the game and had played a few times over the years.

"I already asked you if you knew how to play; I am asking if you *like* to play." Craig glanced quickly, spinning a smirk as he looked away from the road.

"Not really. I never cared for gambling. I'd rather keep my money."

Craig appreciated his honesty. "That's fine. I don't expect you to enjoy it. As a matter of fact, I want you to lose when we play."

"We're going to play poker?"

"Yes. Yes we are..."

United States \ Mexico Border
Tijuana, Baja California, MX
32°32'35.4388"N 117°1'54.311"W

Agent Craig parked his car along the shoulder of the turnaround at the Tijuana border. A uniform-clad border patrol agent flagged Craig down with an aggressively demeaning tone.

"Hey! Hey, you! You can't park that thing here!"

Craig stopped and quietly whispered to the man, pulling his ID from his wallet. The agent quickly stood upright and listened intently to Craig. Luster chuckled under his breath as he watched. "Let's go, Luster," Craig spouted.

They headed toward the narrow cement walkway separating the United States and Mexico. As they walked, the stench of sewage and sulfur crept into their twitching nostrils. Craig made small talk as they continued toward the twirling security gates. They dodged tattered children, all of which were hawking tiny packs of gum and begging for change.

The security turnstile was built with tarnished, solid iron. It creaked as it spun, clacking loudly as the bars fell into place. The gate was designed to only spin in one direction and took a bit of effort to push. Craig went first, poking into Mexico with a shove. Luster soon followed, breathing in the refreshing air of exhaust and feces. Cabbies and vendors yelled for their attention with thick accents and rugged English. Cabs littered the parking lot, while bums sat along the walls attracting more flies than an Ethiopian kid covered in honey. Craig caught the attention of a legitimate-looking cab driver.

"Grand Hotel, por favor," Craig spoke with a perfect Spanish accent.

The cabbie flicked his burning cigarette and opened the backseat doors. Craig took the lead, hopping into the smoky taxi. Their heads jerked unexpectedly as he careened backward. He shifted into drive quickly, sending the transmission and the wide-eyed passengers into shock. They pulled into traffic, bumping over the center divider.

Luster wasn't certain that the loud crash was the curb or a sonic boom from the ascending speedometer. The cabbie's cell rang, illuminating the cab with a horrific rap song. He continued down the freeway, dodging cars like "Frogger" as he laughed wickedly into his phone.

In the time it took for their lives to pass before their eyes, they arrived at the hotel. The driver ended his call and turned around in his seat. He asked for two hundred pesos with an outstretched hand. Craig pulled a folded twenty from his pocket and handed it to him. In broken Spanglish, he asked them if they needed: "...coke, chickas with beeg titties? Weed?" They declined respectfully.

Grand Hotel Tijuana

Tijuana, Baja California, MX
32°30'47.6494"N 117°0'26.944"W

The entrance to the hotel was draped with marble and gold. The concierge was prompt as he greeted them. They checked into the director's suite. The room was large, classy, and sported a view of the golf course that made the brochure photos looks like kindergarten sketches.

Craig unpacked. Six laptops, a phone charger, and a stashed pistol slid from his duffel bag. Pack. Travel. Unpack. Repeat. The process was all too familiar to Craig.

"All right, what are we doing in Mexico?" Luster asked as he eyed the luxurious room. He'd reserved his questions, but curiosity was gaining momentum.

"I need you to play poker, Luster, exactly what I said," Agent Craig replied with grinning subtlety.

"I need a little more than that, Craig. I get the feeling we're up to more than a few flushes."

"'So quick, Luster, again, that is exactly why I hired you."

"Okay, give me something. Why Mexico?" Luster sat in a tall maroon chair. The classiness of the suite spilled from every fixture in the room.

"Mexico, my friend, has different online gambling laws. We, of course, need to obey the rules." Craig opened the laptops. "I need your expertise in programming and I need your lack of expertise in poker." Craig walked to the mirrored bar, popping open a bottle of gin. He explained the computer program as he poured a short glass.

He needed two programs. Both sets of software would be running in an online virtual poker room. One program would simulate a player: a very bad player. While the second would simulate a smart and victorious player. The goal of the operation was for the losing player to transfer money, rather a lot of money, from one player to another. Online gaming watchdogs in the U.S. were savvy to this form of money movement, therefore putting the kibosh on all U.S.-based online gaming. "The losing player needs a random IP bounce," Craig emphasized. He knew that every bank and financial investigation unit tracked the IP address of a losing player.

"In other words, we're laundering money?" Luster understood the point of the operation but didn't care if it was immoral or illegal. Coffee kept him up at night, not shady activities.

"We are not laundering money! Only drug lords and depression-era mobsters launder money. We're creating untraceable money; there is a difference."

Luster appreciated the ambiguous veneer of Craig's operations. He couldn't quite grasp whether this was a legitimate operation or simply a means to filter money. He pondered it for only a blink. Luster cared only about the paycheck.

"Works for me, Craig. Let's get moving."

Craig watched in amazement as Luster created his ring of computers. He'd wired four of the laptops in a circle around the oak desk. Within minutes, scrolling lines of code began spiraling down the screens. Craig paced behind him for a while, feeding him information about the online casino. Eventually, the pitter-patter of typing lulled Agent Craig to sleep on the couch. Luster didn't sleep, working ambitiously through the night. Occasionally, Craig would wake to the sound of room service or a flushing toilet. He loved the anonymity of Mexico. He could finally sleep soundly.

CHAPTER 7

Undisclosed Location in North San Diego County

33°8'5.8696"N 116°58'7.2803"W

Four Weeks Later

The secluded auditorium was perfect for the RC test. The run-down building reeked of stagnant water. It was completely secluded, located far off the beaten path in North County.

The trashcan unit was complete. It had been tested and was fully operational. Nguyen appeared thinner. Her face strained with a look that could only be caused by heavy deadlines and intense stress. Despite her tension, she looked put together and sultry. Craig glanced away from the control panels and diagrams occasionally, specifically to watch her walk or bend down to the trashcan RC.

Luster sat in the office at the apartment, adjusting the controls for the trashcan unit. He'd finished the poker room program weeks ago and was now back on American soil. He'd contributed greatly to the software and programming of the fifteen individual RCs as well as the trashcan housing. Briggs popped open another can of soda, spilling a few fizzy drops on the desk as he answered the radio.

"Briggs, Luster? You ready?" Craig's voice was unmistakable on the radio.

"Ready, Sir."

"Timing is crucial here, boys. Get it right. We only have one shot when it's go time."

"We're on it. We practiced this time." Briggs and Luster spent the last week prepping for the test. They ran through hundreds of scenarios and obstacles. They knew the machines inside and out.

Craig clicked the button on the left side of his watch, setting the countdown. "Start the clock."

Briggs clicked the start button on his screen. The numbers began climbing, beeping every ten seconds.

"Phase one, go." Craig was anxious to see the drones at work.

One by one, the disc-shaped units filed from the trashcan. They exited out of a sliding door on the bottom of the can like an upside-down Pez dispenser. The units quickly moved to their designated, pre-calculated spots in the auditorium. Briggs watched the screens through the eyes of all fifteen units. They were small, but packed a front and rear camera, giving him a 360-degree view of their area. The units stopped and waited in position.

"Twenty seconds, blow the decoy." Craig watched the shiny hands on his watch tick, imagining the scenario. Luster clicked the button on the satellite-operated detonator. A light bulb flashed in the auditorium, signaling that the decoy had been destroyed. "Phase two; go!"

Phase two was trickier. Luster and Briggs needed to drive the smaller, individual units from the trashcan RC, down the jetway to the pilots' cabin. Practicing the stunt was excruciating. The total distance that needed to be manually driven was only ten meters, but time was a crucial factor. Every second that passed was an opportunity for the waiting units to be caught, dismantled, or destroyed.

They quickly drove the first coin-shaped RC to a chalk circle in the far end of the room. Craig smirked as it parked a few feet from him. He noticed a marking on the top of the unit that was not in the plans. He raised his radio. "Automated Vacuum? Nice touch." Briggs grinned. He painted the words: "Automated Vacuum — Please do not touch" on the top of every unit.

One by one, the discs screamed across the floor, zipping to crudely painted circles on the floor, simulating the cabin of the aircraft. "One minute, seven seconds! We can do better than that — AGAIN!" Craig barked. Nguyen cringed as he made the team rework the scenario.

Their boots echoed through the room as they paced, watching the RCs move back into place. After eight attempts, the trashcan unit successfully moved all fifteen mini-units to their designated targets in less than a minute.

Harbor Island Drive

San Diego, CA | 32°43'30.4532"N 117°11'48.1135"W

Two Blocks South of the San Diego International Airport

The alley reeked of spilled liquor and dusty bricks. Briggs pulled the van as far back as possible. The 3:00 a.m. darkness concealed his vehicle nicely. Briggs hopped out and opened the side door on the van. It whooshed open, slamming loudly as it hit its widest point. The trashcan RC was heavy. He shuffled as he moved the unit to the pavement. With a sly thud, the unit met the earth. He sent a text to Luster, closed the van door, and slowly pulled from the alley. His head popped out of the window awkwardly as he waited for the sparse traffic to allow him to pass. He checked his mirrors one final time as he shifted from reverse to drive. The unit was in place and ready for the next phase.

San Diego housed the perfect airport for the mission. It was open 24 hours a day, however, flights rarely flew in past 10:00 p.m. or earlier than 7:00 a.m because of the strict noise laws surrounding the airfield. In the early morning, the building was nearly empty. The only busy portion of the airport was the tarmac, where waiting planes piled together, waiting for the morning rush. "The airport opens in a few hours." Craig's text was blunt. They were on the clock.

Luster moved the trashcan RC forward. It was a delicate, patient process. The unit was two blocks from the airport and needed to remain completely unnoticed. Luster moved the trashcan at a momentum that made standing water look like a hurricane. He watched the speed on the far corner of the screen, allowing a max of less than half a mile per hour. The unit slowed to a stop whenever a vehicle or pedestrian was in sight.

Briggs drove away slowly. He had oodles of time to spare. He dropped off the van and picked up his car from the dark end of the parking lot. On the way back to the apartment, he picked up a burger, a 12-pack of soda, a pack of cigarettes, and a losing lotto ticket.

Minutes turned to hours as the delicate process of driving to the airport dragged on. Luster watched a zombie flick on his left monitor as the RC crept forward. He'd successfully crossed the street to the airport, which was a much quicker process. Luster didn't want to creep across the intersection, in fear that the unit would be struck by a car. He floored it across the pedestrian walkway at 20 miles per hour. Thankfully, no one was around to witness the possessed trashcan.

The parking lot was trickier. Airport employees were constantly pulling into the parking area, forcing the trashcan unit to stop. Groups of coffee shop workers and flight attendants flooded the lots. Luster slowed the RC down as the unit approached the entrance to the building. Millimeters were an excruciating milestone. Electric doors were fast. They opened with a whoosh and closed hard as people passed through. He drove the trashcan near the door, moving silently toward the crowd. Luster watched with intrigue as a maintenance golf cart pulled into view. The man whistled and looked curiously at the can. Luster held his breath as the man reached for the lid. He pulled, stopped, and pulled again at the top of the trashcan. After struggling uselessly, he shook his head, kicked the can, and hopped back into the cart. The room gasped as the tension lifted. Luster moved the RC into the path of the open doors as a group of gift shop employees passed through. An older woman bumped into the can. She cursed loudly and moved it into the airport, unblocking the electric doors. Luster cheered silently as the first of many hurdles was cleared.

“We’re in!” Briggs huffed ecstatically.

Briggs adjusted the cameras and helped direct the unit to the first security gate. They moved the unit into an open elevator and waited for six different groups to enter and exit before they could maneuver the unit without notice. The RC passed undetected through the roped-off section of the unattended airport security section. Ironically, the security line was the easiest obstacle. There weren’t cars, elevators, or electric doors, only black ropes and signs. Luster moved the unit down the dark hallway and parked it in a corner. The airport opened in less than an hour.

Airline pilot Ron Radison walked sleepily down the walkway to the plane. Nancy, a leather-faced flight attendant, hung on his every word. He jabbered about downtown San Diego and his son’s newfound lover. A flamboyant flight attendant opened the cabin door, allowing them into the plane. Nancy giggled like a schoolgirl and took the captain’s bag to his personal baggage hold. She knew that Captain Radison was a slam clicker (a pilot who goes straight to his hotel room, slams the door, and locks it), but she didn’t care. She had a hankering for Ron. More importantly, she had a desire for Ron’s wallet. Ron thanked her and winked back to her as she started getting the plane ready for the first passengers.

Ron plopped into his captain’s chair, greeting the co-pilot with a yawn. The co-pilot, a young man of thirty, handed Ron a coffee and began the checklist:

Parking brake — set.
Throttle — idle.
Battery master switch — on.
Generator switch — on.
Fuel quantity — check.
Flaps — up.

The co-pilot's eyes squinted from the intense flash. As he opened his eyes, the flicker strobed from the belly of a distant plane on the runway. Ron shrieked, shielding his eyes. A deep explosion followed the blistering light. The detonation was strong enough to deafen their ears and shake the plane. Ron pulled his hands away from his face, exposing the red ball of fire and warmth that could be felt through their cockpit window. The 747 billowed balls of fire from every window like a gas burner on a rusted stove. "Holy shit, Ron!" The co-pilot was struggling wildly to get unbuckled.

"Phase one, complete; moving to stage two," Luster said clearly on the radio.

Craig lightly gripped his black coffee as he listened to the radio. He watched the intense explosion on the runway from a seat in terminal two. He raised his hand to his mouth and spoke quietly into his hidden microphone in his sleeve. "Go for phase two."

The trashcan RC opened, kicking out the small round RCs. Each of the discs zipped across the carpet, gliding effortlessly to its target. Luster and Briggs watched in the monitors as each RC reached its destination. Luster grabbed the controls for the first unit. He manually drove down the jetty to the open door of the plane, dodging the screaming flight crews. The large gap between the walkway and the plane caused the RC to jerk and tremble as it hopped into the plane.

Ron held Nancy closely as the small disc-shaped unit rolled into the cockpit. Nancy looked down curiously. "Ron, what is this?" As Luster pressed the button, a screen popped up from the top of the unit. "Pilot. We can see you. Get everyone off the plane, except you and your co-pilot. Once everyone is off and we are alone, I will give you further instructions. If you get off the plane, I will detonate, along with fourteen other planes in the terminal."

Ron looked frantically at Nancy. "Go! Get everyone off the plane!" By the time he ended his sentence, she was already running toward the door. Self-preservation was clearly her motivation. Ron made an announcement to any of the remaining staff. A few yelps and fearful cries were heard as the airplane emptied.

Briggs and Luster repeated the process for all fourteen planes, reaching each plane in less than one minute. "Phase two, complete," Luster announced on the radio.

Ensenada Military Airport
Ensenada Municipality, Baja California, MX
31°47'43"N 116°36'09"W

The phone buzzed loudly on his belt. Lopez looked at the text, picked up his microphone, and called over the loudspeaker in Spanish. Armed military personnel exploded from their tents as the call echoed through the airfield. Lopez watched out his window as three tanks and fourteen jeeps pulled into place.

San Diego International Airport — Airfield
San Diego, CA | 32°43'58.1362"N 117°11'27.4111"W

Fifteen sets of pilots stared at the disc-shaped RCs, waiting eagerly for their next command. Luster and Briggs watched their faces in the monitor as they sent the instructions. The orders were vague. They needed to get the planes in the air and head south. Coordinates would be sent after all of the planes were in formation. Ron read the message and began the flight checklist.

Ron's voice shook as he called to the tower: "U.S. Flight 223-Adam, permission for takeoff, Red Code Flight Adam-Charlie."

The control tower heard his words over the radio with an avalanche of emotion. Tower controllers knew what Red Code Flight Adam-Charlie meant. The transmission could be loosely translated: "We're being hijacked — Oh God, do something!" Controllers now knew that the explosion was not an accident, but an act of terrorism. Wide eyes blazed around the tower and emergency procedures were pulled from dusty binders below their desks. A man bearing a five o'clock shadow jumped up and ran to the center of the room. He lifted a clear plastic shield from a red button labeled "DO NOT PUSH — CODE RED ONLY." He raised the shield and slammed his open palm on the button. The airport immediately began to shut down. Cashier and ticket lines closed. Thick metal shields dropped slowly over the hangar doors. Curious travelers stared at the monitors that once held flight information, reading the evacuation procedures.

Tower personnel spoke calmly to Ron and his co-pilot: "Tower to U.S. Flight 223-Adam, you are not clear for takeoff. Proceed to runway three for evac, copy?"

Ron gripped the radio tightly. "No tower, Flight 223-Adam will blow up if we don't get off the ground! I am taxiing to runway two and taking off. Clear the runway!"

Tower officers frantically placed miniature planes on the glass replica of the airfield as they planned for his takeoff. Seven other pilots called the tower informing the tower of the hijacking. Tower radio operators were overwhelmed, but calmly relayed the "DNF" (do not fly) command, with little cooperation.

Ron drove the plane to the airstrip and pressed the throttle levers. The co-pilot was ghostly white. Ron disregarded the tower's commands and blew past the first set of stripes on the runway. The thunderous roar of the engines rumbled behind Ron as he gained speed. The control tower watched helplessly as Flight 223-Adam raced down the airstrip. The nose lifted, pushing Ron back in his seat. With a sudden sway, the blistering engines lifted the plane from the runway.

Flight 5434-King followed dangerously behind Ron's plane. He too disregarded the tower's instruction and blew across the airfield. Flight 9423-Yellow, 234-07-Henry, and eleven other planes followed, bunching together closely like cattle trying to get through a single gate.

Agent Craig looked at his watch as the final plane was airborne. He sipped his coffee as he walked toward the exit. Nervous passengers and staff filed out of the security gates into the parking lots. He sent a text to Lt. Lopez in Mexico: "FIFTEEN IN THE AIR."

CHAPTER 8

Transportation Security Administration Headquarters

Arlington, VA | 38°51'40.4326"N 77°3'29.1797"W

The ceramic coffee mug made a hollow thump as it tipped on the table. Coffee raged from the mug, spilling a splotch of black liquid onto the director's pant leg. "Damnit, are you fucking kidding me?" the director of the Transportation Security Administration yelled as he received notice of the hijacking. "No, Sir, fifteen planes out of San Diego International." The director's assistant was nervous to deliver the news. The director picked up the phone and called the building operator. "Get me on a secure line and transfer me to the FBI airfare division." He heard a series of beeps and waited on the line. He wiped his pants slowly with a handkerchief while the line rang.

"FBI Office of Aviation Enforcement," the gruff voice announced.

"I need a complete containment on San Diego Airport, Code Yellow."

The man on the other end of the line sighed apprehensively. "I'll send a team from the San Diego office immediately. Thank you. I expect a full report." The phone was abruptly silent as the ranking FBI agent slammed down the phone.

San Diego Harbor Police Headquarters
San Diego, CA | 32°43'50.2085"N 117°11'28.4926"W

The glass doors flicked open like a pinball flipper. Harbor police officers filed from the building with ballistic helmets and tactical gear. Three police cruisers, filled to the brim, sped down the short road to the airport. Their radios chattered loudly as they exploded from their vehicles, running toward the airport. Craig stood by, smoking his cigar, watching the madness ensue. He observed an FBI vehicle, seven transportation security administration trucks, three harbor police cars, and four San Diego SWAT units arrive in less than seven minutes. Impressive, he thought, but useless.

Briggs and Luster relayed coordinates to the fifteen planes. They were to fly a southeast heading to 31°47'43"N 116°36'09"W, a Mexican airport.

The flock of fifteen planes formed a V formation, as instructed. Each of the RC units was emitting a strong radar jamming frequency, which dissuaded the government from tracking their flights. Luster and Briggs relaxed a bit as the planes headed toward the U.S./Mexico border; however, Craig knew the U.S. would retaliate.

San Diego Air Station Miramar (MCAS Miramar)

San Diego, CA | 32°52'04"N 117°08'30"W

Marine airfield officers waved orange wands, directing six FA-18 Super Hornet fighter planes to the runway. The airstrip was buzzing with military personnel, all reacting exactly as they'd been trained. The tint-faced helmets of the pilots gave the tower a thumbs-up and hissed down the runway. Twelve minutes after the planes had been hijacked, the Marines had six fighter planes in the air, headed to intercept the hijacked fleet.

The cramped cockpits of the fighter jets were cold and surprisingly silent. The earth below was a blur as they breached several levels of the sound barrier.

"MCAS Hornet four-niner to command; authorization to down?" the squad leader of the fighter jets called over the airwaves for the rules of engagement. The pilots rarely knew their mission until they were in the air.

"MCAS command tower, ROE (rules of engagement) are as follows: Stop the threat if hijacked civilian planes drop below 2000 feet near civilian population."

The squad leader acknowledged and relayed the message to the other pilots.

From the airport, Craig watched overhead as he heard, and saw, the pack of fighter planes zip past.

The White House
Washington, DC | 38°53'51.61"N 77°2'11.58"W

A voice called from a tan phone on his desk: "Mr. President, the line is ready for you." The President pushed the grey button labeled "speaker" and began to wring his hands.

"Go ahead," he spoke firmly.

"Sir? We need to make a decision on this. Do we have permission to take down the planes over Mexican airspace?"

The President focused on the painting on the wall of the Oval Office. Past President Lincoln stared back without offering a hint of wisdom.

"Sir…we need an answer now, the jets are approaching the strike distance."

The President looked at the fresh letter from the Mexican Ambassador. The letter guaranteed, "Mexican military and law enforcement personnel would handle the situation professionally." Their statement: "We will do our best to bring the U.S. pilots back to safety" was less than reassuring. The letter aggressively continued with, "U.S. troops on (or above) our soil will be considered an act of war, even during these dire circumstances."

"Abort." The President gritted his teeth.

The general on the other end of the line used his words carefully. "Confirming, abort interception of hijacked U.S. planes?"

"Confirmed, abort. But call the ambassador. Make sure he gets us an updated report on our pilots every ten minutes. Don't give him a second to think we're not watching." He clicked the speakerphone off, closing his conversation with the U.S. General. The President knew the cartels had corrupted the Mexican Government. The planes were never to be seen again. He stood, pacing in the Oval Office.

San Diego Marine Corps Air Station Miramar (MCAS Miramar)

San Diego, CA | 32°52'04"N 117°08'30"W

Seconds after the U.S. General hung up with the President, his message spread to computer terminals at MCAS Miramar in San Diego.

"MCAS command tower, Bravo to Hornet Command," the tower called immediately.

"MCAS Hornet four-niner squad leader, go ahead." The pilot's voice was muffled, but understandable.

"Four-niner, abort mission, return to base."

"Copy MCAS, bringing them home." The jets quickly changed directions, turning sharply back toward the base. The mission was over.

Ensenada Military Airport

Ensenada Municipality, Baja California, MX
31°47'43"N 116°36'09"W

Lieutenant Lopez watched callously from behind a pair of sunglasses as the runway danced with activity. Soldiers stood in formation along every entrance to the airfield, ensuring no one got in or out. Lopez twisted his mustache as he heard the first approaching aircraft. The anti-aircraft missile stations were set up along every corner, ensuring that any trailing United States military would be brought down. Lopez already knew the U.S. would whimper when they realized their presence would be considered an invasion.

The first airliner approached the runway. Wings seesawed as it dropped to the ground, creating a massive dust cloud as it touched the tar. Military vehicles led the plane to a far corner of the airstrip. The second plane landed a bit more smoothly. Its wheels were steady as they pillowed onto the tarmac. Lopez counted as they landed, sending periodic text messages to Craig.

Number 11 began its decent a bit early. Lopez gasped as the engines aggressively accelerated. Lopez screamed into the microphone as the plane tipped. The pilots did not intend to become prisoners.

The plane increased to maximum velocity as it reached the airfield. The wings jolted clockwise, spilling a hail of sparks and debris onto the runway. The plane groaned and bounced along the earth. Its hull snapped. Colossal fragments of the jet rolled violently along the tarmac like a rolling pin. Lopez sprinted from the tower as the fragmented metal tumbled, spewing fire from the broken engines. The turbines spun from the wreckage, sending the splintered jets into a group of nearby jeeps. The cockpit snapped from the metal, sloping toward the tower. Lopez hollered into his radio as he broke free from the building. Shock waves shattered windows and deafened the ground crews. Sand, steel, and blips of flame erupted from the building. The tower fell slowly. Steel beams contorted with eerie moans as the structure splashed the pavement. The next four planes followed suit. One after another, the planes kamikazed into the runway, blowing fiery jet fuel along every inch of the cement. The air was thick with heavy smoke, embers, and molten metal. Falling glass rained on the runway like a gentle snowstorm.

"Five airplanes crash, ten no crash." Lopez sent the message to Craig, awaiting instruction.

Lopez barked orders for his troops to put out the fires as he headed for his jeep. He slapped on his seatbelt and wiped the soot from his uniform. He drove to the end of the gravel road, approaching the black SUVs with caution. Twelve tinted SUVs waited. Lopez parked, apprehensively climbing out of the jeep.

The doors of the closest SUV opened, exposing Eric Price, the BlackRiver executive.

"Fine day for a barbeque; eh, Lieutenant?" Price smirked as he watched the distant fires roar.

"We only haf ten planes layft...What'choo want to do?" The deal clearly called for fifteen planes. Lopez was stuck with only ten planes, a global news story, and an airfield covered in smoldering jet fuel.

"I only need seven. The other guy can have the last three." Price motioned to the other set of black SUVs. "But we should hurry; the press will be all over us in less than an hour."

Price followed Lopez to the burning runway. Ten intact planes were huddled together in the nearby field. Distance shielded the aircraft from the explosions, however, tar, dust, and other debris toupeed the jets. Mexican military swiftly escorted the pilots into a waiting prison bus. The pilots were instructed to tell the news reporters: "The hijackers were Asian men dressed in casual clothing, speaking in an indiscernible foreign language."

The planes were stripped clean: identifying numbers removed and replaced with European tracking numbers. The GPS units were found and destroyed. The black boxes and secondary tracking systems were also found and demolished. The crews used welders, ladders, wrenches, paint, metal snips, and twenty-seven minutes to completely re-identify the planes. Price whistled to his patient pilots. Doors opened on the dark SUVs. Seven pilots stepped from their seats. They were dressed in full combat uniforms and sported precision haircuts. Maturity and war crimes were etched deeply in their faces as they shielded their eyes from the Mexican sun. They huddled around Price as he assigned them each a plane. BlackRiver had completely taken over the operation. More doors opened exposing flight staff and take-off coordinators. Rugged laptops sent encrypted signals, disturbing air traffic worldwide. The scrambled transmission allowed a window of safety for the planes to take off and mesh with commercial traffic.

Jürg Becker, the silent buyer, sat behind tinted glass. He, too, waved for his pilots to take the remaining three planes. He relied heavily on BlackRiver's technology to allow him to slip into air traffic. He paid handsomely for the help.

Price slipped back into his truck, calling Agent Craig for the final transaction.

"Agent Craig," he answered after several rings.

"Craig, It's Price. Sixty million each?"

"Always negotiating!" He smiled, despite the fiscal loss of the other five planes.

"I've got kids to feed, wars to fund."

"Sixty-five each. Transfer it when your wheels are off the ground."

"All right, all right, tell you what. I'll buy the other five if you scrape the pilots off the cockpits!" Price snickered.

"You're a sick fuck, Price. And no, they're staying where they are."

"Done deal...always a pleasure, Craig." Price hung up the phone. He closed the SUV door and put on an air-traffic headset. He cleared his staff to jam the American continent's air control database. With a few simple buttons, every screen that tracked airlines in the U.S. and Mexico squirmed with static. Their new planes were cleared for taking off. Wheels bumped over demolished debris as they lifted from the tarmac.

PART TWO

CHAPTER 9

Rochester, MN | 44°1'21.8908"N 92°27'15.1579"W
The Residence of Decklin Marks

"Forks make brilliant back scratchers." Decklin smiled at his simple discovery.

Decklin Marks was a business manager by day and a husband and stepfather by night. His SUV was luxurious...10 years ago. His wife was beautiful, young, and outspoken. His stepson was five: hyper, fighting, singing, running, and not sleeping when asked. He was an adorable, typical boy.

Decklin's life was blissfully ordinary. His wild teenage years gave him experience in alcohol and drug use, while his twenties offered life lessons and bills. For Decklin, the rush of the single life was over and the *3:00 a.m. sick-kid wakeup* had begun. It wasn't bad though, not in the slightest. He happily gave up blonde girls and fast cars for barbeque tongs and bedtime stories. He devoted himself to his bride and her son. The story about her son's father was long, complicated, and normally ended with a disappointing grimace from those who heard it.

Decklin put the fork down on the nightstand, grinning stupidly at the amazing scratching ability of the common fork. It was nearly 7:00 a.m. Their apartment was small enough to hear Pete in the other bedroom. He was eager to start the day, loudly playing with a few action figures, running around in his undies.

"All right, kiddo, we've gotta get moving. Get your clothes on!" Decklin said playfully.

Pete responded with the murmur of simulated gunfire from the action figures. Decklin knew he'd need to ask three or four more times, but it didn't matter. His own routine took fifteen minutes versus Pete's routine which consisted of:

> Play.
> Put an article of clothing on.
> Play a little bit more.
> Fall down on something; pretend to get hurt.
> Get another article of clothing on.
> Brush teeth while goofing around with whatever toy lay on the counter.

It took twenty-two minutes for Decklin and Pete to head out the door. Pete was dressed haphazardly in whatever jeans he found in his drawer and a mismatched sweatshirt Decklin made him wear because of the chilly weather. Pete jumped into his booster seat and immediately started fiddling with the window button. Decklin hopped into the car and turned over the engine. The music was loud, clearly left over from the previous drive home from work. Pete covered his ears and waited for the volume to decrease to a more acceptable level. "So dramatic," Decklin mumbled to himself. They pulled from the parking lot and headed to daycare. Their normal conversations were rarely normal. Pete used his time with Decklin to sing, kick the seat, and ask questions about birds, dinosaurs, and giraffes.

They signed in at daycare and Decklin departed after sharing a hug, a quick wrestle, and a genuine: "I love you, have a great day."

Decklin hopped into his SUV and cranked the tunes. The eight-minute drive to work usually passed rather quickly. He sipped his coffee while mouthing the words to the song. Once at work, it was game time. Greetings were mandatory as he walked into the building. He always had a smile on his face, but was respected as a solid salesman and business partner. His desk was littered with photos of his wife, Angela, as well as funny pictures of Pete and crude drawings that he had accumulated from Pete's years at daycare.

He sighed and opened his laptop. His day had begun. His inbox was stacked with unanswered questions, as usual. One by one, he clicked, answered, and archived the email. Curiously, by 9:30, he reached the top of the list. One of the final emails was of a personal nature, so he ignored it until nearly 11:00. When he finally opened it, he discovered it was from a credit score company. He was pleasantly surprised. His normally low score had jumped nearly 100 points. There are times in life when one questions errors. And others that one should ask no questions and simply smile. This was somewhere in the middle.

Decklin looked over his open accounts and various items on the credit list. He stopped scrolling when he noticed a peculiar line item: NORTH COAST BANK — CA. He clicked the account information and quickly received a branch phone number. The phone rang directly to a teller.

"Hi, I just checked my credit score and I see that I have an account open with you? Can you tell me more about this?" Decklin was inquisitive, but courteous. The woman on the other end asked a few identifying questions, which were strangely correct. I really have an account there? Someone musta stole my ID and opened a ton of credit cards. Decklin wondered as she placed him on hold.

The on-hold music sounded like the ugly baby of a piano bar and a Christmas store. Eventually, she came back on the line: "Hi, Decklin? Are you there?"

"Yes, Ma'am, I am here."

"Hi, Decklin; I'd be happy to go over your account with you."

"Oh, okay. What do I have open with your branch?"

"You have three credit cards and two savings accounts."

Shit! I knew it! Decklin thought. "Three credit cards? How much is owed on each?"

"Well, you've been great on your balance. It seems that you've paid everything off and your limit has been raised!"

The confusion was blinding. Decklin couldn't help but scratch his head. "Paid off? Okay...how much is in the savings accounts?"

"Let me check." Her typing sounded like a battle drum. Decklin wondered if all banks were required to purchase extra-loud keyboards in order to make sure the customers could hear them work. "It looks like...after your transfer yesterday, you have seven hundred eighteen million, four hundred sixty-five thousand, two hundred forty-eight dollars and thirty-two cents."

The earth could have been collapsing behind Decklin and he wouldn't have noticed. He looked down at his scratch pad, glaring at the figure: $718,465,248.32. He could hardly swallow as he asked her the next question: "Can I wire five million into my local account?"

He took the afternoon off, waiting patiently in the bank for the teller to confirm the wire. He sat in an uncomfortable office chair, secluded from the other banking customers. His fingers tapped on the desk in anticipation.

BUZZ! The vibrate function on his cell phone startled him. He pulled out the phone and read: "Hi, babe, how is work?" He closed the phone and put it back in his pocket. He knew his wife would be upset, completely overjoyed, and then upset again because of the *mild* dishonesty of the transfer. An uptight banker walked into the office, smiled falsely, and sat across from him. "Mr...Marks? I have your transfer, but it appears we may have an issue."

Here it comes. The moment of truth. What mess have I gotten myself into? Will mobsters come busting in the doors and drag me off into some fat guy's car to make me sleep with the fishes? Or will a swarm of police cars come busting in at any second? Fuck! What is the problem, banker guy, tell me already! Decklin smiled calmly and asked, "What is the issue, Sir?"

He half-smirked and looked at Decklin with all-knowing eyes. He could judge his soul, knowing that he'd never seen that much money in his life and had no idea how to handle such large transactions, or how to talk to bankers. "We...well...we don't have that much currency in this branch. We'll need to order it from corporate."

Decklin's eyebrows danced an unhappy ballet as he learned for the first time that banks stock money like grocery stores stock soup. "How much do you have here?"

"We have about two million, but I can have the rest here by Friday." He suddenly seemed more willing to help.

"Friday is fine. Can I have the two million today?"

He stood, walked to the teller, pointed, and talked in hushed, banking voices. He returned quickly with a small envelope. "There you go, Sir. May I encourage you to keep at least one million here in a trust or a money market savings account?"

Decklin lifted the small envelope and peered inside. It was heavy, but no wider than a few candy bars. "Is this...is this really two million dollars?" Decklin was stunned. "Two million bucks fits into this little envelope?" He always imagined a silver briefcase filled to the brim. His thoughts remained quiet as he began counting the clusters of hundred-dollar bills. The banker again encouraged investments. It occurred to him that the banker may be getting some heat for allowing a customer to withdraw this much money. He pulled a single bill from the envelope and flicked it across the table. "For your troubles." Decklin grinned like an oil mogul tipping a stripper.

The banker's expression was not the expected gleeful thanks, but instead, he slowly slid the bill back across the table, grinning ear to ear with stuffy arrogance. "Thank you. But I do not accept tips."

The bank staff bid a heartfelt farewell as Decklin walked from the branch office, tightly gripping the jacket pocket containing the envelope, imagining that a gust of wind might blow away his fortune. Quickly entering his car, he locked the doors suspiciously. He pulled out his phone and read Angela's text one more time. His mind raced with the theories of what might happen if he didn't tell her and something were to go wrong. He knew he couldn't tell her. It was a terrible idea. The worst part was, he knew that it was impossible to keep things from her. He prided himself in being independent and completely brutal in the "real world" when needed. But there was something sick that chewed at him when he held onto a secret. He clicked through the keys and sent her a message: "I have 2 million dollars. How's work for you, babe?" He hoped the subtlety would work. The very second he clicked send, the phone buzzed, hissed, rang, and screamed with her caller ID on the screen.

Decklin swirled his drink and looked around the restaurant nervously. His wife was on her way to meet him. Every few seconds, he felt through his jacket for the envelope. *Still there*, followed by a sigh of relief.

She walked in through the front door and looked about the restaurant. He raised an arm casually, calling her to his table. She was thin, short, and as cute as they come. She was a mom, but dressed with a class that could only be found through years of good taste. She seated herself across the booth and told the waiter to get her a glass of red from the cheap side of the list. She didn't waste a second after the waiter left the table.

"What the hell do you mean you have two million dollars?"

Decklin pulled the envelope from his pocket and slid it across the table. As she opened it, her eyes exploded in what could only be described as catastrophic overstimulation.

"Where did you get this, Decklin?" She sounded like she was asking her five-year-old son.

He told her the story...and told her everything. He emphasized the details around having a fresh start, without having to order from the bottom side of the wine list. They wouldn't need to worry about rent, groceries, and daycare. She of course, focused on the obvious.

"Who put seven hundred million dollars into your account? And what made you think that you could pull that money out, even though it clearly wasn't yours?" She continued through various scenarios, all of which ended with Decklin either going to jail, or ending up in a predicament with a bad crowd. Decklin bargained, begged, tried to sell and reached for any story that would somehow allow her to relax. Without success.

Before he could reach the end of his glass, she had pulled him from his seat and out of the restaurant. The short car ride was quiet and tense. They reached the police department in less than five minutes. Once again, Decklin was dragged from his seat and in through the front entrance.

Angela stood in line, waiting for the next counter attendant. The bored officer looked at her with apathy and asked what she needed to report. She spoke with gusto as she told the counter clerk the story. His eyes widened when she whipped out the wad of cash and slid it across the counter. The officer picked up a white phone on the wall and called for a senior officer.

"I can't believe you just took it, Decklin." She scolded, "What were you thinking? You think you can take this much money from an account that clearly isn't yours and have no one notice? You know how much trouble we could be in?" She crossed her legs in the waiting room chair. She was clearly upset. Decklin knew he'd done it. As he had a hundred other times. He didn't think it through and only saw green dollar signs where he should have seen bright red flags.

"Angela Marks?" The door buzzed open and an older, well-built police officer called them into a back room. They followed him through the corridor of interview rooms and offices. They were swiftly seated in a cold room with steel chairs.

"My apologies for the criminal-looking room. Our conference room is being used by the captains today." The officer was kinder than expected. "Tell me about this money. How did you get two million dollars cash?"

Angela glared at Decklin, enticing him to tell the story. After a few uncomfortable stares, he began. He told the officer that his standard credit check uncovered an account in his name, and about the wire transfer, the stuffy local banker, and a few other side notes that may have added to the story. The officer smirked, nodded, and asked appropriate questions at the appropriate times. Decklin ended the story with, "...and then we decided that the right thing to do was to come here and tell you."

Angela, once again, glared in his direction. She knew very well that he would have never reported the money had it not been for her honesty.

After a few minutes of silence, the officer looked over his notes and smugly pushed the envelope across the table. "I've gotta tell you Mr. and Mrs. Marks, I've never heard anything like this." Angela smiled politely, awaiting the officer's resolution. "In Minnesota, we don't have any laws that deny a person rights to their own property. It would seem that there was an error in the banking system and you ended up getting lucky. This is more of a civil matter. No criminal offense has occurred." Decklin sat smugly in his chair.

"May I offer you two some advice? I would put this cash in a safe and see what happens. The banks will most likely contact you about the mistake. Federal law mandates that all financial errors are to be fixed within seven days, or the transaction cannot be reversed."

Decklin perked up. "So you are telling me that if we hold this envelope for seven days and we aren't contacted, or my account isn't reversed, we get to keep it?"

"It would appear that you may be in luck, Mr. Marks. Wait it out and see what happens. If seven days goes by, feel free to pop in and take me out for dinner!" Everyone chuckled. "Of course, I am kidding, we cannot accept any type of gratuity."

Seven days, six minutes, and thirty-six seconds after the transaction, Decklin was sitting on the floor in front of the safe. His eyes were bright as he watched the envelope. His cell phone sat on the floor next to him. It was silent in the room as he contemplated with glee.

Over the course of the next two weeks, Decklin and Angela spent 78,269 dollars. They picked up shiny new cars. They went to fancy dinners, coffee houses, and took a weekend trip to Boston, just to see the city. Their bills were paid, their banks were full, and their smiles were seemingly endless.

They soon were signing papers for a new house on the river. The home was Victorian in style and needed a few repairs, but the two were ecstatic about finding an eclectic home downtown. As Decklin walked from the mortgage office to his car, his phone rang.

"Yellow!" Decklin answered.

"Mr. Marks, this is Officer Kitts from the police department; how are you today?"

Decklin's heart nearly burst with anxiety. "Good afternoon, Officer, what can I do for you?" He leaned on his car, shaking with total fear. Why is he calling me? What does he want? I knew this would happen! I am in so much trouble, he thought.

"Mr. Marks, I had a chance to re-review your case. I've gotta be honest, your story baffled me. I spoke with a colleague about it and he is very interested in looking into your case."

"Sir?" He paused. "We already spent a lot of money...I thought we weren't responsible for the bank error after a week!"

"No, no, you aren't in trouble, the law is the law. You should be completely fine, but it is very unusual. Would you meet with my guy and just tell him about it? He is very curious, I mean, this type of error doesn't happen every day."

Decklin paused. He contemplated turning him down and simply living under a rock with his fortune. The image of Angela's glare set his mind straight. "Sure, I would be happy to meet with him. It is just to tell him my story, right? You promise I am not in trouble?"

"Absolutely, you are not in any danger of criminal charges, Mr. Marks."

Decklin took down the detective's information on the back of an envelope. The conversation ended smoothly, with a courteous farewell. Decklin stared at the number on the paper. He was still shaking, but could tell by the officer's tone that the investigation was simply curiosity. Either way, he knew he needed to play this one by the books.

He slowly dialed the number. The screen blinked, dialed, and soon the crisp sound of a ringing line could be heard.

CHAPTER 10

Charles Unit Investigations

Rochester, MN | 44°3'58.7228"N 92°29'15.3165"W

The investigator's office was tucked between an industrial warehouse and a strip mall. Decklin eyed the address he'd written on the back of an envelope versus the address crudely painted on the door. He knocked on the frosted glass window, waited a few moments and entered. He realized immediately that the investigator was independent, in no way affiliated with the local police.

The waiting room was clean but reminiscent of another era. The walls were lined with wood paneling and the floor was solid oak. A massive brownish-red rug lay in the center of the room, obviously hiding the age of the wood flooring. The brown leather couch was sunburned from sitting in front of the window. He sat, taking in the musty scents of cigarettes and settled dust. The walls were filled with bookshelves and photos. Most of the pictures were images of men in uniforms, standing proudly with their guns. A plethora of certificates and awards crookedly hung on the far wall: Acts of Valor, Lifesaving, and Prestigious Investigations. The wall was a shadowbox of detective work. Decklin fixated on the brass globe that sat along the wall. The world of Ikea clean, modern living eluded the black hole of speakeasy style decorations.

Decklin heard a chair scrape across the floor in the adjacent office. A man's shadow paced toward the waiting room door. With a click of the brass doorknob, the door opened.

Charles Unit stood in the door. His slender, but masculine features overtook the doorway. He was in his late forties, showing a tan adventure along every line of his brow. Charles stretched a hand to Decklin and smiled.

"You must be Decklin Marks, the instant millionaire." Charles had a confident and mysterious air to his words. He wore a tailored mustache, as well as a collared shirt, vest, and suspenders that oozed with old-style tradition.

"Yep. Yes, Sir, I am." Decklin shook his hand, feeling the masculine dryness of his experienced hand.

"Come in, sit down..." Charles opened the door, exposing an unorganized, dark office. "Coffee? Whiskey?"

Decklin felt the oddness of the room as he entered. It was dim, lit by a single green hooded lamp on the desk. Filing cabinets were vomiting paperwork while the end tables held crystal glasses and bottles of brown liquor. The walls were decorated with off-center corkboards and mug shots.

"Coffee would be great, thanks."

"Black?" Charles sauntered over to a tall, antique-style coffee tower. He pulled the silver lever, dripping the steaming java into a glass mug.

"No, I'll have a few scoops of cream and sugar, please. Thanks!"

Charles finished pouring the cup with little grace. He ignored the sugar and cream request, placing the steaming cup on the edge of his massive desk. His eyes glimmered a look that could only be described as a hint of sarcasm that mated with a drill sergeant's snicker.

"Yeah, black is fine, too." Decklin watched as he poured a shot of brown liquor into his own glass.

"I'm glad you came. I heard of your incident and wanted to look into it. It's a civil matter, so the locals can't do a lot about it. But my antennas went up the second I heard."

Decklin sat back in the stiff leather chair across from the investigator. He wasn't necessarily intimidated; he simply felt an alpha presence.

"Where did the money come from?" Charles leaned forward, changing the atmosphere in the room. He commanded attention with his question. His words carried a weight that only a seasoned investigator held.

"Not a clue! Am I in some kind of trouble? The police told me…" Decklin felt immediately defensive. His mind spun with the thoughts: Why did I even come here? This guy thinks I've doing something wrong! I've gotta get the hell outta here!

Charles cut him off before he could finish his sentence. "Hold on, son. No, you aren't in any trouble; I'm just starting at the bottom and working my way to the top. I believe you."

The tension slid from Decklin's body. "You had me worried there for a minute. So, what do you need from me?" Even if he wasn't in trouble, the fight or flight moment took hold; Decklin wanted to leave, badly.

"To cut to the chase, Decklin, I think you've been a victim of identity theft. I would really like to look at the origin of these transfers." Charles slid a form from a folder. "Can you sign here, giving me permission to look at your accounts? I won't raise any flags or let anyone know that you spent their money, if that is what you are worried about."

"Heh, yes, that is exactly what I am worried about! I am uncomfortable with you poking around, raising flags. Right now, no one is bugging me for anything...I don't want you to give anyone ideas."

"Legally, you are already entitled to the money, Decklin. There really isn't anything I can do to bring the heat on you. You're safe. I simply think that your name has been used for something fishy."

"Fishy? Like how?"

Charles shrugged and pointed to the unsigned pieces of paper. Decklin knew exactly what he was telling him. He wouldn't continue the conversation without signatures. He pulled a gold pen from a small stone block and signed on the Xs. One was a confidentiality agreement; another was a release of banking information and a few others that contained more small print than large. He slid the forms across the table. "Okay, so fishy like how?"

Charles looked over the forms for a second, verified the signatures, and said, "You forgot the date here," handing him the pen for one last line. Decklin wasn't thrilled, but signed and asked the question a third time. After Charles reviewed the documents, and acknowledged that they were correct, he responded: "Fishy, as in someone transferring seven hundred eighteen million into your personal savings, then withdrawing it within 72 hours; minus, of course, the five million you snuck out before they had a chance."

Decklin was dumbfounded. "How do you know the exact numbers? Did the police tell you? That was confidential information!"

Without a hint of hesitation, Charles pulled a bank statement from the folder. "It shows up on your bank statement, clear as day." Decklin stood up, pulling the statement from Charles' hand.

"How did you get this?"

"You signed a waiver…I have access to these things."

"I signed the waiver a few minutes ago; this was printed last week!"

"Yes, Sir, I wanted to know what I was getting into before I met with you. I've known you had nothing to do with it from the beginning. I just wanted your consent to look into this one. I have a hunch that this one is *big*." His eyes grew as he became excited with the anticipation of a very large case.

"Wait, so you knew I had nothing to do with this? But you still wanted to talk to me about it?"

"Again, yes, Sir. I needed your permission to go digging into your banking systems; I am always by the book." Charles winked in a way that was casual, playful, and somehow professional. He understood that Decklin was upset, but he also knew that as long as he wasn't going to get in trouble, Decklin could truly care less about the case. He just wanted to keep his money. "You'll hold onto your money, I just want to know where it came from."

Decklin regained his mild composure and sat back down. "Where do you think it came from?"

"The better question is, why you? Why in the hell would someone give money away like that..." Decklin nodded, waiting for the answer. "You have been a victim of what is commonly called *Joe Schmoe money laundering*."

"Joe Schmoe laundering?"

Charles moved the folder off the desk onto a filing cabinet, revealing a revolver, which popped out from its paper graveyard. Decklin's eyes fixated on the gun. Charles couldn't help but notice the change in his demeanor when he spotted the weapon. Charles quickly picked it up, sliding it into a holster on his waist. In the same brisk movement, he pulled a pack of Marlboros from his trousers. Pulling a large brass ashtray from a nearby table and placing it squarely on the desk, he then flipped open his lighter, exposing a tall flame that flickered and spat as he puffed on the fresh smoke. "Yes, Joe Schmoe laundering. It's a very high-level job, not just anyone knows how to do that. It's risky business because of exactly what happened to you. If the wrong person gets picked to launder money through, they might realize it is there and turn out their lights before they have a chance to move the money again."

"Money laundering? High level? Now I'm worried." Decklin watched the lines of smoke fill the room as Charles leaned back in his chair. "What does this mean for me? Are people…you know? Gonna come after me?"

"Maybe. Who knows! But one thing is certain, the people that moved money through your accounts know how to cover their tracks, but I would doubt if you would hear from them." Decklin relaxed a bit after hearing the good news. "But, then again, they might come after you for their five million. It all depends on whose money this is." The comfort subsided.

"Who? Who the fuck might come after me?"

"Well, son, that is exactly why you are sitting there. I'd like to find out."

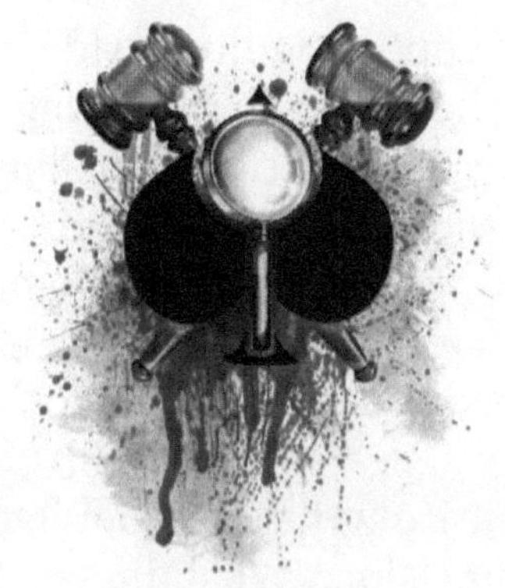

CHAPTER 11

Hotel Circle

San Diego, CA | 32°45'30.8504"N 117°10'59.5247"W

Agent Dominick Craig's Hotel Room

Craig's eyes scanned the laptop screen. Operation Terminal Altitude resulted in ten 747 airliners and a handful of dead pilots. He never anticipated such a human misjudgment on behalf of the pilots. The error was expensive. He flipped to another screen, deducting the total cost of the online casino. He put all of the funds through the poker rooms, pulling 70% from the other end. It was excruciatingly expensive to import money into the U.S.

A knock at the door startled him. His heartbeat doubled as he reached for his weapon. The peephole exposed a bubbled view of Sadie Shae. She stood with a scowl, angrily crossing her arms. Craig bounced his head on the door, weighing his options.

"I can hear you in there, Dom; let me in! We need to talk."

Craig popped the door open. Her foot tapped cynically, waiting for him to open the door wide enough for her to burst in. She pushed past him, closing the door tightly behind her. She paced, frantically looking at Craig. "What the fuck, Dom? I didn't know you were going to blow up my plane! Do you have any idea how many people have asked me questions? CIA, FBI, NSA, locals, literally everyone with a badge has rung my doorbell."

Craig pulled a chair from the small hotel table, sitting down with calculating precision. "What did you tell them, Sadie?"

She pulled her hair over her eyes, burying her face in frustration. "Nothing, Dom, you know that. I told them I knew nothing about it. It's my hangar though; they know I know something." Her glare was piercing.

"They don't know anything, that's the trick. They'll con you into saying anything just to scare you."

"I know, I know." She sat on the bed in front of Craig, shaking from stress. He leaned forward, taking her hand.

"Everything will be fine, as always. I promise."

She nodded, smiled, and then regained her attitude. She pulled her hand from his. "Who was killed on my plane? You killed people! Innocent people!"

"Shhhhh...Sade. Your plane was empty. It was a scare tactic. No one was inside the plane when it detonated."

She looked up, pondering the words. "...and the other pilots? Were those faked?"

Craig gritted his teeth a bit. "No, those were real. We had no way of knowing they would take their own lives."

Unexpectedly, her hand whipped across his cheek, slapping a red print on his face. "They weren't responsible for that, Dominick; they were innocent men and women! What the hell have you turned into?"

"The operation took casualties. It is sad, but a necessary evil to further our operational success." Craig was cold, calm, and collected.

"What operation? Let me guess, you can't tell me? This is the last time I'm doing this for you, Dom, I mean it this time."

"That's fine. I understand." He leaned back, waiting for the standard rebuttal.

"Don't *that's fine* me. I know you! That means, *Shut up, Sadie, I'll call you when I need you and you'll be there*. I mean it this time, Dom. We're done." She stood. Her anxiety was visible in every pore. Her face was a maroon shade of pink. "You know what? I'm serious. That *was* the last time." With intentionally heavy stomps, she reached the door, slamming it behind her.

Craig moved his attention from the door to his watch. He casually counted down from twenty. Precisely 18½ seconds later, the door blew open. "I am so upset!" Sadie snapped, lunging toward him on the chair. She slapped his other cheek, boasting a wrinkled expression, followed by a magnetic embrace. Her lips swiftly moved over his, locking the smoothness of their breath in a single kiss. She pulled back, slapping him again, only to return to his lips with vigor. Craig lifted their bodies from the chair. He staggered three steps, ruggedly dropping their bodies to the mattress. She viciously moved her kiss from his lips to his neck, ripping the collar aside as she moved. He pushed their bodies apart for a panicked moment, tearing his shirt from his chest. Hands scavenged for warmth along his back and biceps. Her dress was thin, pulling easily from her twisting, angry body. Craig's tanned body blanketed her smooth skin. She blindly tugged at his belt, gasping with short kisses and closed eyes. Slyly, he grinned, allowing her to take him again. His chest pushed eagerly against her. Sadie's hands were a gentle grip, holding him closely as she buried her head along his shoulder as the smoothness of his touch penetrated her soul.

As he pressed his face into the pillow, Craig pushed himself deeply inside her, he recalculated their situation. She was an ally. She had become valuable to the operation. He could feel her tensing as he smudged himself upon her. His thoughts relaxed as he confirmed that the act was only adding benefits to the mission. In that moment, the pent-up anger and variables released, climaxing in the comfort of the mission.

Willow Creek Apartment Complex

Lakeside, CA | 32°49'37.8057"N 116°54'15.7692"W

One Day after Operation Terminal Altitude | 0900 hours

Nguyen's eyes flicked open at the sound of the deadbolt. Expectation had built and subsided countless times in the anticipation of this moment. She sprang from her desk, pulling her shirt straight. Craig entered the apartment casually, greeting Nguyen as he closed the door.

"With all due respect, Agent Craig, what the hell were we doing out there?"

Craig's expression remained distant. "Our job, Nguyen! Don't think for a second that this wasn't mission critical. You need to back down." Craig plopped the bags on the floor. He walked past her with a frustrating gaze. He could feel her eyes burning his back as he poured a cup of coffee from the kitchen.

"...and the casualties? How are we going to explain this to the brass? We're prison bound, I know it. You better tell someone that we were only following orders. No one was supposed to die!"

"Stand by to stand by." Craig leaned lazily against his desk as Briggs and Luster entered the room from the back hallway. Both men respectfully acknowledged Craig as they entered the room with the obligatory, "Good morning, Sir."

"Good morning, gentleman." He sipped his coffee. "It has come to my attention that you may be concerned with the outcome of Operation Terminal Altitude." Craig watched as Briggs scratched his head, visibly leery of piping up.

"We are all concerned! I realize we were working on a SWAT mission, but the media and FBI will be all over this. What are we going to do now? No, no! What are *you* going to do now?" questioned Nguyen.

Craig cracked an ominous expression. "What am I going to do?" His coffee lifted to his lips once more, watching her as she hung on his words. "I am going to congratulate my team on a successful operation."

Nguyen and Briggs held an expression that mimicked an open-faced Halloween mask. Luster however, smiled and thanked Craig for the appreciation.

"Operation success? We were responsible for ten American lives, Sir. Those pilots were defending their planes from terrorist hijacking." She shifted uncomfortably. "They were patriots. We were responsible for innocent deaths." She showed a vulnerable worry along her brow. She knew she was stepping a bit over the line, but didn't care. She needed answers for her own morality.

"It is true. Casualties of war, even innocents, are inevitable. The operational success is based on the financing we gained from this operation."

"Financing? Tell that to their families! They don't care that we profited from their deaths!"

"Nguyen, you are stepping way out of line here." Craig slapped his mug on the table. The ceramic thud echoed loudly. He quickly regained his usual composure, paused, and continued. "...Profit was not the motivation. This mission was based on terrorist funding. In this economy we're struggling to pay the bills, let alone finance anti-terrorist operations. If you want to throw a kiddy party for the victims and label them heroes, go ahead, but you are discrediting their names. They are not only heroes for stopping a hijacking, they are patriots for giving their lives to fund the freedom of America. These men gave more than anyone in this room, twice!"

The room was silent. Nguyen stared at Craig. He was suddenly foreign. Unknown. He was a cold enigma of powerful, glittering words that somehow simultaneously put her at ease and brought distrust.

"On that note, you should know that their families will be well compensated. It is unfortunate, but again, a necessary evil in our war." Craig pulled open the first duffel bag. A set of familiar envelopes appeared and were passed among the group. "As promised, your final bonus has been cleared. The mission is complete."

Nguyen and Briggs eyed their bonus. Luster, too, opened his envelope, revealing a six-figure digit on a treasury check as well as a printed note. All of the envelopes also contained a letter of recommendation, transfer paperwork, and a confidentiality agreement, punishable by imprisonment.

"What will happen to the..." Nguyen was full of questions. Craig was in no mood for answers. He interrupted: "The mission is complete, Nguyen. Your letter to your previous commanding officer is signed and confirmed. You will revert back to your previous assignments. Sign the forms, calm down, and resume your previous command."

Nguyen was struck with a mixture of denial and inquisitive anger. She quickly walked to her laptop, packing it into her bags with obvious aggression. Briggs thanked Craig and began to pack his computer, soda, and other desktop essentials. Luster sat at his desk. Unlike the others, he received a note instructing him to stay behind to complete the details of the mission.

Just as quickly as it began, it ended. Nguyen walked from the apartment, casually saying her good-byes to the others. Briggs made an excuse for a salute and left.

Craig looked over the empty desks. He felt a glimpse of satisfaction as yet another operation finalized. Luster popped open a few screens, calling Craig to their progress. Luster knew that he was crucial to the operation, at least from a financial standpoint. Craig knew little of the money transfers. He didn't care. Quite simply, he needed the funds to be clean, transferred, and available. Craig ordered a full report by morning. Luster acknowledged, popped in a set of tiny earphones, and began to work.

CHAPTER 12

Willow Creek Apartment Complex
Lakeside, CA | 32°49'37.8057"N 116°54'15.7692"W

Morning rose quickly. Luster sipped his green tea as he prepared the final reports. Craig arrived punctually, as usual.

Craig and Luster spent a majority of the morning scanning the profit reports and general ledgers from the operation. The funds passed through a variety of cleaning schemes. Poker rooms were used to transfer a majority of the funds from overseas. Once the funds landed in the U.S., Luster used several creative means to clean the money including gift cards, identity embezzling, and the purchase of gold and silver via an online auction site. The bonuses were repaid to the treasury. The RC parts were repaid with preloaded credit cards and Lt. Lopez received his obligatory cut of the meat.

"Everything has been moved, however, I noticed a small glitch in the system, Craig." Luster casually pointed to a red box on the spreadsheet.

"Five million dollars is no glitch! That is a major collapse! Banking error?" Craig moved closer to the screen, watching the box with a squinted glare.

Luster laughed. "No, Sir, this is no banking glitch. Get a load of this." Luster popped up a scan of the withdrawal slip made from one of their anonymous accounts. "I already pulled everything else from his account."

Craig took a step back, expanding every possibility in his circling mind. "Forget it. Just another casualty of the operation. Call the bank. Tell them we transferred the funds into the wrong account." Craig backed off, ignoring the issue. Five million U.S. dollars was a drop in the pot compared to their margin.

"Banks have a fraud alert on the account, Craig. If we call, there will be a lot of questions."

"A fraud alert? Who put a fraud alert on an account that gained that much money?"

"It appears that there was a police report issued that contains these account numbers." Luster typed furiously, gaining access to the local police department's confidential records. In less than a minute, Luster presented a scan of a signed report from the Rochester, Minnesota police department. The report was rigid, as all police reports are. The facts were present, without all the jargon and personal narration. Luster and Craig read the report, line by line.

On August 23, at approximately 1750 hours, Decklin Marks, of 683 East Center Street, Rochester, MN, reported a bank *error in which he received the sum of $718,465,248.32 into his personal bank account (bank account number XXXXXX8593).*

Marks immediately withdrew $5,000,000 from the account at the Rochester branch of Sterlight State Bank located at 1365 Shanes Road, Rochester, MN.

Decklin Marks, and his wife, Angela Marks, reported the banking error to the Rochester Police Department, several hours after the withdrawal.

Luster and Craig read the three-page report from end to end. As they completed the quick read, Luster looked to Craig for orders.

Craig quietly contemplated their options. After an eternal silence, Craig spoke: "We have a major problem here, Luster." He nodded, weighing the consequences. Craig continued after a brief thought. "If we contact the banks, they will know it was a government transfer. We cannot have them poking around in our business. If we contact Marks, he will know that he has been used as a money mule. There is a solid possibility that he would update the locals." Craig sighed loudly, pulling a cigar from his pocket. He refused to smoke indoors if women were present, however, Nguyen was gone and Luster didn't give two shits and a martini what Craig did.

He puffed a ring of smoke as he pondered the unfortunate circumstances. Craig knew the process of general law enforcement investigations. He wasn't concerned with a few mustaches digging into the labyrinth of webs they laid for the funds; it was the banks that concerned him. The NSA financial crimes division was a worthy adversary. He knew that in time, they would track the funds. It might take years, centuries...or, a few days. It was all dependent on the thickness of the computer geek's glasses. Craig knew he needed to end the investigation. As it stood, they were okay. A typical fraud alert raises a flag the size of an ant on the general radar, however, if this guy were to report any additional information, it could get ugly.

"We need to minimize the damage, Luster. We're going to contact Decklin Marks and make sure he doesn't dig us any deeper than we already are."

"How? This guy's already spent half of it, I'm sure."

"How? Simple. We give him five million to replace the error and call it a night."

"He's going to ask questions."

"We're governmental officials, Luster. We'll flash our IDs, write him a check, and call it quits. In and out, stop the threat."

Charles Unit Investigations

Rochester, MN | 44°4'4.8282"N 92°30'13.7157"W

Charles scanned the bank statements. The amount was too great for an average bank error. He'd worked in the financial crimes division for a season or two and had never come across such a blatant error. He knew the money was jaded, however, *how* jaded was the question. He followed the transfer from an offshore holding company to Decklin's bank. The funds were transferred anonymously, via account number. The Swiss perfected the art of blind money transfers.

The account number for the holding company was long. It looked more like a car's VIN number. He spent three hours researching the company, coming up with little more than an address and a voided phone number. A bank that held millions should have at least held a solid website. Charles phoned the cantonal police in Switzerland. After a choppy, short phone call, the conversing pair decided that email would be the best conversational tool. Charles wrote a short narrative. Instead of explaining the situation, Charles changed tactics. He carefully designed the email. It read:

...I recently inherited a large sum of money. Due to the volatility of the U.S. market, I am looking to deposit my funds into the Shins Holdings Bank in Switzerland. After much research, I've found little on the institution. I am a retired U.S. policeman and would appreciate a bit of professional courtesy. Can you stop into the following address and verify that the bank is legitimate?

Shins Holding AG
Swartzstrasse 536-4
Postfach
4002 Basel, Schweiz

Thank you again for your assistance.

After a quick proof, he clicked send. Charles quickly shut his laptop. He was from the school of hard knocks and paper trails, not Google and emails. He despised technology, but embraced it because of its ever-growing ability to track people. Despite technological advantages, Charles usually caught his crooks with good old-fashioned elbow grease.

He spent the next few hours looking over other cases. He smoked casually, mumbling while he wrote details on a piece of torn scratch paper. His coffee was cold, but drinkable nonetheless. The coffee drizzled down his chin as the "ding" from the computer startled him. His computer volume was perpetually too loud, however, he lacked the technical skills required to turn it down. He wiped the coffee with his pocket-handkerchief, flipping the screen so that he could read the response.

Much to his surprise, the email was simple, rugged, and filled with broken English. Regardless of its choppy grammar, the translation was unmistakable.

> *Dear Ser,*
>
> *We don't like to tell you our findings, but the banks is an empty warehouse in not good side of the town. You take your money to real bank. They will handle correctly. Is anything else we do for you?*

He read the email four times, ensuring nothing was lost in translation. The trail was cold. The email confirmed the funds were transferred under unsavory circumstances. Charles immediately picked up his cordless phone, dialing Decklin's telephone number. Decklin picked up quickly, nearly yelling into the phone over the blowing wind. Charles took a millisecond to mourn the days before loud cell phones and public phone calls. "Decklin, can you pop into my office today?"

Decklin mumbled something loudly into the phone. It was nearly indiscernible. Charles spoke louder: "Decklin, can you hear me? I think you should come down and see me today; I've got a little bit more information on your case."

"Charles! Charles, are you there?"

"Yes." - *Sigh* - "I am here, did you hear me, Decklin?" His subtle annoyance began to seep into his tone.

"Good, Charles, I think I need to come down and see you today! I got a call from someone about the money. They want to meet with me tomorrow!"

The Capitol Building — Washington, DC
38°53'24.5917"N 77°0'33.3641"W

Senator Royce walked casually up the stairwell. His entourage carried briefcases and buzzing cell phones, walking with purpose toward the Senate Chamber. The RC Act (prohibiting the use of electronic, remotely operated vehicles to execute criminal activities) was attaining certain scrutiny by the House. Senator Royce pushed the lobbyists to make the bill into a priority with a strong pocketbook. The formal draft had been submitted, discussed, and further adjusted. The second reading was ridiculously scrutinized. Intricate amendments were inserted, as well as a lengthy addition to the proposed verbiage. Today, Senator Royce faced the toughest challenge of his career. He'd planned for years with Agent Craig to pass this specific bill.

Crowds gathered outside of the Capitol Building. Hippy picketers held signs that read: "What about the kids! The RC Act only protects the banks, not the schools!" Conservative picketers held signs that stated boldly: "Pass The RC Act! Protect us from Terrorism!"

Senator Royce and his colleagues argued for hours, pushing for the bill to pass. The oak-laden Senate Chambers were buzzing with overachieving language and counterpoints. Hundreds of senators chimed in with different patriotic influence. The volume of their shouts was absurd for a crowd of government officials.

A few senators presented one of many angles of the bank explosion footage, driving home the point of devastation. The opposition showed similar videos from the casino. They pushed vigorously to prove that the vehicles were used inappropriately, however, were a safer robbery method than gun-waving criminals. The opposition moved to gag the crimes. They intended to simply destroy the footage, quietly passing a hush order on the incident. They insisted that legislation banning the use of remotely operated vehicles (for criminal activity) would occur in the upcoming years; however, the U.S. simply couldn't afford to pay for the countering devices. As always, the pro-RC Act committee pushed back. The cost of the robberies was extensive. The cost to install barriers in the banks and buildings was minimal in comparison to the costs that the FDIC would shell out in paybacks. As always, sleep worthy spreadsheets, graphs, and diagrams followed.

Seven hours of deliberation slid through the chamber. Senator Royce was tired, standing only to promote a point. Hours of debate had taken a toll on every suit in the building. The process of passing a bill was strategic, lengthy, and designed to completely smother the opposition through exhaustion. At hour seven and a half, Senator Royce popped a few odd-shaped pills and sniffed a casual line of cocaine in the bathroom. Suddenly, his energy was replenished.

Senator Royce reentered the chambers. He stood with confidence. His explanations were rushed, deliberate, and solid. After a thirty-six minute speech, the chambers hushed with a finale of irritation and decisions.

Following a long deliberation, the bill was moved forward. Senator Royce was ecstatic. Strung out and optimistic, he stared at the final draft of the bill. He focused darkly at the two most important sections:

The RC Act defines the law as:
Any person, group, or organization [Law does not apply to peace officers, authorized security personnel, and United States military personnel in the course of active duty] who willingly and knowingly uses an automated, remotely operated machine, vessel, vehicle, or mechanical device to carry out any violation of the law, is guilty of a felony. Sentence: 10 to 30 years in a maximum security, federal prison.

The RC Act also grants funding from the United States Treasury in the following way:
As a result of recent remotely operated, mobile vehicle domestic terrorism and federal robbery, the United States will award the Patriot Barrier Corporation the duty of preserving the security to banks, financial institutions, and other federal, state, and local buildings. The U.S. grants $352,000 per installation, ensuring protection to each institution from mobile attacks.

Royce's cell phone screen was bright against his tired eyes. He punched the keys with victorious rhythm. "Craig, the RC Act has passed so far...waiting on final signatures."

Rochester International Airport

Rochester, MN | 43°54'30"N 92°30'00"W

First class was packed. Agent Craig sat uncomfortably next to Luster, who apparently neglected to mention that his snoring was louder than the jet engines. Luster bounced awake as the plane touched down on the runway. He wiped the drool from his face. "Are we here?" he questioned.

"Yes, it appears we are." Craig wondered where else the two could be, but he neglected to make a fuss over Luster's idiotic question.

The flight attendants were walking about the cabin before the seatbelt sign clicked off. Moments later, a familiar ding sounded, notifying the passengers that the safe removal of their seatbelts was permitted. In a flash, the entire cabin erupted with sounds of clicking belts and muffled voices. He checked his watch when the door finally opened. The passengers stood in a hunched stupor for seven minutes and thirty-two seconds, waiting impatiently for the door to open.

The crowd moved slowly from the first class cabin. They inched along the crowded path like slow-motion lemmings. Craig stood, only when the aisle was clear. He moved through the airplane while Luster paced behind.

The Rochester International Airport was small. The walls and carpeting were reminiscent of an uncivilized era in decor. They used entirely too much bleach, Craig thought as he passed the crude, 1970's-looking bathrooms. He noted the intense, disturbing smell of cleaning solutions as he passed.

The Minnesota accent was thick. They waited at the baggage claim, forced to listen to tales of fishing and vacation hotspots. Beards and hunting apparel was a staple among passengers. Luster and Craig moved through the line at the rental car company, finding themselves safely tucked into a rental car within minutes. Craig lit a fat cigar. He pulled in the sweet smoke with a childish grin. The flight was long, nicotine free, and dreadfully bumpy. He enjoyed the smooth texture of the bold flavor with his eyes closed. Luster scrambled to open his window. The SUV was filling with white lines of smoke. Eventually, Craig opened his window as well. They pulled out of the parking structure, heading toward the city.

Rochester was an odd town. The skyline was modern, mixed with the industrial architecture of the early century. Dirty brick buildings held antique Pepsi advertisements while the adjoining buildings were new, modernized, and bustling with laptop-laden patrons. The city was home to a few major businesses: The Mayo Clinic, which employed one third of the city's population and an IBM headquarters. It was a clean town, littered with new cars, doctors, and Midwestern smiles.

Luster and Craig checked into their hotel, located in the heart of the city. The building design was the essence of old class and eccentricity. They reached the top floor, reserved for Arab kings, pop stars, and government officials. The small doorman popped the door open with a bow, allowing them into the room with politeness. Almost immediately, Luster was scavenging for an outlet. He found one, next to the tall marble fireplace. Within moments, he plugged in his laptop, monitors, and other equipment. Craig, too, started unpacking. He was a light traveler. He brought only the equipment he needed. His small carry-on bag consisted of a laptop, Oxford shirts, his duty pistol, magazines, a first-aid kit, two cell phones, and a few bathroom supplies.

Nearly an hour passed before any mention of Decklin or the money was discussed. Craig tried to arrange a meeting with Decklin earlier in the day, without success. A simple chat, nothing more, and nothing less, minus, of course, any resolve. Craig's cell phone rang, showing "Decklin Marks" on the caller ID. Craig picked up the phone, answering politely. General niceties were exchanged, offering nothing more than a few blank moments of curiosity for both parties.

CHAPTER 13

Charles Unit Investigations

Rochester, MN | 44°4'4.8282"N 92°30'13.7157"W

Charles sat across from Decklin, listening to the call on speakerphone. Charles could tell that the man on the other end of the phone was educated, concise, and as trustworthy as a tack on a chair. Thankfully, Decklin was doing a good job of sticking to the script. Charles went over the conversation rules and topics to avoid before they dialed the number.

Charles pointed to a sheet of paper containing the words "Paneran Coffee Shop, 6:30 p.m. this evening." Craig and Decklin agreed on the time and place, hanging up with the same polite niceties.

Decklin ended the call with a quick swipe on the screen of his phone. They both stared at the phone on the desk. Charles leaned back in his chair, taking in the lasting impression from the conversation.

"He sounded calm," Decklin said curiously.

"He was calm. That could be good or bad." Charles flicked open a rusted Zippo lighter, igniting the tip of his cigarette.

"What have you found out about these guys?"

"Nothing solid, but there is definitely something funky with this group."

"What do you mean?" Decklin moved uncomfortably in his chair. "I mean, it's *my* money now, right? I waited the legal amount of time for possession."

Charles snickered heartily. "Well, it is your money now, but I am sure they aren't too concerned with politeness or legalities. It all depends on whose money it was before you came along. On the flip side, they may be legitimate detectives. If that is the case, you need to be calm and cooperate."

Charles and Decklin discussed all of their options for the meeting. At the forefront of Decklin's mind was the question: *Do I need to pay them back?* While the first thing Charles pondered was: *What do they want, and how hard will they try to get it?* Decklin finished his creamless coffee and left after their lengthy chat; Charles had much work to do before the meeting.

The door creaked behind Decklin as he walked from the office. Charles began pouring over the bank receipts, emails, and history of the case. Buried under his leather brow hid a quiet fear of the men who wanted to meet with Decklin. He couldn't put his finger on it, but he knew deep down, something was amiss.

He paced the office, murmuring at the paperwork. He stared at mug shots on the wall, hoping something would brandish an idea. The case was a dead end, with loopholes along every lead. The steady beat of the clock on the wall was the only sound for an eternity. He sat, stood, paced, leaned, and pondered. He slugged back another drink, taking the edge off his desire to find answers without patience. A tingle slithered up his spine as the booze warmed his chest. He sat back in his chair, scrambling through the paperwork for his lighter and cigarettes. A grin grew as he found the pack, buried amidst the clutter. As he sparked the flint on the simple lighter, he paused. He held the flame an inch from the grille of his cigarette as he stared in awe at the local newspaper. The cigarette fell from his lip as he pulled the paper from the mess, exposing the headline: "Hijacked!" The image on the front page was large, blinding the reader with an image of a flaming commercial plane. He flicked the paper open, reading the article from the first line.

"Fifteen commercial aircraft were hijacked in San Diego, California. The planes were flown south along the West Coast, landing in Mexico..."

His finger traced the words, rereading "...over nine hundred million dollars in stolen jetliners." It was more than coincidence, but far less than solid proof. His watch read 5:43 p.m., only forty-five minutes until Decklin was to meet with the investigators. Where did the time go? Charles wondered. He was suddenly in a panic to reach Decklin. The phone popped off the cradle, sending a pile of paperwork to the floor.

Decklin paced in the small living room. Angela was nervous, too. In less than an hour, they would find out if their miracle money would be yanked out from under them by none other than the U.S. Government.

“We’ll be fine either way. Don’t stress, hun.” Her words were deflected as Decklin walked in worry. She heaved herself from the deep couch, stopping Decklin with a gentle touch. She smiled lovingly, pulling his tense body close for a caring embrace. Her arms wrapped around him tenderly, hugging away a sliver of the anxiety.

“What if they want us to pay it back? Do you know how long that will take us?” He shook his head on her shoulder.

Her voice was muffled as she spoke into his chest: “It’s only money. We’ll be fine.”

The phone lit up Decklin’s pocket before the ringer announced the call. He pulled back from her tight grip, answering curtly.

“Decklin? Are you there?” Charles’ voice was unusually energetic. He normally spoke in a deep clarity only heard in late show radio personalities and psychologists. This was different.

“Yes, I am here. What is going on? Are you okay?” Angela pulled her head to the opposing side of the phone, listening intently.

“Have you left yet?”

“No. No? I haven’t, what is wrong?”

“I’ll explain at your place. I am headed there now.”

The doorbell rang as Decklin ended the call. “That was crazy fast! What’s going on, honey?” Angela said quickly, anxiousness ripening her voice. She let go of his arms, squeezing his elbow once to show one final sign of calming affection as she hurried to the door. The peephole showed the distorted view of a police officer. "Can I help you?" she announced.

"Yes, Ma'am, it's Officer Kitts from the Rochester Police Department. Charles told me to meet him here."

She spun the deadbolt. The door opened, exposing the weathered but sharp officer. She stretched a welcoming arm for him to enter.

As he walked into the apartment, he looked around. Pete barreled out of his room with toys in hand to see what visitor was there to see him. "Hey, buddy! Would you like a sticker?" Officer Kitts kneeled down, sliding his hand in his breast pocket of his uniform. He pulled out a metallic-badge sticker, handing it to the bright-eyed Pete.

Pete quickly peeled the back from the sticker, slapping it on his chest with pride.

"What do you say, bud?" Decklin's fatherly tone poured from his tongue.

"Thank you!" His young voice was cute, soft, and appreciative. Officer Kitts smiled.

After Pete flew back down the hallway, Decklin questioned, "What are you doing here? What did Charles tell you?"

Angela pulled the group to the living room, sitting in an "L" along the sectional couches. "He didn't tell me much, just to meet him here. Have you talked to him? I haven't heard that tone from him in years." Officer Kitts sat tall on the couch as he spoke.

"No no, he hasn't told me anything. I thought you would know something." Decklin's nerves were an electrical storm of worry and impatience. "Am I in some kind of trouble? Is that why you're here?"

Officer Kitts shrugged. "I'm not sure. All I know is that Charles wouldn't get excited if a tornado was headed right at him. He's rock solid. Concrete. If he's excited, everyone should be, and that is why I'm here!"

Decklin hummed a disappointed sigh. "Have you gotten anything back on our case?"

"Nothing." It became clearer that Officer Kitts was anxious and not entirely up for conversation. They waited twelve minutes for Charles to arrive. Ten of which were filled with meaningless chatter about police procedure while two minutes were used up with smiles and silence.

The buzzer surprised them. Angela hopped up, quickly buzzing in Charles. He entered their apartment ambitiously. Decklin, Angela, and Officer Kitts stared at him, waiting with urgency.

Charles pulled off his pea coat, sliding it on a peg by the door. Without a moment's hesitation, he paced the living room floor. "Kitts, I think I know where the money came from; I need you to run a trace on the phone number, GPS location, owner of the phone, their personal information, the works!" Officer Kitts slid out a notepad, jotting down notes as Charles spewed information. Charles pointed haphazardly at Decklin. "I need you to call them. Reschedule. Tell them anything! Car accident, kid is sick? Whatever, just put this thing off until tomorrow morning."

Decklin was worried. He watched as Charles commanded the room. The silence from a few minutes ago turned into pure adrenaline as Charles paced the carpet. "Wait, wait! What is going on here?"

Charles stopped, mentally snickering at his enthusiasm. "Ah, right. You don't know anything." Charles proceeded to tell Decklin, Angela, and Officer Kitts about the hijackings, as well as the faux-bank that was used to cleverly transfer the money into Decklin's account. He'd loosely linked the hijacking to the international money transfer. The room was stiff with uneasiness.

"Wait, so you're telling me that some guys hijacked fifteen planes, by force, flew them to Mexico and laundered the money through my account?" Decklin was red. Beet red.

"I knew it! I knew something was very wrong from the beginning! Dammit, Decklin, I told you we should return the money!" Angela was a blended cocktail of anger, fear, and worry.

"Wait, wait! How did you figure this out? How do you know the money came from those robberies?" Officer Kitts believed Charles, however, the policeman in him asked for facts.

"Three robberies in a row, all using a mechanized machine cannot be coincidence. Someone is ahead of the game with technology. Clearly the government thinks so too." Charles slapped down a freshly printed copy of the RC Act, straight from the U.S. Senate website. "The Senate is trying desperately to stop this before it becomes widespread, but these guys made hundreds of millions in no time."

"So, how the hell did it end up in my account? Why me?" Decklin was worried about his safety...and of course the safety of his precious money.

"You are a nobody!" Charles held out a polite hand. "No offense. You don't have a lot of debt. You don't check your accounts. You are the perfect target for a laundering scheme."

"Or so they thought anyway," Angela piped in. "Who is the investigator that Decklin is meeting?"

Charles shrugged. "I am not sure. They could be true U.S. investigators; however, I am sure they haven't had enough time to start tracking the funds yet. It takes weeks for them to track movement like that. These funds were transferred right after the hijacking. They need warrants, documentation."

Decklin popped into the kitchen, clanking a mug from the cupboard. "Coffee, anyone?"

The group was a bit put off by the haphazard need to have coffee in the midst of this crucial conversation. "Yes, please," Charles responded. Angela was surprised that he took up the random offer for a beverage.

Officer Kitts continued, avoiding the odd request for java. "He's right. Even if they were investigators, they wouldn't go after Decklin. He is small time. Clearly not a player in the robberies. He has solid proof that he was working at the time of the robberies...right?" He glanced to Decklin, who nodded appropriately.

"So we're not in trouble?" Angela questioned.

"We get to keep the money, right?" Decklin walked back into the room, curiously holding the coffees. He handed Charles a fully creamed coffee, stacked with sugar. Despite the situation, Decklin leapt at the chance to give Charles a creamy coffee. Not black.

"Not sure...What I am sure of is that we need more time. We need everything documented. Kitts, we need your help with setting up the case. This could be a career maker for you." Charles knew that Officer Kitts had been trying for years to gain the rank of sergeant, without success. He sipped the coffee.

"First off, you need to make the call." Charles pointed to Decklin's cell phone on the table. "Calmly."

Decklin flicked on his phone, dialing Craig's number. The room went silent, adding unintentional stress to Decklin's phone call.

"Decklin, what a surprise! What can I do for you?" Dominick Craig sounded cool and cautious.

"I'm sorry, but can we reschedule? Our kid's been throwing up all afternoon."

"Oh, what a tragedy." Craig's emotionless voice crept into the phone without a smudge of genuine intent. "What works for you, Decklin? Later tonight?"

Decklin's nerves were tight, but he mustered, "Actually, can we meet for lunch tomorrow? Same place? Maybe 11:30?"

A long pause broke. Craig wrote the information on a sheet of paper at the hotel. Decklin tapped his fingers nervously as he waited for any type of response. "Yes. Yes, that works."

"Great, see you there. Thanks again."

"No problem."

Decklin ended the call. He set the phone down gently. Nerves and adrenaline surged from the jarring call.

"Good. Now that that is done, we all need to get moving. There are only a few hours between now and tomorrow morning. Let's make them count." Charles began to lay out what needed to be done. Everyone had a task list when Charles finished. Decklin and Angela were to write down everything that has happened since the transfer. Count every dollar spent and calculate exactly how long it would take to repay the money. Of course, only if they were required to do so. Charles needed everything: bank employee descriptions, exact times, addresses of the bank, and even the color of the envelope that the money came in. He was precise. Charles asked Kitts to prepare a report, which could mean a break in the federal hijacking case; therefore, he needed it to be perfect.

Charles casually mentioned to Kitts that Decklin was to be wearing a wire during the meeting. Time stopped as the wrath of Decklin's wife spoke. "He *IS* in danger, I knew it! No! Not happening."

"We can't say if he is or isn't in danger, Mrs. Marks," Charles spoke calmly.

"A very politically correct answer, Mr. Investigator. I don't give a shit about odds; I only care about his safety!" Angela was stern. Her tiny stature hid a colossal punch. "Is he in danger or not?"

Officer Kitts and Charles looked at each other, searching for the right words.

“That’s what I thought. Not happening.” She’d put her foot down. It was enough to scare a cop, a seasoned investigator, and her husband. Even her son heard the commotion in the other room and stopped playing with his toys.

“This puts a damper on the plan, Ma’am,” Charles said politely.

“Damper or no damper, he isn’t going. We can call them back and tell them to meet you instead. That won’t be an issue if it truly is as harmless as you hope it is.”

Officer Kitts adjusted himself in his chair. Charles lifted his head in surprise. “Yes, you are right! I will meet them instead!” This created confusion in the room. “I’ll show up as Decklin! It’s perfect.”

“They’ll know you aren’t me. They’re government guys. They’ll know.” Decklin sat back, watching to ensure he didn’t spill his coffee.

“They will know. You’re very right, Decklin.” Charles pointed to Officer Kitts. “TIP. It’s perfect.”

Officer Kitts struggled with comfort again as he raised an eyebrow. “No, this doesn’t warrant TIP. We need more than a hunch.”

Angela raised her hand like a school kid with a question. “Um, TIP? What is TIP? Pardon us normees with zero police knowledge.”

"Temporary identity placement," Officer Kitts said grumpily.

"A *TIP* is when we swap an informant out with someone else. That way, a police officer..." Charles thumbed to himself "...or an investigator can go into any situation with the identity of their informant. It's hard to train informants about what to ask and what to do. We know how to ask the questions and when to ask them. It's perfect, really."

"Why are they going to think you are me? I mean, I've talked to them already. They are going to figure it out." Decklin was skeptical.

"They've *only* talked to you on the phone. I'll tell them I have a cold. Besides, by the time they know something is fishy, they'll either be legitimate investigators, or they'll have given us enough information to put them behind bars."

Angela smiled. She liked it. Officer Kitts on the other hand, was skeptical. "These things take time, Charles, you know that! You expect me to walk up to a judge tonight, and ask for a full TIP? We'll need solid facts, proof! What do we have? Definitely not enough to get a judge's signature."

"How bad do you want to be a sergeant next quarter?" Charles knew he hit close to home. Officer Kitts refrained from replying, but the answer was evident. He shrugged and agreed with a nod. Charles asked for all forms of government-issued ID from Decklin. They walked to their back room where Decklin pulled out his stuffed billfold. Hundred-dollar bills were pouring from every seam of the torn billfold.

"Looks like you're keeping a lot of cash on you!" Charles blurted as he looked at the wallet.

"Yeah, I keep a few grand on me. I've got the rest sitting in my safe." Decklin pointed to a small grey safe in the walk-in closet. His fingers quickly returned to the wallet, pulling his Minnesota driver's license from its sheath.

"Birth certificate? Sorry, I need everything," Charles said hesitantly. Decklin walked to the safe, opening it with a turn of the dial. He sifted through paperwork, stacks of hundred-dollar bills, diplomas, and pictures. He finally slid a tattered, folded birth certificate from the pile. He handed the certificate to Charles. It didn't feel right. He'd never surrendered his identity. Charles took the certificate, slurped a sip of creamed coffee and walked back to the living room.

Officer Kitts looked over his list. He carried the burden of convincing a judge to swap the IDs. Mildly overwhelmed, he said his good-byes quickly.

CHAPTER 14

4th Street Southeast
Rochester, MN | 44°1'9.587"N 92°27'35.1264"W

His radio beeped as he called dispatch to inform them that he would be busy for the remainder of the day. He drove a few blocks, contemplating the identity swap. Ethics and procedure crept into his thoughts as he toiled over his options. TIP was tricky. He knew the judge would ask a lot of questions. Questions he didn't have answers to. He knew how to swap IDs, he'd done it a hundred other times. He thought about what could happen if he skipped the court order for the ID change. He could simply break protocol, changing the identities for 24 hours. Who would know? he pondered. If he were to get caught using the system for an investigation without proper documentation, he could be in serious heat.

He clicked the garage door opener. The large grey door opened, revealing the belly of the government center. He pulled into the underground garage, parking next to the endless row of police cruisers. He flipped the door locks and passed through the dimly lit garage to the barred door. His keys jingled, pushing into the door handle with smooth precision. Brightness from the fluorescent lighting blinded him for a moment. Endless hallways eventually led him to his office. His chair squeaked as he sat in the silence of the room. He stared at the blank monitor, contemplating procedure versus speed.

The circular motion of his mouse woke up the monitors, exposing the graphic of a shield. He entered the password, clicking through the screens to the TIP system. He glared irrationally at the empty box that stated "judge approving the request." His foot tapped on the floor. His eyes darted from the keyboard to the screen. Six minutes and thirty-four seconds later, he entered "N/A" in the box, clicking the submit button. The TIP screen flickered, exposing the DMV screen. He entered Decklin's information. He convinced himself that his actions were legitimate. I mean, this is a big case. I can't wait for the courts to do everything. Sometimes we need to rely on our gut for exigent circumstances, he told himself as he submitted the information.

The card printer hummed and wobbled as the Minnesota driver's license slowly printed from the machine. He whipped it out, blowing on the fresh ink. Charles' picture was perfectly aligned on the identification card. His address, license number, and birth date were adjusted to Decklin's. He slid it into an envelope, flipping through the administration processes of swapping IDs. Department of Motor Vehicles was updated. Hospital records were updated, spitting a birth certificate from the printer. The process for birth certificates was more difficult because of the quality of the paper as it fed through the printer. They used distressed, torn paper to add the appearance of age to the certificates. It added credibility for the officers as they worked through cases involving multiple identities.

At least two hours passed. Form after tedious form was stuffed into two full-sized manila envelopes. He sighed loudly, releasing a breath of anxiety when the paperwork was completed. Their identities were completely swapped. Decklin was no longer Decklin and Charles wasn't Charles any longer. He locked the screen, whipping the two envelopes off the desk as he stood.

"Kitts!" The door swung open, exposing the lieutenant.

"Yes, Sir, what can I do for you?" Officer Kitts nervously held the envelopes as he addressed his superior.

"What's the verdict of the Banello case? I've got his family on the phone." The lieutenant leaned on the door handle as he asked the seemingly important question.

"Banello? In custody. We brought him in last night."

"Good. Thanks." The lieutenant closed the door, walking away quickly. Kitts' hand was shaking, wiggling the envelopes. He was paralyzed. He knew he went against procedure. It was either a career-making or a career-ending move.

He barely noticed his feet moving as he passed through the halls. He pulled the door to the garage, nearly knocking over a female officer. Politeness was unnoticed as he briskly passed her. He pulled the handle to his patrol unit, realizing the doors were locked. Wild distractions engulfed his mind as he slithered through the underground tunnels of the garage. He pulled into traffic, ignoring the constant chatter of the radio.

Angela buzzed Officer Kitts into their apartment. He looked a bit frazzled. His stance was hunched. His smile was fake. She greeted him with nothing more than a rushed response. Kitts handed her the envelope containing Decklin's new identity. It was a requirement by the state always to provide an identity for anyone in the program. It was a program no-no to leave a witness or informant without a government ID. The program usually offered a variety of fake identities, however, it had become common to simply swap IDs with the opposing party. The paperwork was simply easier to track.

Angela took the envelope, peeking inside with curiosity. Before she could address him further, he left.

"That was odd," Angela said loudly to Decklin, who was playing with Pete, casually swinging a miniature sword. She slapped down a new driver's license and stack of papers right between the two of them. Decklin picked up the new ID. He was impressed. The plastic card and holograms were perfect. He bent it, checking the thickness with the tip of his thumb.

"This is amazing, hun. Look at this thing!" His eyes fixated on the moving holograms.

Angela sat next to him on the floor. The oddness of the situation fell from her thoughts as she appreciated the simplicity of her husband. He was somewhat concerned about the money, but was so easily distracted by the quality of the simple things. She loved his easygoing nature. She loved his distracted enjoyment of life. She looked into his eyes, enjoying the familiar beauty of the man she'd known for so long.

"Let's go out tonight. Let's ignore all of this for one final night." She moved her hand over his, pulling the wooden sword from his grasp.

"Tonight? Shouldn't we be getting ready for tomorrow?" He had no idea what to expect for the following day.

She too was concerned with the outcome; however, she desperately needed a break from the madness of their life. "Let's text the neighbor. She would be happy to watch Pete."

"You know? That sounds amazing!" Decklin put down the toys, and hopped up from the floor.

After the quick set of texts, their neighbor, Monica, knocked on the door. They'd shared a hallway for several years and trusted her completely. She entered with her usual rosy smile, kindness pouring from her dimples as she greeted Pete. Decklin went over the basics with her: the time they'd be home, their routine at bedtime, the works. Angela prepared frantically in the bathroom. Her hair straightener wove a perfect pattern around her head as she prepped for the evening. She emerged a few minutes later. Decklin's heart stopped for a moment. His eyes scanned her tight dress and primped features. "Wow, baby. You...You...You look absolutely amazing." He couldn't help himself. He slid across the room, running his hands up the side of her dress. Her petite body pressed delicately against the curves of every stitch. She thanked him, brushing him off to scavenge for a set of heels that matched her outfit. She kneeled in the closet, sifting through piles of shoes, hangers, and other lost garments.

The pair of red pumps pushed her calves into a delicately strong form. Decklin was awestruck. Parenthood and schedules often mask the true beauty of moms, but in a thirty-minute prep session, she managed to turn herself back into the princess that took his breath away.

They said their good-byes. Pete needed several hugs and kisses before he could allow them to leave. Thankfully, both Decklin and Angela were more than willing to give him the extra attention on their way out.

"I already miss him. He'll be okay, right?" Angela said as she pulled the SUV's door shut.

"Yeah, he'll be fine, hun." Decklin gently kissed her cheek. The motherly worry spread across her face down to her fidgeting hands.

"Right. Right." She paused, looking out the window with a blatantly worried expression. "I know he will be. You trust Monica with him, right?"

Decklin smiled, sliding his hand over hers. "Of course. He is in good hands."

Kahl Hotel

Rochester, MN | 44°1'21.8353"N 92°27'53.2023"W

Craig's cell phone was bright in the dimly lit suite. Computer screens and fireplaces illuminated the room with bouncing shadows. Craig leaned back in his chair, watching the fire. Luster slept on the couch. Jerky movements abruptly woke him. He wiped his face and checked his watch. "How long have I been out?"

"An hour and twenty-five minutes," Craig answered without checking his watch. Luster sat up, eyeing the dim room. He sensed something odd with Craig.

"Sir? Everything all right?" Luster straightened his clothes waiting for Craig's response.

"Do you know why we dropped the bomb in Japan, Luster?" Craig didn't move, blink, or flinch. Luster tilted his head, completely baffled by the odd question. He knew there was something behind it. There always was. Luster simply didn't have his wits about him enough to answer the question with any deep acknowledgment.

"Sir? Hiroshima?" He paused, watching the nod that Craig let off. "Sure. We needed to retaliate. We showed them who had superior force by using shock. It's how we won the war."

Craig nodded. "Yes, but do you think Americans agreed with it? Do you think we went too far in defending our country?"

"No, Sir. I think it was brutal, but needed to be done. Sometimes we need to do something that people may think is terrible to keep our country safe."

Craig turned his expressionless face to Luster and nodded. His cell phone remained illuminated. His cheeks showed the hint of a dimple as he spoke. "Exactly. There are times when we've needed to make sacrifices to protect the best interest of the country. We need to ask ourselves: How far would we go? His finger pressed the green send button on his phone, dialing the number that had been sitting on his screen for over an hour.

Old Sea World Drive

San Diego, CA | 32°45'37.1517"N 117°13'23.746"W

The warm San Diego air blew through the open windows on the small car. Nguyen wasn't particularly happy to be sitting in tight quarters with Briggs, but an order is an order. "What time did he say he was going to call?" Briggs asked. He knew the answer but wanted to break the silence in the car.

"Anytime now. He should have called half an hour ago." Nguyen was annoyed. Craig was never late. She was confused as to why they needed to be parked at the beach for the call. She toyed with the idea of phone tracking or blending in, but in the end, she figured if Craig set it up, he had a reason.

"Why the hell does he need us together? I thought the missions were complete?" Briggs chugged the final sip of his soda, throwing the can out the window.

"Are you really going to litter? Right in front of me?" Nguyen was annoyed. She dealt with it during the mission but her patience had been worn to a pulp. Briggs was about to open the car door to pick up the can when Nguyen interjected, "Wait! That is him. I'll put him on speaker." Nguyen reached for her phone. She dug for a few brief seconds through the barrage of lipgloss, wallets, pens, and other purse-cluttering memorabilia. She lifted her phone from the purse, looking at the odd number on the screen. She slid her finger across the screen, speaking clearly: "This is Nguyen."

Craig watched the face of his phone, listening to the quiet voice of Nguyen on the other end. He turned his attention to Luster once again. "...That is the American way." He pressed number eight on his keypad.

Nguyen heard Craig's muffled voice, followed by the blip of the tone. Nguyen had only a millisecond to process the twisting metal and flame that engulfed the passenger compartment of the car. The explosion ripped the doors open, breathing a pressurized swirl of flame in every direction. The car split like tin foil, belching fragments of Nguyen, glass, and cell phone parts. Her body unhinged, vaporizing into moist fire. Surrounding buildings spit fragments of pressurized glass as the force rippled through the cool air. Briggs catapulted from the car. The intensity of the blast curled his bones into mushy fragments. His burning body flopped lifelessly against the cement. He came to rest a full block from the remains of the car.

Craig looked at his phone. "Call lost," blinked on his screen. His brow rose momentarily as he released a subtle sigh.

"Everything okay, Craig?" Luster asked curiously.

"Absolutely, Luster. Everything is right on schedule."

Steakhouse Bar and Grille

Rochester, MN | 44°0'20.587"N 92°27'51.696"W

She sat delicately. Decklin gently pushed her chair in true gentleman's style. "I love this place." Decklin peeked around the restaurant as he sat. She reached across the table, pulling the warmth of his hand in hers. "I love you." She spoke softly against the loud background. He blinked, taking in the sight of her beauty. She was in a league of her own. Her face was perfect. An angel couldn't mimic her radiance. Her skin was flawless. He followed the line of her eyes to her supple, smiling lips, down to her fragile neck and chest. "I love you more." He was in awe of his beautiful wife. She was loving, generous, stern, tough, and absolutely perfect. Decklin often wondered what cupid was thinking when he struck Angela with his arrow, but it didn't matter. They both felt like the most fortunate couple on the planet.

"Evening! Would you like a drink? Appetizer?" The waiter was distracted, but courteous.

Decklin flipped over the drink menu, ordering a lager for himself and a light beer for his wife. He placed his finger on the menu, pointing to a deep-fried onion and dip. "Also, can I get one of these onions?" The waiter nodded, jotting down their order on a small piece of paper.

"Onion? Wait...no, no. You know how many calories are in those, baby?" Angela was always concerned with fat content.

"Why not splurge a few calories? You look great, relax." He knew she wouldn't. She was more annoyingly health conscious than a fitness model.

"Rock ya for it." She knew he would go for it. In their relationship, there was only one way to settle disputes. Decklin pulled his hand from his knee, holding it out on the table in a classic "rock, paper, scissors" formation. The waiter rolled his eyes and shifted his weight as he patiently awaited their decision. Their eyes met. The challenge was on. They pumped their fists three times, flashing their paper and scissors at the finale. Decklin won, grinning ear to ear over his victory. He held his scissor fingers to the waiter and said, "We will take the onions!" The waiter scribbled the order and walked away.

"I don't know why you even try. Clearly, my game is *far* superior to yours." He gleefully wove a tapestry of sarcasm into his tone.

"Oh, you think so? Are you sure I am not just letting you win?" She too had perfected the playful sarcasm. Decklin quietly pondered her response. He knew it was very possible that she knew him well enough to let him win, or, was she completely full of it? Either way, he won. He rubbed it in as hard as he could. They frequently challenged each other. It was one of the many sweet spots in their marriage.

They flirted and chatted as they waited for the drinks and onions. It was a simple joy to be out of the house, away from children's toys, computers, and the daily coffee grind. The money changed things, but not as much as some would imagine. They still woke up, dressed, and headed out the door in the same hurry as always.

The onion arrived on an oversized plate. Fingers of sliced onion were drenched in batter, steaming the aroma of perfection. Decklin snatched the first bite. He pulled off an enormous chunk, shoving it partially into his mouth. Angela reached across the table, poking the remaining bits into his overly stuffed mouth. "Squirrel cheeks! That's your new nickname. Just for tonight!" she lightheartedly mocked. He kindly grinned, showing her his middle finger first, followed by the food in his open mouth.

They ordered steaks. Rare. The cracked-pepper goodness filled their bellies with the warmth of juicy deliciousness. Angela finished half of her steak, patted her slender belly, and belched. Decklin laughed, clenching his gut silently. "That's my girl!"

They chugged their beer, silently challenging each other to yet another race. She finished first, slamming the frothy glass on the table. Ridiculous cheering belted from her mouth as she pumped her fists gleefully. He set his down, accepting a quiet defeat. "No, no, dear. You need to finish it!" Decklin sneered, finishing the glass.

They managed to slam three more drinks before heading out the door. They considered driving, but the keys were far too blurry. He laughed, hiccupping with unexpected power. She slipped off her heels and gave him *the eye*. Every man lives for the eye. Women possess a skill no man can match: the raw sensuality of a look, a simple glimmer. She grabbed his shirt, pulling him close. Passion shivered along his lips as her tongue flicked his tender skin. Swaying affection slid hurriedly, gliding along the pleasure of their partner's kiss. She grabbed him fiercely as she whispered, "I love you…" Teasing hands shoved him away. His dazed gaze was priceless. "Let's go home."

He wrapped her hand tightly as they paced down the sidewalk. Decklin walked barefoot while Angela stepped drunkenly into his mammoth shoes. Kisses were charmingly exchanged as they walked. Decklin's hands couldn't resist roaming along the tender lines of her back as he felt her lips against his.

By the time they reached the door to their apartment, they were rigid with desire. He pressed her body against the entry, holding her arms above her head. Hands wandered through the slit in her dress, sliding up the warmth of her thigh. Their open mouths hummed deep breaths of excitement. In a hurried slide, he plugged the key into the doorknob. They tumbled through the door, racing to the bedroom.

"You're home!" The sound of their neighbor's voice surprised them. Angela chuckled, bolting into the bathroom while she covered her slender body with the twisted dress. "Your little man is asleep!"

"Yeah, we're home! Thanks, here you go!" Decklin pitched her a twenty-dollar bill and rushed her to the door. He loved his neighbor; she was an absolute sweetheart, but chatting was not on his list of current priorities. The deadbolt flipped with an audible click.

"Is she gone?" Angela questioned from behind the bathroom door. "Absolutely." Decklin slid the rest of his clothes off, jogging to the bed. He pounced onto the soft comforter awaiting his prize.

Hall lights silhouetted her seductive, sauntering naked body. Slyly, she arched her back as she slid on top of Decklin. The warmth of her chest tingled as she writhed up his body. Smooth lips touched his ear. "Decklin, I don't care if we're millionaires, broke, or somewhere in the middle. I'm crazy about you." She pulled her face back an inch, brushing her nose against his. They paused, gleaming at one another.

"Ditto," he whispered. Her body nestled against his chest as she reached his lips.

Their bodies moved slowly. Moist pressure of ecstasy rubbed along their skin. Decklin pushed his body deeply into hers, blissfully retrieving the closeness they cherished.

Raised bumps along her skin tingled as Decklin wrapped his arms around her. They moved in harmony, perfected only by years of intimacy. Their sighs grew louder, shaking the posts along the wall. Her body tensed around him as her nails dug blissfully into his back. Their grips tightened, releasing a perfect flow of groans. Collapsed bodies dripped sweat as they relaxed. She kissed him with a smile, winking sweetly. "Tonight was amazing."

CHAPTER 15

Marks Residence

Rochester, MN | 44°1'21.8908"N 92°27'15.1579"W

The buzzer was violently loud. Decklin sat up hastily, pulling himself from the intertwined legs of his wife. Angela rolled over, searching for the alarm clock with a matted tuft of hair strewn across her face. Decklin hopped up, feeling the rage of his headache. He rubbed his brow and scanned the room for a pair of pants. The dark blue jeans from the previous day lay crookedly along the edge of the bed. The door buzzer sounded again. "All right, all right," he mumbled. Mischievous pant legs were a conundrum, choosing to make his morning difficult.

He popped open the door, revealing the bushy-eyed face of Charles Unit. "Good morning, Decklin, can I come in?"

Decklin yelled back to Angela, informing her of the visitor. More importantly, it was a sly reminder to put on some clothes before trudging out from the bedroom. Pete was barely awake. He too stumbled from his colorful bedroom. He immediately gained his familiarity with awareness, jogging to the living room to play with his new action figures. Charles eyed the apartment with an odd curiosity. The curtains were ruffled. Toys flooded every corner of the room while frilly panties hung casually over a dining room chair.

"Long night, Decklin?" Charles snickered.

Decklin respectfully ignored the question, redirecting the conversation to: "Coffee? Extra cream, right?" Charles accepted, completely sidestepping the cream comment. He knew Decklin would pour it anyway.

"Are you just waking up? It's late!" Charles could tell by the lines across Decklin's face that he'd recently woken from a long night.

"Late? By late, do you mean our definition of late, or yours?" Decklin dripped water from the pot into the back of the coffee maker. As always, it dribbled ridiculously on the counter as he poured.

"That is beside the point. We've got the meeting in a few hours. I wanted to brief you."

"Brief me?" Decklin picked up his shirt from the floor, pulling it over his head with great difficulty.

"Yes, brief you. You didn't think I was just going to take over completely? You need to know what is going on." Charles was a bit put off by Decklin's lack of reliability. Charles was assuming all of the burden, all the danger, and all of the risk while Decklin sat at home drinking coffee with his young wife.

"Well, no. Of course not. What do you need me for though?"

Charles pulled open the small black bag he carried into the house. "You're my backup. Since the police department can't have anything to do with private investigations, I'm counting on you to pay attention during the meeting."

Decklin watched as Charles pulled a small mountain of wires and radios from the bag. He lifted a radio, presenting it to Decklin with a shameless expression. "You'll be listening to the whole thing."

"Wait, listening? What do I need to do? I can't exactly storm in there if things get froggy!" Decklin was confused. He wondered why he needed to pay attention. Then again, he also knew that it was in his personality to shy away from things he wasn't directly tasked with doing.

"We're going to run through a training scenario." Charles untangled a small wire. His top button popped open with a flick of his fingers. The microphone stuck snugly to his chest, draping a snake of wires down to the radio. "Nothing beats a little training bright and early in the morning!"

Angela walked out of the bedroom wiping the sleep from her eyes. She'd found a hooded sweatshirt and a pair of pajama pants to throw on before greeting Charles. "Good morning, is it already time?"

"Good morning, Ma'am! Yes, it's almost time. Your husband and I were just discussing how he is going to help."

Angela walked to the bag of electronics, peering inside with a touch. Charles flipped on the radio. A squelching shriek popped from the speaker, followed by three beeps. Charles looked distracted, flipping the radio from on to off.

"I assume we are going to listen to your conversation this morning?" Clearly, her wits were stronger than her hangover.

Decklin looked astoundingly to Angela. She never ceased to amaze him with her quick-witted knowledge. "That is exactly what we're going to do, honey." Decklin picked up a radio, fumbling with the controls. Charles scowled, snipping the radio from his hands.

"You should be able to listen from anywhere in town…except…" Charles flicked the power buttons again, releasing only a muffled buzz. "Except, the batteries are toast." Charles pulled the batteries from the radio, eyeing their orientation. "We might have a few of those in the junk drawer, Charles, let me check." Angela rummaged through the drawer in the kitchen, finding nothing. Decklin followed quickly behind, pouring three cups of coffee, all containing an exuberant amount of creamer. He handed one to Angela, took one for himself, and offered the other to Charles, who took it, setting it down with little interest.

"I'll run back to the office. I know I have some there." Charles began to stand. Angela held out a polite arm. "No, you're our guest. Decklin will go pick up a few. He needs to get the truck anyway and I'd love to hear more about what you've found on our case." Angela whipped her pointed finger in the direction of the door, instructing Decklin to go.

"Sure, right. I'll do that. What size are they? Triple A?" Decklin leaned into the battery compartment of the radio, eyeing the specs of the batteries. Charles nodded, pocketing the dead batteries.

"That's great, Decklin. I really appreciate that." He took a large sip of the creamed coffee and smiled. Decklin rolled his eyes, kissed his wife, and headed out the door.

Broadway Avenue
Rochester, MN | 44°1'24.24"N 92°27'46.62"W

The light changed from green to yellow. Craig smoothly accelerated through the intersection. Wind blew in Craig's window, sucking the smoke from the tiny compartment. Craig puffed smoothly on the cigar. His fingers slid along the wheel as they turned past the coffee shop.

"We're not going to the coffee shop?" Luster asked. History taught him that Craig was twenty miles ahead of the plan, but it often left Luster in the dark.

"Yeah. Coffee shops are too crowded. I hate discussing business in public." A smirk rose from his cheek.

Luster shrugged. "Diplomacy failed yesterday with the meeting. I think we should scare him a little more than we would have. Throw a lot of legal jargon at him." Luster played out the situation. The small town Minnesota man was no match for their government knowledge. "What do we know about him?"

Without hesitation, Craig spilled a stream of knowledge. "He's married, with a stepson from a deadbeat dad. He works at a small company outside of town and owns two vehicles because his wife has a credit score of 508." Luster arched an eyebrow. It wasn't surprising, yet remained impressive. "Run a full record search for Decklin Marks, including recent banking transactions." Craig pointed to the laptop in the backseat. Luster leaned to the back, straining against the seatbelt. He popped open the computer, running lines of code along the edge of the screen. Only seconds were needed for Luster to pull Decklin's banking reports and a full copy of his state record. He snapped an image of the screen, transferring it to Craig's cell phone. The phone fit snugly in the cup holder next to Craig's arm. Luster noticed a familiar bulge from under Craig's oxford.

"Are you wearing a vest?"

"Yes." Craig watched the road, unaffected. "I always wear it to meetings; don't worry about it." Craig didn't waver. Luster knew he didn't wear them often. It drew a sliver of concern.

"Ten seconds out." Craig looked particularly determined. It was a motivation Luster hadn't seen since the RC operation. Luster prepared himself mentally for the meeting, dismissing the odd use of a bulletproof vest. He knew he could scare the living shit out of Decklin with the distinct fear of legal repercussion. He wouldn't think to tell anyone where he got the money, or spend another dime. He knew Craig had a plan to disguise the money, but wasn't sure of exactly how he would pull it from Decklin Marks. Craig turned left onto Decklin's street. He reached into his pocket, pulling another cell phone. As he looked to the screen, a black SUV pulled from a parking space, cutting off their path. Craig dropped the phone and nervously stomped on the brake. Their bodies jerked forward, sending the phone to the floor. Craig gritted his teeth as the car came to a stop. The driver of the truck waved and drove away carelessly. Craig shook his head in annoyance as he pulled in between the poorly painted lines on the side street. His arm stretched to the far end of the floor mat, retrieving his cell phone. Craig dialed a set of three numbers and lifted the phone to his ear. The high-pitched voice of a dispatcher sounded through the speaker.

"Rochester police. What is your emergency?"

Craig paused, clearing his throat. "Oh fuck, oh my God! Someone is shooting! Someone is shooting people!"

"Sir, where are you?" The demeanor of the police dispatcher was cooler than a penguin in a freezer.

"Oh, God! It's terrible! We're...we're in the mall parking lot! Oh God, please hurry!" Craig hung up the phone, sliding it back in his pocket. He flicked his cigar and checked his watch.

"What the hell was that?" Luster asked, baffled by the unexpected call.

"Let me teach you something." Craig rolled down the window. "Listen." He pointed outside, pausing. Luster stared nervously, waiting for something to happen. Nothing. Silence.

Just as Luster was about to repeat the question, the sound of multiple, citywide police sirens blasted down the nearby streets. Craig opened the door, popping his investigator's badge onto his belt. "Distractions, Luster. Always create a distraction." Luster hesitantly acknowledged. Racing thoughts were clouding his rationality. Craig leapt from his seat, tenaciously walking toward the apartments. "Are you coming?"

CHAPTER 16

Rochester, MN
The intersection of 6th Avenue SE & 4th Street SE
En route to the gas station

He walked a few blocks before the weight of the meeting truly sunk in. He realized how fortunate he'd been with the money. He also pondered how devastating it would be if they had to give it back. Were the investigators good, crooked, or somewhere in between? His mind bounced on every step.

The walk was brisk. Decklin reached his SUV faster than he'd expected. Mirrors reflected the shrinking image of the steakhouse as he pulled from the lot. Several blocks and a bad song on the radio passed; he'd reach his apartment in record time. He stepped from the car, clicking the alarm as he headed toward the front door. Decklin stopped, bowing his head in geeky shame. "Jeez, dude, really?" He mocked himself as he swiveled back to his truck. He'd forgotten the batteries. Thoughts of the meeting consumed him to the point of completely ignoring the reason for the trip. He could hear Angela's voice in his head, mocking him for the blonde move. He beeped his alarm again, reaching for the door handle.

Decklin slammed the door to his SUV with a groan. He adjusted himself in the seat, turning over the ignition. Preoccupied, he skipped checking the mirrors. Heart pounding surprise woke him from his routine as the horn sounded from the car behind him. He pressed hard on the brake, sending his chest tightly against the seatbelt. He waved a polite apology, checked his mirror and smiled at the passengers. Cautiously, he pulled from the side of the street.

His mind was leaping between thoughts as he watched the houses pass. He wondered what Charles would say when he sat down at the meeting. He bounced between scenarios, pondering them like scenes in a movie. An audible tone rang from his dash, telling him to "stop thinking about Charles and the meeting and put on your seatbelt." He ignored the warning, turning quickly into the gas station.

The store was nearly empty. Decklin walked with purpose, aiming directly toward the battery aisle. He respectfully grinned as he passed the clerk, giving a rushed wave. Towering down aisle three stood a rack of batteries. He scanned the brands, pricing, and sizes. His eyes wandered harshly in curiosity as he tried to remember the battery size. "Triple A," he whispered under his breath. He pulled a pack from the rack, eyeing the brand name. He strolled back toward the counter, stopping to answer his cell phone.

Charles swirled the remains of his coffee. He sat quietly while Pete and Angela played on the living room floor. Pete flicked a toy car across a racetrack of books, crudely crashing into his mom's leg. She laughed, flicking the cars back toward Pete, who picked up a car, stopping for a moment as the lights flickered. Charles looked up, eyeing the sudden adjustment in lighting. The bulbs flickered, and died. "Well, that's wonderful," Angela said, pushing the cluster of cars and books from her lap. "I'm sorry, I have no idea what happened! I am sure we paid the bills. May be an outage." Angela walked to the breaker box, popping it open without result. "Not a breaker," she hollered from the hallway.

"It could just be an outage, Mrs. Marks; I am not worried about it." Charles swigged the last of his coffee, checking the time. The meeting was in less than an hour. He knew he needed to ask just the right questions, fishing for just the right answers. The meeting was a final building block to the start of a solid investigation.

"I'll call Decklin; maybe he forgot to pay the electric company. He's a bit ditzy sometimes." Angela flicked open her dated cell phone, dialing Decklin's number. She paced the living room, "shusshing" Pete as she walked.

"Hey, babe, what's up?" Decklin answered quickly.

"Did you get the batteries?"

"Yep, got 'em in my hand. I am about to check out; why, what's up?" He could hear that she was irritated. The subtle tone in her voice revealed a bit of annoyance.

"Good. Hey, did you pay the electric company this month?"

Craig walked with purpose. He turned, speaking a few uneasy words. "You are a soldier, Adam Luster; are you not?" They stopped, just feet from the entrance to the apartment.

"Yes, Sir, I am." Luster stood tall. He'd grown accustomed to informality with Craig, however, he was briskly reminded of his militaristic formality.

"Good. Keep your mouth shut and follow my lead. Your career depends on it." Craig's eyes were blank. Cold. His body moved meticulously, popping the lock on the outer door with frightening speed. He put the small lock pick back in his pocket, holding the door for Luster. Craig's feet barely touched the steps as he zipped down the stairs. He stopped, opening the grey breaker box. He counted a few numbers under his breath. He slid the seventeenth breaker to the off position, clicking audibly as the power was cut from Decklin's apartment. Luster was silently nervous, but followed quickly behind as Craig flew up the stairwell.

"Unit 17," Craig whispered. "Angela, Decklin, and Pete." He continued mumbling as he pressed his ear to the door. A woman's voice murmured behind the wood. Slightly disturbed, Luster took a step back, watching the cold efficiency of Craig. Five — Craig's hand signaled the countdown. Four. Three. Two. One. Craig heaved his weight back, kicking the doorknob with the force of a sledgehammer. The doorframe exploded, flailing fragments of wood through the air. Craig drew his pistol from behind the waistband of his pants, shoving it in the doorway. Luster took two steps back, fearfully edging away from the intensity.

"What the fuck? Oh my God, Decklin, someone is breaking in!" Angela screamed into the phone. Charles leapt to his feet as the door disintegrated.

"U.S. Intelligence, let me see your hands!" Bold words left Craig's mouth.

Charles put his hands out in front of him. "Hands! See my hands?" Charles shouted. "Take it easy, guys, we're not armed." The burn of the first round ripped through Charles' body. Blood popped from his chest. Craig held the pistol precisely, shooting three more rounds into Charles' body: two in the chest, and as a finale, one in the head.

"Run, Angela..." Charles spoke his last words. His limp body plummeted to the floor.

Craig quickly turned his attention to Angela as she sprinted toward the back of the apartment.

Luster screamed, "What the fuck are you doing?"

Craig flicked his attention from Angela long enough to slide his pistol full circle, releasing two rounds into Luster's chest. Luster choked, gurgling as he fell to the ground. "Finishing the operation," Craig spoke clearly, pulling the trigger a third time. The last bullet tore a hole into Luster's forehead, drenching the wall with ripe, oxygenated blood.

The pistol quickly swept toward the back of the apartment. Angela shrieked for her son, gripping a baseball bat. Craig smiled devilishly, pointing the barrel at her face. Pete rounded the corner, fearful for his mom. Craig turned his head, looking at the little boy.

"Please! Please! Let him go! Kill me! I don't care! Just let my son go...I'll do anything! ANYTHING!" Craig tilted his head, pondering the consequence of a living witness. "You're doing a good thing for your country, Mrs. Marks." He pulled the trigger, dropping Angela into a heap of nothingness. Pete ran dreadfully to his fallen mother, sobbing uncontrollably. "You too, son. You're so young to be doing such a great service." Pete opened his throat, yelling at a ferocious level. The pistol popped again. The yelling stopped.

Craig walked through the narrow hallway to the living room. He stopped, listening to the odd silence. Fingers slid deeply into his pocket, rustling his cell phone. Records of Angela, Decklin, and Pete appeared on the small screen. He verified their photos against their DMV records, holding the images next to their lifeless faces.

His arms flicked, popping his perfectly white sleeve from his shiny watch. He looked at the time, making note of how quickly the operation ended. A new record, he thought smugly. The shine from his shoes glistened as he stepped over the hunched body of Adam Luster. A pattern of numbers appeared on his cell phone as he pushed the keys. He tossed it into the room carelessly. He turned off the light, locked the door, and walked from the apartment.

The air was cool and moist. He wondered if rain would fall. The keyless entry of the rental car beeped as he walked. As he sat down in the car, he checked his watch, turned on the radio, and counted down from seven. He turned the volume knob slowly, raising the symphonic tones to ear popping levels. ...Three, two, one.

The apartment flashed, sending an audible pressure wave through the windows. He blinked as the fireball spun from the windows. Thick black smoke rolled from every opening.

Angela screamed into the phone. A pounding sweat broke along Decklin's brow. His heart stopped. "Someone is breaking in?" The batteries fell from his hand, hitting the floor with an inaudible prance. His feet were thunder along the pavement toward his truck. Helplessly, he listened to the terror in his wife's voice. "I'm coming, honey, I'm coming!"

He turned over the ignition, slapping the truck into drive. He could hear the roar of a man's voice yelling; he could only make out the words: "U.S. Intelligence." His hands slid wildly across the steering wheel as he sped over the curb, rocking his truck like a drunken seesaw. Rocks pelted his wheel wells as the tires screeched, leaving a path of black rubber. "Hands, see my hands," Charles yelled gruffly in the background of the call. The dull thud of gunfire rattled Decklin into a frenzy. His truck growled, pushing the engine to new limits. "Run, Angela!" ... The sound of gunfire again tore a hole into his reality. His mind was in catastrophic shock. His eyes were tunneled, seeing only the whipping road ahead. His ears were acute, desperately trying to decipher every note that chattered through his earpiece. Another whisper of words was exchanged. Decklin pushed the phone to his head, nearly crushing the case with force. He startled as gunpowder clapped in his ear. He pulled the phone from his head, sobbing with frustration. He screamed into the phone, desperately trying to distract the shooter: "Angela? No! Angela!"

Angela's distressed voice echoed through the phone. The sound of the engine silenced. Wind and whipping rocks were soundless. Decklin heard the words of his dear wife through the phone, pleading for her life. His mouth opened, screaming into the emptiness. He couldn't hear himself, only the distant shots that rang through hell on the receiver. His eyes blurred with hate and tears. Dripping sweat drenched his neck as he punched through the neighborhoods. The phone was silent.

Rapidly, he approached the apartment complex. His truck jumped the median, swimming over the curb to his backyard. He wept angrily, feeling the roller coaster of adrenaline. The truck stopped a few feet short of the building. Decklin flashed from the truck, bolting to the back door. Unexpected force met his chest. His eyes closed from the explosive wind. Dirt met his face as the blast shoved him to the ground before he could reach the door. Gruesome waves of fire rolled from the windows, blowing the door from its hinges. He lay along the grass, watching the smoke and twirling fire blow over his head. Darkness consumed him as he slipped from consciousness.

PART THREE

CHAPTER 17

Kahl Hotel
Rochester, MN | 44°1'21.8353"N 92°27'53.2023"W

Agent Craig stepped from the elevator at the hotel. Two suitcases, filled with Luster's equipment trailed behind him. The slender, bubble-faced hostess at the counter greeted him with dimples and Midwestern warmth. He handed her the room key and waited for his checkout paperwork. She typed effortlessly, blankly gazing at the computer screen. He pulled the papers across the counter, eyeing the charges. Swirly curves accentuated his name as he signed.

He dragged the rolling luggage down the marble corridor toward the exit. Electric doors opened, revealing a black sedan and a suited driver. "Afternoon, Sir. Do you need to stop anywhere before we go to the airport?" The man was portly and appeared to have shaved with a dull rock. "No. Thank you. Please just get me to the airport." Craig was impatient. He noted every wrinkle in the man's suit. Sloppy, he thought as the chauffeur shut the door.

Craig gazed out the window, ignoring the useless small talk on their drive to the airfield. The trip felt like an eternity. He had work to do and was incapable of working in the car, especially with a jabbering driver. Craig tipped the man with a crisp five-dollar bill as they pulled to the drop-off point. The man thanked him under his breath, cursing the rude- mannered businessman.

Craig wheeled his massive baggage through the terminal. The airport was still distasteful and tragic. He despised the sights and smells of small town living. He pulled his tickets from his pocket, offering them to a hefty security guard. The man eyed the tickets and Craig's government identification.

"Has anyone given you anything to travel with today?" The guard's speech was rehearsed. Dry. Craig could tell he'd checked out, mentally dreaming of football scores and bottles of beer.

"No. No one has given me anything, Sir."

"Did anyone pack for you or do your bags have someone else's belongings in them?" It was painful for Craig to listen to the drawn out, slow speech of the man.

"No, everything is mine. Please check me in; I am on official U.S. business." Craig whipped his right arm from his side, checking his watch impatiently. He was seventeen minutes and thirty-four seconds from takeoff. The man handed him his ID and the tickets, clearing him with an effortless wave. Craig walked briskly, pulling both suitcases behind him as he walked.

The plane was early. It parked in front of the large bay window, nearly shoving the nose into the glass. Craig dragged the luggage to the counter, checking them as government carry-on. Even on official business, Craig was charged for the extra bag.

He ducked as he walked through the cabin door. The flight attendant greeted him with a sterile, "Hi, welcome." He nodded, walking past her to the first-class section. He let out a quiet grunt as he packed the luggage above his seat. Craig removed his laptop from the collage of travel bags and sat in his assigned seat at the end of first class. The last row was separated by a wall, quietly protecting his confidentiality while he worked. He opened the tray table setting his laptop on the wobbly desk. The screen flickered on, revealing a complex series of passwords and identity checks. He typed his password and flipped through security questions designed to verify his identity. Digital information triggered a U.S. satellite to move gently in orbit, creating a secure link from his laptop to the *Military Intelligence Operations* Intranet. Most of the agents called the program MIO for short.

MIO - *Military Intelligence Operations* glowed in green at the top of the screen. He moved the cursor to the button labeled "Operation Red Line." He clicked on the button, revealing an intricate web of windows. At the top of the screen, a box with the number $1,463,236,745.25 flashed. The number represented the amount of profit the U.S. Government achieved from the mission. *Operation Red Line* was categorized as an economic operation, authorizing high-ranking agents to do anything necessary to boost the economy. Craig planned the RC operation for years before implementation.

He clicked on a small box toward the bottom of the screen labeled "Grey List." A window opened, revealing a name and social security entry field. He entered Adam Luster's information, clicking the submit button after the last number of his social security number was entered. MIO Grey List was a Level 9 confidential system, allowing Craig to document mission casualties and manipulate the cause of death. An hourglass spun in the center of the screen, bringing up Luster's complete file. Craig entered the cause of death as *mission casualty*.

A plethora of other checkboxes appeared. Craig clicked through the appropriate selections and continued. He pulled the U.S. Treasury bonuses from his personal accounts, re-depositing them into U.S. hands. Savings, checking, and retirement accounts were also emptied. He reached the bottom of the screen and checked the boxes next to *Honorary Discharge* and *Medal of Valor.* Craig mentally saluted Luster for his dedication during the RC missions. He appreciated what Luster gave to his country to assist with *Operation Red Line*. His death was necessary for the confidentiality of the mission. He completed the form, clicking the final button labeled *Seal medical, dental, military, and personal records and complete MIO Grey List entry*.

Craig watched as the system whipped through records, deleting and altering international records. Craig grinned, thinking, Adam Luster was a hero. He died to protect the wellbeing of the United States.

"Entry complete — Would you like to add another?" MIO asked. Craig clicked, "Yes," entering the information for Nguyen and Briggs. Awards and medals of merit were given for their selflessness to the greater cause. Decklin, Angela, and Pete were entered next. Civilians were much simpler. He cleared their deaths as an accident.

> Cause of death: Smoke inhalation
> Reason: Accidental home fire

"Sir, we are getting ready for takeoff. Please put your tray table in the upright position," the flight attendant barked.

Annoyance crossed his brow. He nodded. "One minute, Ma'am."

"Thank you, Sir. Have a nice flight." She walked to the next passenger, stating: "Sir, we're getting ready for takeoff. Can you please fasten your seatbelt?"

Craig clicked through a few more required screens for Angela, Decklin, and Pete. Things like insurance policy approval and next of kin property transfers were always required fields. He didn't wince as he entered their dates of death. Callously, he finalized the death certificates.

He closed his laptop, sliding the table into position. The mission was a success. He'd earned more money than any other agent. Phase one of *Operation Red Line* was complete. Phase two was less stressful and more administrative. He'd set up the Patriot Barrier Corporation months earlier. Once the RC Act took hold, the Senate would grant millions for his company to build curbs, barriers, and posts to protect installations and public buildings from remotely operated threats. He pulled his seat back, closing his eyes. What a country, Craig thought. They're paying me to protect themselves from a threat I created.

Mayo Clinic Hospital

Rochester, MN | 44°1'24.24"N 92°27'55"W

Dull pain swelled in Decklin's back. His eyes flicked open, revealing the blazing, fluorescent light in his hospital room. Confusion blossomed long enough for him to sit up, reaping the pain from his lower back. He bellowed a groan as he realized that he was not home.

Where am I? Decklin pondered curiously. The faded hospital gown pulled on his skin as he cringed, painfully reminding him of how and why he was at the hospital. The horrific memory of his wife screaming for her life flashed through his brain. He swung his legs from the bed. Cold steel dug into his ankle. He whipped off the blankets, revealing a shackle, holding him captive to the hospital bed. Panic struck. His wife. His stepson. Were they alive? What happened after the blast?

He yelled, "Hello? Somebody! Please!" His voice trailed with tears and fear. "Angela? Are you here?" The door swung open slowly. The nurse didn't look at him, didn't smile. She reviewed the chart, walking to his bedside without a word.

"What the hell is going on? Is my wife okay? Angela Marks? Is she here?" Decklin pleaded.

The nurse looked up, posing with a condescending smile. "Hello, Charles. How are you feeling?" She put the clipboard on the desk, sitting in a chair across the room.

"What happened to my wife?" Decklin screamed, pulling aggressively against his shackled leg.

"I'm not sure, Charles. The police will tell you what you need to know. Now, can you calm down a bit so I can check your vitals?" She crossed her arms smugly, smiling from a safe distance. Decklin pulled on the chain, moving the bed with a moan.

"Where is Angela? Why am I handcuffed to the bed? Stop calling me Charles! My name is Decklin — Decklin Marks! *Help me!*" he yelled, violently pulling on the chain. His heart fluttered with fear, anger, and worry. The nurse quickly reached for the call button, pressing it with a pop. A buzzer sounded, sending thunderous footsteps down the hall. Two security guards burst through the door. They muscled Decklin to the bed, holding his legs and arms as he cried for help. A doctor sauntered into the room wielding a needle. "Get the fuck away from me with that! Where is Angela? Where is Pete?"

"Calm down, buddy, I'll send the police in soon. Right now you need to relax." The doctor pushed the cold needle into his wriggling arm, sliding the liquid into his body. The calm was instant and blinding. The face of his wife circled in his mind as the room went dark. "There you go. See! Nice and easy." The doctor's voice echoed as Decklin passed out.

The world spun in a narcotic darkness until a quiet conversation sounded a crescendo in his ears. His eyes opened, revealing Officer Kitts and a chatty nurse. Decklin wiped the drool from his cheek and tried to sit up. The sharp edge of the shackle caught his leg once more.

He mumbled, "Angela? Where is Angela?"

Officer Kitts waved the nurse out of the room, pulling a chair to the bedside. "You're awake. Thank God!"

"Where is my wife?" Decklin sat up, feeling the burn from his back.

Officer Kitts didn't move. His eyes scanned the floorboards, looking for words that could never be said right. "I'm so sorry, Decklin. Your wife...Your wife didn't make it. I am terribly sorry." He put his hand on Decklin's shoulder. Decklin's eyes welled, holding back the flood of devastation.

"Didn't make it? How? Died? My wife is *dead*?" He glared at Officer Kitts. His fists clenched forcefully as a ball of tears ripped down his cheek.

"I'm so sorry, Decklin. She died in the explosion."

"It wasn't the explosion! Someone killed her! I heard it!" Decklin sobbed without control, pulling his face into a bed sheet. "...and Pete? Please God, tell me he is okay?"

Officer Kitts shook his head somberly, whispering, "I'm sorry, Decklin."

Memories of his family danced in his thoughts. Aching muscles clenched around his heart. The smiles of his wife, the laughter. The joyous feeling of Christmas morning with Pete. Gone. He cried out, struggling for a breath as he slumped in the bed.

"I heard it! I heard everything!" Decklin sniffled. "I heard her calling for me! There was nothing I could do!"

"You heard her calling for you? How?"

Decklin wept somberly. "On the phone. She called me. I could hear her yelling for help! I tried...I tried to get there. I didn't make it in time." Decklin was completely exhausted. He whimpered, mouthing the words, "I couldn't make it" in between breaths.

"You don't need this." Officer Kitts pulled the blankets from Decklin's whimpering body. The leg shackle clicked as he inserted the key and twisted it.

"Why? Why was I cuffed? I didn't do anything!"

"I know. You were at the wrong place at the wrong time. You were listed as the arson suspect. I'll clear you in the report after you sign a few things on your way out." Officer Kitts was concerned. It was a shame that Decklin came into the hospital as a detainee. "Sorry for the formalities."

A nurse arrived, pushing a cart of food and paperwork. "How are you feeling, Charles?" She smiled, unlike the previous nurse. Decklin didn't smile back. He didn't move. Numbness overcame him. "Charles? Why are you calling me that?" She ignored his question, wrapping a blood pressure cuff around his sleeve. She checked his blood pressure, temperature, and heart rate, all while jotting numbers into his chart.

Decklin wiped his tears, mumbling, "Stop, wait! My name is not Charles! My name is Decklin Marks; m-a-r-k-s!" He spelled it, hoping the quick alphabet lesson would jog her memory. The nurse rolled her eyes, checked the chart, and held the papers in front of Decklin's face.

"Sir, you checked in as Charles Unit. I'll call you Decklin if that is what you prefer?" Decklin pulled the paperwork from her, gazing at the name. In printed letters, the words "*Unit, Charles*" appeared.

"No! No, wait...that isn't me! My identity was switched because of the investigation..." His voice trailed as he watched the nurse pull back his chart. Her raised brow expressed her thoughts: she thought he was crazy.

"Sir, I am sure the police officer would love to hear about that. I have better things to do." She signed the release form and handed it to Officer Kitts. She walked out, glancing back with a snicker.

"C'mon, I'll give you a ride." Officer Kitts held out his hand, offering to help Decklin up.

"A ride? To where? Everything is gone…" Decklin began to whimper. "…everything."

"I found a nice place for you to stay for a while. I'll show you. It's the least I can do."

Decklin was difficult to move. His body was limp as Kitts helped him from the bed into the wheelchair. Decklin slumped over, staring at the ground as he was pushed from the room. People in scrubs, gowns, and lab coats filled the long hallways. Decklin didn't see a soul. His eyes focused on the wiggling tire on the front of the wheelchair. Every few moments, the sounds of his wife and stepson stabbed his memory. He'd cringe uncomfortably and weep under his breath. His body jerked forward as the wheelchair rumbled over the elevator threshold. Officer Kitts grabbed Decklin's shoulder, gently helping to push him back into the chair.

The elevator beeped rhythmically as it descended. The doors groaned open, revealing the waxed flooring of the lobby. It was busy, densely populated with hospital staff, and visitors holding balloons. Officer Kitts carefully wound through the corridor to the parking structure. Decklin didn't speak. He didn't move.

Black and white paint caught the corner of Decklin's eye as they rounded the corner of the parking ramp. Officer Kitts' police car was parked deep in the garage, nestled tightly between a red sports car and a rusty station wagon. He parked the wheelchair a few feet behind his cruiser and clicked the parking brake. Bags and paperwork littered the passenger seat. He scooped the forms from the seat, stuffing them into his duffel bag.

With a shrug, Kitts heaved Decklin from the chair to the passenger seat. Decklin didn't flinch as he landed. Blinking lights, a laptop, and the glowing switch panels were ignored. He sat in silence after Kitts closed the door. He stared at the side of the laptop. A dull roar of thoughts circled in his head. He was furious, terrified, lost, and completely overcome with sadness.

Kitts opened his door, climbing into the seat with a gasp. He tried making conversation about the weather or the hotel he had chosen for Decklin, but he was just a blank slate. Kitts turned the knob on his radio, tuning in a rock station just above audible. He told dispatch that he was unavailable, generously giving his lunch break to help Decklin get to the hotel. He peeked at his passenger, feeling terrible. Decklin's head rested against the glass, as he watched the painted lane lines .

Kitts pulled into the hotel, stopping at the door. He left Decklin in the car as he entered the hotel lobby. A short, bearded man checked him in, handing him a key and a hotel map.

It was more difficult to pull Decklin from the car than it was to get him in. Sweat gathered along Kitts' brow as he picked Decklin up. He grabbed the duffel bag, swinging it over the other shoulder. Decklin's legs were rubber, bouncing along the ground as Kitts propped his weight on his shoulder. Kitts leaned against the wall as he popped the hotel key into the door.

Decklin flopped on the bed, mumbling something to Kitts. He asked for clarification, but Decklin waved him off with a limp hand. He left his card on the dresser, circling his cell phone number. Kitts pulled soup cans and plastic containers from the duffel bag. "If you need anything, Decklin, please call me. The room is paid up for two weeks and there should be enough soup, crackers, and sandwich meat here to sustain ya for a few days."

Decklin waved again, miserably acknowledging the gesture.

CHAPTER 18

The White House

Washington, DC | 38°53'51.61"N 77°2'11.58"W

"Sir, one final note on the RC Act." The President's aide added another document to the overflowing compilation of papers, folders, and forms. The RC Act was edging up on the 10-day window to be signed.

"Thank you." The President signed the form, authorizing the passing of the bill. "That will be all for tonight." His signature was fluid, clean, and professional. He lifted the page, handing it to his aide without breaking eye contact with the next form on his desk.

He took the sheet from the President, sliding it gently into a white envelope. "Thank you, Sir, have a wonderful evening. I'll get this out right away." The aide dismissed himself, respectfully edging out of the Oval Office.

The hallways leading from his office were packed with litigation teams, military personnel, and administration secretaries. He handed the envelope to a sharply dressed woman behind a desk. She pulled her headset off, greeting the President's aide. "Priority delivery to the Senate Administration Building." His words were hushed and direct. She nodded, pushing the envelope into a briefcase. As the aide turned, she buzzed the military courier, informing him via loudspeaker of the urgent delivery.

The courier station was buried in the basement of the White House. Sitting behind a steel desk and a computer, the courier acknowledged the page. He hopped to his feet, checking the creases in his uniform. The labyrinth of secure hallways under the White House were checkered with security checkpoints. The courier stopped six times to flash his ID and verify his thumbprint. He reached the desk in excellent time, grabbing the briefcase with a polite wave.

Exiting the White House was a bit trickier. Blast doors and security checkpoints were plentiful, however, within a few minutes the armored security car came into view. Glistening badges were tightly pressed together on the driver's uniform. Decorated soldiers were generally used for White House operations, ensuring their retirement was simple and safe. The car drove for several minutes before reaching the Senate Administration Building. He walked down the long path, past the gardens, to the front doors. As he approached, a uniformed police officer checked his ID, calling into his radio for verification. After a bit, the voice on the other end cleared him to enter the building. The tall glass doors opened. The woman behind the counter approached him, taking the briefcase with little ambition for conversation. She headed immediately to the rear chambers. Her small knuckles rapped on the door. The muffled words, "Come," rang through the door. As she opened the door, an elderly administrator smiled, taking the briefcase from her. He too didn't have time for niceties. Before she could blink, the door shut.

The briefcase was opened, exposing the freshly signed bill. The experienced senate admin scanned the document, sending the bill over a secure connection to eight different email addresses.

The Capitol Building — Private Senate Chambers

Washington, DC | 38.889°N 77.0072°W

Senator Royce's eye caught the flicker of the *"new email"* icon in the upper right corner of his computer. His mouse moved to the icon, clicking with anticipation. A scanned image of the signed, official copy of the RC Act stared back at him. He let out a sigh, ecstatically laughing with glee. Confidentiality was ignored, forwarding the image to Agent Craig's cell phone. *The RC Act — Passed. See attached.*

San Diego Freeway

Freeway 8 (West) San Diego, CA | 32°45'00"N 117°11'45"W

Agent Craig held the steering wheel with one hand. Eighty miles per hour was the standard as he zipped along the freeway. He squinted to read the small text on his cell phone. *The RC Act — Passed. See attached.* He clicked the small icon shaped like a paperclip. The scanned image of the bill slid down his screen. The corner of his mouth tilted into a tiny smirk. He clicked out of the screen, dialing a lengthy phone number.

"Good afternoon, Agent Craig, what can I do for you?" a man's voice came through the speaker.

"Good afternoon. Are you in your office?"

"Always, you know how it is. Are you ready to sign?" The man was energetic, filled with anticipation.

"I think I am ready to sign today. Is the paperwork in line?" Craig sifted through his breast pocket as he spoke, driving shakily with his knee.

"Absolutely! You sign the form and the building is all yours! How soon will you be here?"

Craig pulled a cigar from his pocket, pausing the conversation to light the tip with a puff. "I am exactly eight minutes away. I'll see you then."

"All right! Great! I'll see you in…" Craig hung up the phone. He didn't care much for the gratification from a real estate broker.

Douglas Real Estate

San Diego, CA | 32°45'57"N 117°11'50"W

Palm trees and a cluttered parking lot surrounded the building. Agent Craig walked into the unmarked building to the small set of stairs. Douglas Real Estate was a private company, operated by a few business major types. The firm only worked with commercial properties or quiet government buyouts. They were the definition of silent acquisition.

"Good afternoon, Officer Craig!" the broker said enthusiastically as he walked into the room.

"*Agent* Craig. I believe I've told you this before." Craig spoke clearly, holding out a hand to emphasize the sentence.

"Right, right, right! I remember! Well then, *Agent* Craig, let's go see the property!"

"Why? I've seen it. Unless something has changed, I much prefer a quick turn on this transaction." Craig was annoyed. Not by the man's inappropriate use of "officer," but by the process. He knew what the building looked like. He knew the cost. He knew the dimensions and the square footage. Craig had studied the building with a microscope.

"Right. Of course, Sir." The broker grinned showing his blazing white teeth. He rustled through his clipboard, pulling a small stack of deeds, papers, and forms. He laid out the packet, pointing to the spots where Craig needed to sign. Again, Craig's annoyance grew. The pages already contained small red stickers that stated "sign here." The coaching was a bit unneeded.

He signed thirty-six arduous times, ensuring his signature was mildly legible. "Okay, I think we're done here. Can I have the keys?" Craig stretched an impatient hand to the broker.

"Keys, right." He chuckled uncomfortably. "I've never turned a transaction this quickly. You must be in some rush to get in there, eh?" Craig didn't respond. His hand remained up, waiting for the keys. The man dug through his drawer, pulling a small ring of keys from a lockbox. Craig counted the seconds as he waited. Exactly twenty seconds later, the broker pulled the keys from the ring, placing them gently in his hand.

"Well...I guess that is everything! It was a pleasure working with you, *Agent* Craig."

"Indeed. I'll be in touch if I need anything." He pocketed the keys without looking at them. He was completely detached from the transaction. His signature transferred millions to the broker, officially making the Patriot Barrier Corporation the proud new owner of a commercial building off Interstate 5. Craig's mind simply checked off the sale as an item completed.

Swedish Springs Hotel

Rochester, MN | 44°1'24.24"N 92°27'46.62"W

He tried not to knock loudly, despite his training. Officer Kitts stood outside the hotel room door, waiting for Decklin to answer. The stir of bottles and footsteps approached the opposing side of the entry. Decklin opened the door a few inches, squinting at the sun. His skin was pale, holding the solid outline of an unshaven scruff.

"What do you want?" Decklin asked through the sliver of space.

"I wanted to check on you. How are you holding up?" Pungent aromas of booze and sweat wafted from the room.

"I'm fine. Thank you." Decklin started to shut the door in his face. Officer Kitts stuck his boot in the door, wedging his foot tightly. Decklin sneered at him drunkenly.

"I have something for you, Decklin, please...let me in? I won't stay long." Officer Kitts had seen a thousand deaths: car crashes, heart attacks, just about everything. He felt very little in the face of on-duty tragedy; however, he held a special hurt for Decklin.

Decklin walked away from the door, mumbling for Kitts to enter. He swung open the door, revealing what could only be described as a depressed disaster. Wastebaskets were full of drunken vomit. Tables were littered with empty bottles. A few wallet-sized pictures of Angela and Pete were hung on the broken mirror. Officer Kitts didn't mention the mess. He turned back to retrieve the blackened remains of Decklin's safe. "I thought you might want this." Decklin slouched into the chair, raising an eyebrow in disinterest. Officer Kitts gripped the heavy safe, walking it slowly to the side of the dresser. "I'll leave this here. I'm sure it has something inside that you want." Kitts was out of words, choosing retreat over awkward conversation. He paced to the door when Decklin spoke clearly for the first time in days.

"The funeral." His words were simple, but treacherous. "I had a funeral." Decklin held up the local paper. An image of Angela, Decklin, and Pete made the front page, titled: "They will be missed."

"You were unconscious, Decklin. I'm sorry. You were late to your own funeral." Kitts tried to chuckle, lacking the poise he'd hoped for.

“I missed *her* funeral,” Decklin said, slamming the paper on the table. His hand swiped the brown bottle of rum. Warm alcohol poured down his face and throat as he guzzled.

“I'm sorry, Decklin.” Kitts looked to the floor, trying to empathize. “Do you need anything? I can bring you anything you need. Like I said, you have quite a while before you need to leave the hotel.” Kitts smiled, only to quickly dodge the whizzing bottle of rum flying over his shoulder. Glass smashed against the wall.

“I want my family!” With his face in his hands, switching from infuriated anger to uncontrollable crying, Decklin mumbled, “I want them back.” Trying to offer a bit of sympathy, Kitts reached out to Decklin's shoulder, when he snapped back, flicking Kitts' arm away. “Leave me alone! I just want to be alone!”

Officer Kitts reached his limit. He knew Decklin was fragile, but he could only give so much. “Okay, Decklin, I'll see you soon. Please be careful.” He motioned to the bottles surrounding the room. “I am always here if you need me.” The door closed quietly.

Stillness was heavy in the lonely room. Decklin picked up another bottle, sipping the vivid liquor from the tip, eyeing the safe with the blur of his glazed eyes. The charred exterior was battered and dented. Recalling the last time he opened it, sent the burn of misery deeper into his chest. The chair rocked backward as he stood. Unbalanced was the method he used to pace across the room, plopping to the floor without coordination. His weary hand rubbed the soot from the combination, revealing the steel numbers along the dial, turning it slowly, and edging through the digits. The door popped with a squeak, revealing the clutter of small boxes, envelopes, cash, and photo albums. He gasped when he saw the tip of the red album titled

"Decklin and Angela's Honeymoon." Loose bills flopped to the floor as he vigorously snatched the book, flipping the pages somberly. Angela's smile echoed through the pages. The first four pages were official wedding photos, forcing them to pose unnaturally. Page five revealed her lips pressed against the side of his face in a nameless restaurant. He closed his eyes, replaying the moments leading up to the picture. They were laughing, joking about something only they would understand. She told him to smile, whipping her camera from her pocket. Decklin couldn't react quickly enough. The picture captured a drip of sauce along his cheek, as well as her grinning lips as they pressed against his jaw line.

Decklin smiled. Cried. Whimpered and warmly held the album to his chest. She was gone. He lay on the floor, gazing at the ceiling. "I miss you, babe," he said quietly. "What am I going to do without you?"

CHAPTER 19

Patriot Barrier Corporation

San Diego, CA | 32°44'57"N 117°11'50"W

The heat was unbearable. Sunbaked construction workers leaned lazily while they waited for orders. Craig pulled up, parking in a freshly painted parking slot. He scanned the group of torn t-shirt wearing construction types. He parked, sliding on his mirrored sunglasses as he stepped from his car. The foreman, an older bearded Irishman, walked to his car. "Afternoon, Dominick! How's business?" He was friendly and harmless, yet Craig still loathed his casual nature.

"Sir, address me as Mr. Craig," he stated, while standing motionless, sternly correcting the foreman.

"Oh damn, my apologies, Sir. I get so used to construction fellas that I completely forget my manners." He meant no disrespect. He was a bit shocked at the custom, but didn't care. He had a job to do.

"Good. Let's get these guys on the clock. Have the building plans been explained?"

"Yepper, of course. In detail. We've got it covered, Mr. Craig."

"Good. Have your boys start as soon as possible." Craig shook his hand, feeling the grit of his harsh palm. Craig walked away, confident that the Irishman could handle the workload. The foreman whistled loudly, calling to the group. The train of workers headed into the building, closely behind Craig. They immediately started drilling, sawing, and measuring the spaces for cubicles and offices. Craig walked through sawdust-laden hallways to his office.

He closed the door, blocking the sound of hammers and tools. Casually, Craig wandered to the chair at his new desk. One by one, cutting through the pile of envelopes that filled his inbox, he sifted through the junk until reaching the bottom envelope. He opened it carefully, ensuring he didn't damage its contents. "United States Treasury — Contract Division" was printed neatly across the check. It was the first bulk sum from the RC Act contract. The Patriot Barrier Corporation would be paid handsomely to ensure federal buildings, airports, and banks were free from threat. Craig was content.

"Sir, the ceremony starts in one hour. Do you need your suit jacket?" his new assistant screeched over his phone intercom.

He had forgotten about the ribbon cutting. He reached for the phone to respond, eyeing the plethora of buttons. The top button buzzed, clearly warning him of the mistake.

After a few tries, he responded, "Yes, please bring my coat to me. Also Mary, is the new CEO in the building?"

She paused a few moments, and then replied, "Yes, would you like me to send him in?"

"Yes, please." Craig snuffed his cigar and opened his laptop. He opened the MIO program, logging the final details of his operation. Following the approval of the RC Act, Craig's mission was nearly complete. He needed to ensure the Patriot Barrier Corporation was running smoothly prior to moving away from Operation Red Line. Craig was ready to move forward, anxious to strategize for the next operation. He slowly typed the details, ensuring every element and cost was logged.

"Mr. Craig? Busy?" The new CEO popped his head into Craig's office.

"Yes, Sir, come in. Sit down." Craig closed his laptop quickly as Mick Zimmer entered the room. Mick reeked of business. His suit was pressed to perfection while his shoes glared a brilliant shine. He wore a wavy hairstyle that had been out of date since the eighties. Most importantly, he was as clean as a whistle and willing to operate the company according to Craig's needs.

Mick sat down. It was his second day on the job at the Patriot Barrier Corporation. He knew only that Craig was a government liaison. Not only was the job new, but Craig was
an intimidating figure.

"Today we officially open. After the ceremony, I need you to make sure the first job goes smoothly." Craig leaned over the desk, open handed and confident in every pore.

“Yes, Sir. I’ve got crews headed to the first site as we speak.”

“Good. I am counting on you. I plan on being hands-off in a few days.”

“You can be confident in my abilities. I’ve run seven companies, all of which…” Mick stopped abruptly as Craig held up his hand, motioning for him to stop.

“I know your history, Zimmer. I picked you because of it. Just get it done.”

“Yes, Sir, Mr. Craig. I will.”

“I know you will. Do you have a speech prepared for the opening ceremony?”

“Absolutely.”

“Good. Let’s get out there before the press.”

Swedish Springs Hotel

Rochester, MN | 44°1'24.24"N 92°27'46.62"W

Decklin pushed the button on the hotel phone. The front desk answered after three rings. “Front desk — What can I do for you, Charles?” Decklin pulled the phone from his ear, glaring at the receiver. The idea of being called Charles sickened him.

“I need a cab.” Decklin’s voice was weary.

"Yes, absolutely. I'll call one right away. I'll call you when it has arrived."

"Thanks." Decklin slid the phone back on the cradle. He buried his face in open palms, letting out a tear. The trip made him nervous, almost sick. He'd seen black and white pictures in the paper, but he never dreamed he'd be visiting his wife and stepson's grave. The ball in his heart grew, sliding into the pit of his stomach. His belly twitched, sending him into a frenzy to reach the bathroom. Face down, he knelt over the toilet, releasing his nerves into the bowl. He wiped his face, washing away the spit and vomit. His hand reached wearily to the counter, pulling himself up to the sink. Cold water rushed over his face. He stopped, looking at himself in the mirror. "You can do this," he mumbled.

He paced from the bathroom to the living room and back. The brown bottle swayed as he walked, occasionally sliding to his lips for another sip. He stared at the phone, waiting for the red light to flash. He paced. He guzzled three more mouthfuls of liquor. The phone rang.

"Hello?" He swallowed hard.

"Charles, your taxi is here."

Decklin hung up the phone hard, knocking a bottle from the nightstand. He turned, looking at himself in the mirror and said, "You can do this, c'mon," and walked from the hotel room.

He squinted at the sun, instantly raising a hand to shield his eyes. As he walked toward the lobby, he felt his heart fumbling. He stopped, wiped the water from his eyes, and turned the corner to the lobby.

The cabbie was young, dark, and appeared to be of Middle Eastern origin. Decklin stepped to the side of the cab, taking a deep breath. He pulled on the door handle, getting into the backseat. As he closed the door, he sprung the small bottle of booze from his pocket.

"You no drink in my cab, asshole; put it away. Now, where do you need go again?" His tattered English was thick and vile. Decklin took a drink, sliding the bottle back into his pocket. He spoke the address softly, reading it from the wrinkled article in the paper. The cabbie glared at him in the mirror, pushed the button on his fare counter, and pulled out from the hotel. Decklin slumped in the backseat, watching the cars drive by. He wondered about the people in the cars. Had they lost someone? Did they know real pain? What did he do to deserve such a misfortune?

The trip was a quick blur. Suddenly, the cab slammed to a stop. "Twelve dollars!" the man yelled, turning in his seat. Decklin pulled out his billfold, spilling currency all over his lap. The cabbie's eyes widened. "Fuck man, you rich! Give me big tip!"

Decklin didn't look at him. The rude voice was a distant sound in his whizzing mind. He pulled a twenty-dollar bill, handing it to the driver. "Keep it, but wait here."

The cabbie pulled the bill quickly from his hand. "I wait, but be fast. You aren't only customer today, you know!"

Decklin ignored him, stepping from the car without a word more. The wind was colder at the entrance to the cemetery. Lines of stones filled his sight. His feet were heavy as he stepped toward the entrance. His legs burned, aching from the emotional heaviness. Row after row, he walked toward section B-25, as mentioned in the paper. He puffed up his chest, holding back the sorrow. He told himself repeatedly, "You can do this."

He approached section B. Graves filled his vision as three clean stones drew near. The dirt was fresh. The flowers were bright. He slowed, gasping for a deep breath as he grew closer. Marbled grey stone, etched deeply with familiar names looked new and solid. Modest rock presented their earthly titles: Angela Marks, Pete Joan, and Decklin Marks. Flustered tears crept as he looked to the heavens. His legs collapsed into the fresh dirt. His mouth opened, blaring sobs of dread as he knelt before his wife. Beautiful Angela, buried in the ground. He embraced the stone, dripping tears along the top of the cold rock. He unsheathed the bottle of booze and pulled two pictures from his pocket. He guzzled furiously, spilling liquid down his shirt. Tears and liquor formed a V along his neckline. Decklin wiped his face with his sleeve, solemnly peering at the pictures. The first portrait held an image of Angela and Decklin's kiss. He stared at the image, his stomach knotting as he gripped the photo harder. He set the print at the base of her headstone. Attention turned to Pete's grave. Pete and Decklin wrestled in the second photograph. It wasn't a fancy shot, less planned than most. He peered into the image, revering Pete's laughter. Pete was his son, blood or not. He set the picture at the base of his grave and wrapped his arms around the two icy headstones. Fire cut through his chest as he sobbed. He pulled an arm free, finishing the small bottle. Relief in a bottle is what he craved. He desired numbness.

The third marbled rock caught his attention. There, covered in flowers, stood a tall gravestone labeled "Decklin Marks." Primal anger masked his sorrow. "This didn't happen! How did this happen?" he yelled, flinging the bottle against his monument. The glass shattered, sending bitter shards through the air. His balance faltered, landing him on a brown chip of glass. Dull pain drizzled from his hand.

"Is this what she would want?" Officer Kitts walked up the path. He'd been watching Decklin's drunken show.

"What the fuck are you doing here?" Decklin gripped his bleeding hand, stumbling to his feet. Balance was lost again, landing him against Angela's tombstone.

"I called the motel. They said you called a cab. It wasn't too difficult to find you." Kitts held out a helping hand for Decklin to stand.

"You shouldn't have followed me. This is your fault! I'm stuck with a new name, no family, and a shitty hotel!" Decklin refused his hand, kneeling instead.

"Decklin. This is not my fault." Kitts knew Decklin was fragile, but he didn't want to take the drunken blame. "No one is at fault here. It was just bad luck."

Decklin angrily turned, mumbling, "Bad luck? This isn't bad luck. This is Hell!" Blood oozed from the wound, dripping past his elbow.

"Look at you, Decklin! Is this what she would want you to do? Is this what *you* want?"

"Fuck you. Of course this isn't what I want! I want my family back!"

"I know. That isn't what I meant. I mean, do you think this is what Angela would want you to do?"

"No! She would want me to find the fucker that hurt her son..." Fantasy blocked his conscience. Finding her murderer consumed his rage. Ecstasy of revenge swirled, deepening his thoughts of stringing her killer in horrific ways.

"Well, I can't help you with that. Your case has been blacklisted by powers much higher than me! I can't even open the file anymore." Kitts wasn't impressed with Decklin's new vengeful ambition. The last thing Kitts needed was a drunken vigilante.

Decklin's eyes flashed with sobriety in a moment of clarity. "You can help me! Can't you? We can find whoever did this!" Decklin walked on his knees to Officer Kitts, grabbing the pressed seam on his police-issued pants. "Please help me; I want to make these assholes pay for what they took from me."

Officer Kitts peered down at Decklin. His face glowed red from crying. His beard was far past a 5 o'clock shadow. He smelled of liquor and a lack of bathing. Kitts felt sorry for him, but knew vengeance would solve nothing. As Kitts stared into his eyes, he thought of his own family. Officer Kitts had children. A wife. A dog. A home. What would he do if they were taken from him in the blink of an eye? Going after these guys would be arduous, dangerous, and inevitably lead to more crime. Again, he was placed in a position where he knew the letter of the law disagreed with the right thing to do. He toiled, questioning: was this the right thing to do? As he considered the consequences, Decklin begged again. "I'd help you, Decklin, but really. The reports are sealed. Someone with power sealed your files — may be political. I really have no idea who can even do that. There is nothing I can give you!"

"Anything? Something! I need this! I need to make them feel what they've done," Decklin pleaded. He'd found new purpose.

"I don't have anything, Decklin, I'm sorry. But...I know Charles did."

"Charles? Charles is dead!"

Officer Kitts shook his head. "Decklin, you *are* Charles! His office is yours now. He didn't have family here and didn't really make a name for himself in this town. No one even knows he died! Go to his office, look through his reports. That is where I would start." Morality and ethics clouded his thoughts as he told Decklin of the details.

"Yes, you're right. I am Charles now. An investigator...but, I don't know the first thing about investigations."

"You'll learn, Decklin. But, I've gotta warn you. Whoever these people are, if they even smell that you are still alive, they'd take you out — no questions asked."

Patriot Barrier Corporation

San Diego, CA | 32°44'57"N 117°11'50"W

Press gathered around the podium, snapping pictures of the new CEO. The audience was small, but filled with political and business influence. The Patriot Barrier Corporation was the latest in government contract news. It was a difficult task obtaining a bid, let alone the sole holder of a contract. Patriot Barrier Corporation was to install cement curbs around the nation, creating a massive increase in the Southern California economy. Mick Zimmer stood proudly, waiting for a lull in the camera flashes.

"Good evening, San Diego! It is an honor to take part in such a monumental event." He paused, clearing his throat. Craig watched the CEO as he began to speak. He noticed the small things. His hands shifted on the podium. His left foot tapped against the stage. He was nervous. A weak speaker, but a solid puppet for the operation.

Mick continued, "A few months ago, we were devastated by a new type of domestic threat. We'll never forget the horrific images of the explosion at the Luxemburg Bank. We were awestruck at the reports of the casino robbery and felt sorrow for the pilots who lost their lives in an effort to fight terrorism. But, the Senate took action. Their swift, stern hand quickly put the hammer down on these acts of tyranny. They challenged companies across the nation to develop a defense against criminal drones..." He paused dramatically, smiling with confidence. "...and we met that challenge!"

"Automated vehicle terrorism will no longer be a threat. We won the contracts because of our integrity. We achieved this honor because of our diligence and we gained your respect by support from the community. We will deliver the safety the public deserves." He smiled, showing rows of white teeth. Ridiculously large scissors rose toward the ribbon. "The Patriot Barrier Corporation is officially open. Together, let's make our country safer!"

He turned from the podium, sliding the scissors over the wide ribbon. He posed momentarily, allowing the press to take pictures. *Snip!* The ribbon twisted in the wind as it fell. Strobes of camera flashes were blinding, but empowered Mick Zimmer.

Craig stood to the side of the stage, quietly scrutinizing the speech. He turned from the wind, lighting another cigar. The smoke wafted on stage, catching the attention of Zimmer. "Come on up here, Mr. Craig. Get a picture with me!" Craig shook his head sternly. Before he could stop him, Zimmer walked from the stage, put his arm around Craig and posed. Cameras flashed. Craig was less than thrilled. Purple spots glimmered in his vision as Zimmer shook hands and smiled to the audience.

Craig sucked on his cigar and peered over the crowd. Tall legs walked through a path in the mob. Craig squinted, watching her approach. Sadie Shae emerged, heading straight for Craig.

"Isn't this a surprise, Ms. Shae." Craig wasn't displeased to see her, but he didn't care to mix business events with pleasure.

"Surprised to see me? I thought you'd know I was coming from a mile away. What, you don't have my car bugged anymore?" She winked.

"That was a long time ago, Sadie." He dropped the cigar, grinding it into the pavement. "What are you doing here?"

"I saw your name in the paper and knew you were up to trouble. I just wanted to show up and make sure you stayed in line." She motioned to the door. "Everyone is going into the conference room to celebrate. Care to invite me in?"

Craig's presence wasn't needed at the celebratory party. Politicians, press, civilians, and city council members could open the bottles of champagne on their own. "Yes, Ma'am. Come in. I need to stop in my office first." He motioned for her to follow. They slid through the crowd, past the doorway and around the conference room.

He opened the door, extending a polite arm for her to enter first. She walked in, surprised at the simplicity of the office. She put her finger on the nameplate on the door: "*Mr.* Craig. Hmmm. That's a new one." Her hands traced his jaw as he closed the door. "What exactly is your involvement with the Patriot Barrier Corporation anyway? Nothing to do with planes, I'm sure."

Agent Craig lifted a single finger, pressing it to her lips. "Shhhh, enough about planes." He pulled her into his lips, kissing her with the passion she needed to stop talking. Of course, she melted, wrapping her arms around his shoulders. She leaned against him, pressing his weight to the cluttered desk. One swift wipe of his hand threw the folders and paperwork to the floor. Strong hands pulled her to his lap. Loud sighs trickled into his ear, while she wrestled with his belt. She fumbled with the buckle, eventually pulling it free from his waist. Gentle skin graced his fingertips as his hands explored. Silky fabric slid effortlessly as Craig lifted the dress above her hips. Heat from her smooth thighs sat restlessly on his unbuttoned pants.

She kissed him furiously, sliding her panties to the floor. Warm skin radiated on her hands as she tugged at his fly. Her delicate fingers danced along his excited body. He pulled her close, sliding his body into hers. Arching anxiously, Sadie felt the slippery girth of Craig as she relaxed around him. She lifted herself slowly, feeling every inch of his raw sexuality. As she dropped, pushing her depth to the brink, she let out a quiet moan. Her manicured fingernails dug into Craig's arms as she bobbed in his grasp. His eyes closed, satisfying hidden desires. Their movements gained in rhythmic speed.

Despite the ecstasy, he was conflicted. Their attraction was fire, but she was a conflict of interest to the mission. She was the only asset remaining with information on Operation Red Line. He pulled her off, sliding himself from her body with a slick pop. He gazed into her eyes for a split second, contemplating the very real fear that he may need to terminate her records in order to preserve the mission.

Confused, she gently asked, "What's wrong, baby?" He said nothing, but grabbed her waist hastily. He shoved her over the desk, pressing her chest to the hard oak. Hands wandered up her dress, pulling the soft fabric above her bellybutton. He dove inside her without gentility. She moaned, feeling the sudden bliss of fullness. Her body went limp as he held her tightly, shaking the desk with an increased cadence. Her hands reached for the edges of the desk, gripping tightly as Craig rocked inside her body. Moist skin slithered between their thighs, pressing a crescendo of moans as Craig slowed to a gentle pace. Blush-colored cheeks sweetened her smile. Craig pulled himself from her peaceful hold, kissing her forehead as he pulled up his trousers. He'd missed her.

Charles Unit Investigations

Rochester, MN | 44°4'4.8282"N 92°30'13.7157"W

Officer Kitts pulled into the parking stall in front of Charles Unit Investigations. "Thank you for the help, Officer Kitts." He was kind enough to give him a ride to Charles' office. Kitts simply grinned, fearfully enjoying the new spark in Decklin's eye. "Here are the keys; I pulled them from

Charles' belongings at the morgue. Everything you need should be in there."

"I appreciate everything you've done for me, really." Decklin grabbed the key.

"You're welcome, Decklin. But..." Officer Kitts offered a serious look. "No one, and I mean *no one*, can know that I've helped you."

"You have my word."

He waved as Kitts drove away. He turned his attention to the keys, sitting squarely in the palm of his hand. Odd feelings swept over him. The keys he held were his, but not justly. He'd acquired a fresh world overnight.

Tumblers clicked as the key turned. The knob squeaked as the door opened. Decklin pocketed the keys, walking into the silent waiting room. He switched on a lamp, illuminating the dusty corners. Silence hung in the room as he approached the office door. It too was locked. He sifted through his keys, finding the proper fit on his last attempt. The green lamp brightened only a fraction of the office, leaving quiet shadows along the walls and file cabinets. An unfamiliar hum buzzed from the lamp, whispering away the silence. Creaking floorboards welcomed his steps as he sat behind the desk. Cigarette butts and paperwork quilted the surface, leaving only a few inches of visible wood.

Charles Unit Investigations LLC belonged to him now. He smirked; everything in the building was his. The green lamp. Ruffled papers. Assorted collared shirts hanging on the cabinets. The lonely plastic plant that sat in the corner; everything was his. Crystal reflections from the decanter glimmered in the muted light. He reached for the stylish bottle, pouring a three-finger glass. The alcohol was bitter, pursing his lips. The desk held three drawers per side. The top drawer was difficult to open. Paperwork bloomed from the open drawer as it popped free. He quickly closed it, moving to the next drawer. It opened more smoothly. A revolver and a pack of unfiltered cigarettes slid into view. He gasped at the sight of the gun, sliding the drawer closed instantaneously. Screams echoed in his head, playing back the sounds of his wife and stepson. He covered his ears, gritting his teeth at the thoughts. He slid open the drawer, sliding the revolver from the musty drawer. He looked at it, fantasizing about a chance at shooting the killer. The drawer slid closed, less the revolver that lay neatly on the desk.

Weathered leather squeaked as he stood from the chair. Framed prints, wanted posters, and shadowboxes plagued the walls. A thin door on the west wall opened into a bathroom. The toilet and sink were pearly clean, while the tile flooring was a brown shade of age. Curiously, he lifted his arm to sniff his armpit. He realized in that moment what an unbathed, drunken man smells like after a few weeks. He slipped off his shirt, revealing weeks of grease. Warm water from the faucet poured over his face. He eyed the bowl of bathroom utensils on the counter. Clearly, Charles spent too much time at the office. He had an entire bathroom set sitting a precise arm's length from the sink.

He reached for the straight razor first. Within the pearl handle popped the dreadfully sharp razor. His finger tested the edge, finding the blade to be fittingly razor sharp. He pulled the brush and soap from the bowl, setting them in the sink. He'd seen people in movies shave with a straight razor and foam lather, but never attempted it in real life. Foam, soap, and hot water rushed over his face, followed by the slim edge of the razor. His skin was frail as the blade scraped cleanly over the surface. Three knicks and five minutes later, his face was as smooth as a bowling ball. Next, he rinsed his chest. Special attention was paid to the armpit zones, washing away the sweetened smell of aged sweat. A splash of aftershave slapped onto his raw skin, stinging wildly as it burned along his pores.

Decklin dried himself with a miniature hand towel. He tossed his soiled shirt in the small garbage can under the desk. He replaced it with one of the many hanging dress shirts. His sense of purpose was in overdrive. Clean and ready, he sat at Charles' desk, sifting through the mess of folders. Three stacks of paperwork were at the top of his mountain of forms. Each folder had a name scribbled across the top. He recited the names, hoping to recall something, anything that would trigger a clue. He quickly realized that the names were completely foreign to him. Setting the folders aside, he popped open the computer. Several, painful minutes passed as the computer booted up. The dated PC finally opened to the main screen, revealing a packed desktop of icons. It became vividly clear that Charles was not computer savvy. Decklin's eyes lit up as the folder "Decklin Marks" appeared on the far right corner of the monitor. He clicked it. The hourglass spun slowly. The folder opened for a moment, teasing him with a preview as the hourglass spun again. Finally, the icons appeared. "Two files? Only two files?" Decklin mumbled.

The first file was labeled with "foreign banking." The second: "Decklin Marks." He clicked the "foreign banking" file, revealing a copy of a string of emails. He read through the text. Disappointment set in as he read Charles' notes.

Summary of Findings: Shins Holdings Bank in Switzerland is not a legitimate bank. Follow the money from D. Marks.

He clicked the printer icon and moved the cursor to the other file. It opened, revealing a transcript from their original interview. A few notes were added in red to their conversation. Charles noted: "Decklin appears to be nervous, but he's oblivious to the origin of the funds." It was oddly comforting; however, it still didn't help him find anything on his suspect. He jumped as the printer began humming behind him. Paper loudly squirmed out of the bottom tray. Pages slowly printed, creating more racket than a bulldozer. Decklin shook his head and thought, I've gotta go shopping. This isn't going to work.

CHAPTER 20

U.S. Army Military Intelligence Station
San Diego, CA | Undisclosed coordinates

Attack dogs barked from behind the barricade. Uniformed military personnel brandishing assault rifles slowly approached Craig's car. Craig knew the drill. He'd been in and out of the administration buildings more times than he could count. Craig apathetically held his ID out the open window. The closest guard pulled his ID card, reviewing the information. He slid the card through a laptop, testing the authenticity of the ID. A shrill beep bounced from the computer.

"Good afternoon, Sir. Who are you meeting today?" The guards always asked the same questions.

"I have a meeting at thirteen hundred hours with General Tanning."

The guard nodded, handing the card back to Craig. "Have a good afternoon, Sir." He clicked a button on his belt, sending the signal to the gate operator to open the barrier. Craig drove up the zigzagged path to the building. He stepped from his car, checking his manicured uniform. He cherished his oxford shirts and suits, however, he felt at home in digital camouflage.

High-ranking officers walked casually in the courtyard. He avoided saluting by steering clear of direct eye contact. It was completely inefficient to stop every ten feet, salute, greet the person, and move along.

He slid his keycard in the slot to the right of the door. Lights blinked from red to green, clicking loudly as the lock opened. As he entered, a man at a podium immediately greeted him. He questioned Craig, ensuring he was at the right place at the right time. As always, he was. Blue Room 2 was several doors down from the entrance. Oddities in room titles were common. The room was not blue, nor was there a "Blue Room 1" in the building.

Agent Craig sat alone in the room for several minutes. His hands rested neatly in his lap. He sat straight, poised, and motionless.

The door whipped open. A young officer entered yelling, "Attention on deck." Craig stood quickly, standing at attention as General Tanning entered the room. "At ease, Agent Craig," the general said calmly, taking the seat at the end of the table. "You've got ten minutes. Please tell me you've wrapped things up." The general was tall and weathered. His stars were crisp, glimmering in the lighting. He sat comfortably, leaning back in the chair with a dominating presence.

Craig opened his laptop and plugged in the projector. He clicked through a few screens, ensuring the projected image was crisp. He opened a spreadsheet containing financial information about *Operation Red Line.*

"Thank you for meeting me, Sir. I've completed the operation with profitable results." Agent Craig walked to the wall, pointing to the image of the numbers. "The mission's total cost was originally over budget."

"Wait, wait! How far over budget?" the general interrupted.

Craig looked at him squarely. "Eleven million, three hundred twenty thousand, eight hundred seventy-three dollars, and twelve cents over budget." The general was displeased, but surprised by Craig's ability to recall the exact number. "During the operation, we had a few unexpected setbacks."

"Setbacks? Stop being so fucking political, Dominick. We've known each other for how long now? Twenty years? For God's sake, shoot me straight. I read the report on MIO. Flying planes into Mexico for a profit? That was ballsy, but expensive."

"Yes, Sir. The military response alone cut five million into the budget. It's not cheap getting an entire nation's military at their feet."

"No shit it's not! I had to pull in favors from across the board to clear that mess. We had media all over us. Please, oh please tell me it was worth it."

"Yes, Sir it was. I've prepared a full breakdown on our sizable investment." Craig previously prepared the slideshow of numbers, calculations, and mission details. The first few slides detailed the price of the Luxemburg Bank explosion. The cost of the fake footage was low, but had the desired media effect he needed to make a fearful public impact. The slides progressed to the bonuses paid to three, unnamed military personnel. Craig carried on about price tags and guidance systems for the RC unit. The overall cost to build the remotely operated drone was staggering. General Tanning paid close attention to the details, jotting information down in a notebook. After ten pages, Craig reached the slide detailing the theft at the casino, in which the sub-mission was merely to bring in a few more bucks to pay off the Mexican military for the airline landing. The casino slides were quickly followed by the costs of the second set of remotely operated drones. They too were wildly expensive, reaching into the millions to build, test, and operate.

The airport mission was more comprehensive. General Tanning asked questions about the operation, undoubtedly to cover the incident with the President and Mexican officials. Craig noted the profits from the mission, quickly skimming over the portion of the narrative that mentioned that five planes crashed violently on the tarmac.

Money laundering was next. The intricate web of fake banks, *Joe Schmoe* account transfers, and offshore accounts were expensive, but highly lucrative. The fees involved in cleaning money rose annually; a curious margin that law enforcement agencies never anticipated. Transfers, transactions, and ledger sheets flooded the page.

"What is that? There...on the left?" General Tanning pointed.

"We had a security breach. One of the accounts became aware of the funds."

"Is the account a threat?" He was not thrilled with the idea of civilians holding classified knowledge, let alone a chunk of money that belonged to the U.S. Government.

"No, Sir, the account and any witnesses have been hushed. They are not a threat."

The general knew exactly what Craig meant when he said "hushed." They'd worked together in dozens of operations. Tanning also realized that collateral damage was an unfortunate part of any solid operation. He asked Craig to continue without further discussion.

A graph appeared, showing the growing profits for the Patriot Barrier Corporation. All costs, variables, and operating expenditures were documented thoroughly, of course. The RC Act was a major part of the operation from the beginning, all to ensure the Patriot Barrier Corporation maintained years of growing profits.

He concluded the presentation with one final page of operating expenditures and petty bills. Senator Royce needed bribes. Airlines needed to be paid for travel, and lunches were purchased. He documented every dime spent.

"Ridiculously meticulous, as always, Dominick. But, what is the bottom line?" He checked his watch, realizing his ten minute window had come and gone. Craig flicked to the next screen, showing a ten-digit number.

"I estimate we should be sitting just over two billion by the end of the second quarter." Craig pointed to the number on the screen.

"Excellent. Especially today, I needed good news. Have the funds been transferred to the Treasury?"

"The transfer was complete this morning, Sir. Everything will be available tomorrow."

"Excellent. Send me a copy of the report. You've earned some leave." The general reached across the table, shaking Craig's hand. "You should actually take your leave this time."

"I'll think about it, Sir. I've got another operation in the Middle East next week. Maybe I'll take a day or two." Craig had no intention of taking the time off. His next operation needed much preparation and detailed planning.

"Until we meet again, Craig. Be safe out there."

Swedish Springs Hotel

Rochester, MN | 44°1'24.24"N 92°27'46.62"W

Decklin slammed the door to the cab, per the driver's instruction. He'd told the cab driver to wait while he ran into his hotel room. An unconvincing nod, followed by an unintelligible murmur was the cabbie's only response.

Decklin quickly made his way to the room. Upon entry, he was blasted with a combination of vomit and body odor. He cringed. What a mess, he thought. The dark room brought back the ball in the pit of his stomach. Angela reemerged in his memory. *Stop, I need to move forward.* He needed to do what she would want him to do. His goal was clear and motivating.

He popped open the safe, yet again, spilling pictures and bills onto the floor as the door swung outward. Pockets filled with a handful of strapped hundreds. Cold steel met his hand as he reached into his pocket. He pulled out the revolver, looking at it with a sense of awe. He'd never owned a gun. He'd never needed to. Vengefully, he smiled, sliding the pistol back into his pocket.

Angela caught his eye. Beautiful eyes shattered him. He sighed, dripping a few tears onto the glossy photograph. He slid the picture into his breast pocket, shut the safe, and walked from the room. He wiped his eyes before reentering the cab, regaining his composure gracefully.

First stop on his list: the car lot. He didn't dare try to track down his SUV. Off the radar is where he belonged. The car lot was only a few miles up the highway, greeting him with tall flags and skyward balloons. He tipped the cab driver well and thanked him for waiting for him at the hotel. He sped off, leaving Decklin to his shopping. The first row was bare. Second row, nothing interesting. The third row, however, housed a sporty black four-door coupe. The windows were tinted. The wheels were shiny. Clearly, the most appealing in the row. The doors were unlocked, revealing a clean, dark interior.

"Afternoon, pal! You like this one, ah? What can I do to set you up with some financing?" The energetic salesman was grinning from ear to ear. Decklin didn't pay much attention to him. He was busy opening the small compartments scattered around the interior. "We can take it for a spin. Would you like that?" It was like talking to a wall. "It's got a V8, plenty of horsepower under the hood. Wanna take it for a ride, bud? I'll let you open 'er up on the highway!" Decklin continued peeking around the interior of the car, without responding. He was intensely evaluating the comfort of the seat and the gadgets around the dash. One last attempt from the salesman: "Sir? Is there something I can..."

"I'll take it," Decklin said, finally making eye contact.

The salesman's eyes widened. "Wait, really? You don't want to drive it first?"

"Nah, I like it. I've heard they are pretty awesome." Decklin got out of the car, peeking at the price tag for the first time.

"Okay. Well. Ah, let's get inside and get the credit application started!" He waved for Decklin to follow. He was ecstatic. It was his first sale of the month.

"I've got cash. Do you accept cash?" Decklin followed behind him, entertaining himself with the salesman's continuous stream of surprise reactions.

"Cash? Like, a credit card? ...or like cash-cash?"

Decklin pulled out a thick stack of strapped hundred-dollar bills, ensuring the pistol didn't accidentally fall from his pocket. "Cash-cash."

Decklin whipped through the paperwork inside the dealership. Unnaturally, he signed the paperwork with *Charles Unit.* The smiling salesman handed him the keys.

The engine turned over, grunting the deep romance of the V8 engine. He smiled, yanked on the shifter, and pulled from the parking lot. Next stop: the electronics store. He admired the smell of the new car on the short drive. The transmission was tight. The interior was prime. It was a sexy beast of an automobile.

He parked in the second row at the electronics store. *Beep!* Decklin enjoyed clicking the alarm for the first time. He walked straight for the computer section. Endless rows of laptops were somewhat overwhelming at first. Numbers and specs were printed cryptically on price cards below the laptop displays. After an hour of searching, Decklin picked one. He pushed his cart through the narrow computer monitor row, brutally pulling three of the biggest monitors from their slot. Cart wheels squeaked as he moved through the aisles to the digital camera section. Again, he picked the best one. He grinned as he read through the specs on the box.

The cart was getting heavier. Patiently, he pushed it through the winding line to the front counter. A jovial high school student rang up his pile of electronics, stating the total clearly. Decklin pulled a wad full of loose cash, casually handing him the balance.

He scanned his new keys for the trunk release. He found it, popping the trunk with a click. The boxes filled the large trunk, spewing electronics from every corner. He was dreading the next errand: shopping for clothing was never his strong suit. His style was blissfully bland. Exactly how he liked it.

He tested the new engine on the highway. It purred as the speedometer rushed to eighty miles per hour. At that speed, it took only minutes to reach the department store. Decklin rushed in, hoping to get through his list quickly. He picked out a few sweatshirts, a stack of t-shirts, a few cheap watches and a few bags of socks and boxers. He heard a voice in the back of his head, bringing his heart to a quiver. Angela spoke in his memory. "Why don't you buy these? These would look great on you!" Decklin's smile turned somber as he realized he would never hear her bug him about trendy clothing again. Her fashion advice, unwanted or not, was still a part of her he'd miss. He took a deep breath. As he exhaled, he stood straight and courageous. You can do this, Decklin — you'll find them, he thought.

He wheeled the cart through the mess of shoppers to the men's suit section. He selected a classy black jacket and pants. He slid a few ties and dress shirts in his cart, adding to the pile of cotton rubble. A sigh of relief struck as he checked out. Shopping for clothing ranked right up there with being punched in the groin.

Flowers by Kerry, a floral shop, was only a few blocks away. He stopped in, selecting a beautiful bouquet with all of Angela's favorite colors. He used delicate care as he set them on the passenger seat, not to protect the new upholstery, but to ensure they stayed fresh and beautiful.

Again, he kicked the accelerator, enjoying the first true smile he'd felt in quite some time. He reached the hotel, pulling only the suit from the pile of plastic bags. He covered his nose as he entered his room. The musty space was still dark, resonating with his recent depression. Decklin stripped naked and turned on the shower. He tested the water, ensuring it was somewhere between scalding and warm. With one bare foot at a time, he climbed into the water. The clean warmth was brilliant. He felt soot wash from his body. He closed his eyes, feeling the trickling splash cleanliness. The complimentary soap was tiny, but smelled decent. He cleaned for an eternity. The mirror was completely fogged over when he pulled open the curtain. The rough hotel towel worked well, but left his skin feeling like it'd been through a belt sander. He shaved again, catching any of the remaining spots that he'd missed.

He pulled his legs through the crisp suit pants. The jacket and dress shirt weren't a perfect fit, but Decklin didn't know the difference. The room contained nothing of his, except the safe. He kneeled down, picking it up with a loud grunt. Of course, the door posed a challenge. He set the far end of the safe on the table, stretching his arm to the doorknob.

His walk was staggering. He carefully carried the safe to the backseat, ensuring his suit stayed clean. The car shook as he plopped the heavy metal onto the fabric. After locking the doors, he headed to the hotel lobby. His checkout was simple enough. He needed only to sign his name on a printed receipt. He realized then how much Officer Kitts had done for him. Kitts set up the hotel, drove him around, pulled him from his drunken stupor, and cared for him. Merely caring was enough to earn a medal. He made a mental note to properly thank Officer Kitts.

Maplewood Cemetery

Rochester, MN | 44°1'35.1381"N 92°27'20.2948"W

He slowly pulled through the stone archway. Vicious hurt lingered in the depth of his heart. He bit his lip, watching the passing stones through watering eyes. He pressed the brake, stopping a short walk from their gravesite. He pulled the flowers from the cushion.

Slowly, he moved one foot in front of the other. Angela's smile. Her laugh. He missed it. Pete's giggle. His playful heart. Decklin's breath became choppy as he wept. He stumbled as the crash of emotion rushed through his veins. His eyes closed, pulling strength from his upcoming vengeance. He approached the headstones, choking back the rain of tears.

“Hi, babe,” he said softly. His voice quivered and cracked. He paused, coughed, and spoke again: “I sure miss you.” He broke again. His throat was tight. “I, ah…I think about you all the time. I would do anything to see you and Pete again.” His knees wobbled. He wiped his cheek. “I’m…well…I’m going to do something now, that you may or may not want me to do. I want to make sure these guys don’t take anyone else’s family.” He could feel the heavy scratch in his voice. “I want to get them, babe, for taking you from me.” His knees buckled. His new pants dug into the earth as he cried. “I miss you so much,” he sniffled. “I am going to get these bastards, no matter what it takes.” He set the flowers between mother and son, wiping their names clean from the blowing dust. “I love you both, more than you will ever know.” The cold rock pressed against his cheek as he hugged Angela’s gravestone. He leaned to Pete, hugging him tightly. “I love you too, son.”

CHAPTER 21

Charles Unit Investigations

Rochester, MN | 44°4'4.8282"N 92°30'13.7157"W

Decklin felt a new sense of duty. His vengeful determination was immeasurable. He walked into the investigation office without flinching. The desk was cleared carefully, ensuring each pile of paperwork was moved without disrupting its order. Decklin emptied his car, piling his new purchases on a chair in the corner of the room. The computer equipment was opened first. Styrofoam and clear tape littered the floor as he unpacked the laptop and monitors. He carefully arranged the equipment on the desk, ensuring every monitor was visible from his chair. Wiring was a twisted mess along the floor and far side of the desk. He plugged in the new camera, powered on the computer, and watched the screens come alive.

Decklin sat on the floor, carefully creating three stacks of folders and forms. Clearly, Charles left very little for him to go on, but Decklin was banking on a missed clue. He knew there had to be some small amount of information printed on one of the forms that would help him. Sticky notes were dispersed, assigning a yes, no, and maybe pile.

The first folder he looked over was labeled "1996 — Toni Kaboloni shooting." He flipped through the pages. A few color photographs slid from the folder exposing the man's brain and a few other miscellaneous injuries. ...ick, Jesus, I don't think this is my guy, Decklin thought, sliding the folder safely into the "no" pile. The second file seemed promising. A corrupt police officer and an accountant were listed in the report. It appeared they were involved in embezzling millions from a local credit union. He nodded as he read, enjoying the thought of finding this bad apple cop. Sadly, as he reached the last page of the report, he read, "both suspects in custody — sentenced to 30 years." He tossed it in the "no" pile.

After thirteen more folders, only two found their way into the "maybe" pile. They were both a far cry from promising, but they were something. The next file was labeled "Abaz Narabi — Wanted fugitive AUE." Decklin read the print. The man was wanted in six countries for murder, money laundering, illegal distributing of firearms, and for manufacturing cocaine. He read the short report. Charles only had one line jotted below the man's photograph. *Seen last week in Wisconsin — 1536 Apple Place — Milwaukee.* Decklin's eyebrows rose, glaring anxiously at the man's picture. He slid the folder into the lonely "yes" pile. He resisted the urge to immediately jump on a plane to Wisconsin. He needed to plan. Brash actions could get him caught, or even worse, killed.

A few more folders containing useless information made their way to the growing "no" pile. Decklin adjusted his posture frequently. The floor was less than comfortable. He lifted the top file from a new pile. The folder was light, containing only a few newspaper clippings. He read the heading to the first paper: *Domestic terrorism on the rise*. The article documented the robberies in San Diego, California. It rambled for three long columns, reviewing in detail a bank explosion and casino robbery. Interestingly, the robberies were done with some kind of radio-controlled contraption. Decklin smirked at the ingenuity of the robbers. He flipped to the next clipping. Two names were circled below the heading: Agent Dominick Craig and Mick Zimmer. He read the first few paragraphs, which were political and less than electrifying. The text ran below the seam into the second half of the paper. Decklin gently flipped the page, exposing a color photograph of two men, shaking hands. His fingers gripped the page with growing force as a memory flipped through his mind. He recognized him.

He flashed back to the day when his wife was taken. Flooding images ran through his thoughts. On that day, when he pulled out from the parking space, he heard a car horn. He peered into his mirror. The man on the newspaper was the driver. "No way!" he mumbled. He gazed at the image with fury. "This is him. Right here. I told you I'd find him."

He pulled the rest of the clippings from the file. Thumbtacks pushed into the clippings, propping them up in a pattern along a blank spot on the wall. His new laptop flicked on, revealing three screens of search windows. "Agent Dominick Craig — San Diego" was entered into the search. Not a second passed before all three windows were filled with results. He clicked the first link, opening a narrative about Dominick Craig. A color image of Agent Craig appeared on the screen. Again, his mind pulsed with rage. He printed the photograph and tacked it next to the articles. The story ranted about Craig's military history. He'd been in seven tours: the Middle East, Africa, South America, the list was endless. He'd received sixteen awards and twelve medals. Undoubtedly, a decorated military hero. Why was he there? What role did he have? Decklin asked himself. He continued his search for answers.

Hours passed as the printed collage of articles were tacked on the wall. He had a plethora of pictures, mostly portraying a uniform-clad war hero. Decklin cringed at his sight, but needed to burn all of his information into his mind. Personal information though, was nonexistent. Dominick Craig had no trace of family, no address, no contact information. He was a ghost. Any leads that surfaced led to *dot gov* networks, closely guarded with passwords and encrypted information. Agent Craig had zilch listed for the past two years. Clearly, Decklin wasn't the only person who labeled Craig as an enemy.

The second face in the car squirmed in a blur down Decklin's memory. He looked at the images of Mick Zimmer. *Was he the other man in the car? He had to be.* Clearing another spot on the wall for Zimmer, Decklin began his search in the obvious places. Within moments, he found mountains of information on Mick Zimmer. He had no military affiliation, no political agenda. He had been thriving in Fortune 500 companies for the last 20 years. His personal address, work address, emails, and phone numbers were all readily available. Zimmer even posted his personal schedule on the Patriot Barrier Corporation website.

Decklin stood back, looking at the madness he'd created along his office wall.

"I am going to need a suitcase."

The stores were busier than earlier in the day. He quickly picked out a few travel essentials and prepaid credit cards, flying through the checkout line in just minutes. The cell phone store caught his attention as he passed through the mall parking lot. He ran in, purchasing the most expensive, most technologically sound smartphone. He left just as hastily as he arrived.

He returned to the investigation office, packing a week's worth of clothing. He booked a private flight from Rochester to San Diego. He pocketed the printed tickets and went over a checklist of things he needed. He decided not to bring the wall of printouts and newspaper clippings. Instead, he took a photo. The camera resolution was strong enough to zoom into the letter on any one of the clippings.

"Clothes, bathroom stuff, shoes, camera, phone, laptop..." He went over the list, stopping as he felt his pocket. He pulled the revolver from its quiet spot in his pants. "...gun." He held the pistol, feeling the authority of the steel. He now had a face to imagine at the end of the barrel. He dreamt of finding Dominick Craig and Mick Zimmer, pulling the trigger against their heads. Of course, he needed something to say before he killed them. He pondered what tagline to use as the last words of their life. Maybe: *This is for my wife and son*. He felt silly rehearsing, but it felt good. Good enough to bring a smile to his face.

He packed his car, quickly tiring of the constant packing and unpacking. He left the office in a blur, driving directly to the airport. Thirty minutes before check-in, he thought. I can make it.

He pulled into the valet parking ramp. A young blonde attendant greeted him. He saw Angela for a moment. Her hair? Eyes? Something reminded him of her. He took another deep breath and tossed her the keys.

He walked hurriedly to his gate. The luggage dragged behind him. His eye caught an odd sight. A suited man held a sign stating "Charles Unit." He'd never taken a private jet and was baffled by the service. The man greeted him: "Good afternoon, Charles! May I take your luggage?" Decklin still wasn't used to the name. He wondered if he ever would be.

The airline chauffeur walked him to a side door near the rear of the airport. As they opened the door, an overwhelming sound of jet engines filled their ears. The wind was strong as they walked down the runway. The crew to his jet stood outside the plane, greeting him as he approached. Decklin was stunned. He'd never received such service. Curiously, he pulled the tickets from his pocket to review the price. He shouldn't have checked.

The plane was small, but luxurious. He sat on what could only be described as a couch with seatbelts. The flight attendant poured him a glass of champagne as soon as he was seated. She offered a three-course meal, a full bar, and even a cigar. He happily said yes...to everything.

The captain addressed Charles by name, telling him about the weather conditions. It was strange, but wonderful. The plane took off gently, pushing a solid altitude in less than a few minutes. Decklin enjoyed the first entrée, but couldn't stomach the second or third round. Weeks of boozing had taken its toll on his appetite. Coffee was also served. He sipped it, staring out the window into the tufts of moving clouds. He couldn't help but think of Angela. She'd never taken the opportunity to fly. He tried desperately to take her on trips, but her feet were firmly planted on the ground. She would have enjoyed this luxury, even though she would say something along the lines of, "This is way over the top; we didn't need to spend all this money." She was still in him, living and breathing in his memories.

The landing was smooth. Clearly, the best pilots worked on private airliners. Decklin walked down the steps onto the blistering tarmac. The Southern California sun was dry, holding a solid ninety degrees. Limousine personnel greeted him at the bottom of the steps, walking him through the terminal to his waiting car. They thought of everything! he thought as he waved good-bye to the airplane staff.

The limo driver opened his door, packed his luggage, and drove him to the San Diego Master Hotel, which was tall and elegant. He chose the junior suite on the thirty-eighth floor. The hotel staff treated him like royalty, wheeling his bags to his room. He tipped the bellhop with a twenty, receiving a quaint nod of appreciation.

Wrinkles plagued his new t-shirts and jeans as he pulled them from the luggage. His laptop followed suit, sliding from the baggage onto the desk in the corner of the room. He plugged it in, powered it on, and called the front desk.

"Master Hotel," a woman's voice sounded from the receiver.

"Hey, this is Charles from thirty-eight-oh-five. I need a rental car and dry cleaning service; can you set that up for me?"

"Absolutely, Charles, I'll send someone up to pick up your laundry and reserve a car right away. Is there anything else I can do for you?"

Decklin paused, looking at his laptop. He twisted the cord in his fingers as he spoke: "Actually, yeah. Do you have a printer I can use?"

The hotel staff printed his pictures on high gloss, extra-large posterboard. When he questioned them about why they had a commercial-sized printer, they simply replied: "Why not?" He tacked the images in the corner of the room next to his desk. Mick Zimmer's address placed him in the center of a luxurious neighborhood in La Jolla, a suburb of San Diego. Hotel notepads filled quickly with his personal information. Meticulous notes were taken on Zimmer's schedule. Decklin plotted his drive to and from work, including travel time and even traffic conditions. He knew exactly where Zimmer would be over the next 48 hours. Finding him alone would be tough because he surrounded himself with employees and conferences. Decklin needed secluded time with Zimmer.

Decklin creatively used an investigative tactic he'd learned from a popular TV crime show. He logged onto a social media website, creating two new accounts. The first was created to mimic a businessman from Los Angeles. Decklin took special care to ensure he looked the part. He stole a profile picture from a Russian CEO; no one would know the difference. The second was created out of lust. If Zimmer resisted adding the businessman, he would surely add the bleach blonde bombshell. Her fake name was Jennifer Albright, a Russian foreign exchange student. Her profile pictures showed numerous bikinis, wet t-shirt contests, and other scandalous activities. He knew Zimmer would take the bait. He sent the friend requests with personalized notes.

Decklin moved to the bed. He studied his notes like flashcards. Exhaustion met his eyelids as he reached the last page. He blinked heavily. Within moments, sleep overcame him. His body relaxed, dropping the notes onto the comforter.

The darkness of his dreams drifted into a slideshow of memories. Satin sheets brushed against his face as he snuggled with her. The smell of her skin was bliss. A dangerous murmur could be heard in another room. Decklin already knew who it was. His body was frozen, horrifyingly unable to move. He held Angela's body closely as the door flung open revealing Agent Dominick Craig and Mick Zimmer. He cried out, furiously yelling for help. His voice was agonizingly mute.

"Dry cleaning is ready, Sir." The voice woke him from his dream. Decklin fumbled with the pistol, pointing it sleepily at the housekeeper. The young Latina's eyes widened at the sight of the gun. "Please, don't shoot, I'm sorry, I should have knocked louder! I'm so sorry to disturb you!" Decklin lowered the gun, feeling the surge of adrenaline pass through his veins. The housekeeper backed out of the room slowly, closing the door behind her.

"Three hours," he muttered. "Shit, I slept for three hours!" He leapt out of bed, flinging the pistol on the pillow.

Decklin flipped through screens, reaching the social media website in moments. Zimmer took the bait; however, he did the opposite of what Decklin expected: he denied the blonde and accepted the businessman. Decklin smirked as he looked over Zimmer's profile. The latest update showed him checking in at a construction site with "Job number one — Checking in with the construction crew" posted above the link. The posting was twelve minutes old. Decklin needed to hurry.

Decklin struggled with his jeans. He was moving too quickly to master a quick slither into the freshly washed pants. He slid into a white t-shirt and jogged out the door.

The hotel staff issued his rental car quickly, feeling the pressure of his impatient rush. The rental car was parked a few spaces from the front door. Decklin ran to the car, whipping the keys into the ignition. His GPS beeped and flashed through menus as he entered the address to the construction site. The revolving globe icon took forever, spinning the words — *loading real-time GPS location.* Eventually, the route appeared. Gas pumped into the engine as he ripped from the parking lot.

National Bank and Trust

San Diego, CA | 32°49'14.4366"N 117°10'28.7029"W

Yellow hardhats sat in a row along the trailer. Zimmer picked one up, sentimentally charged with the excitement of the first job. He pulled the straps snugly below his chin and walked to the foreman.

"Afternoon! How are we doing?" Mick Zimmer stretched a hand to the foreman. He shook his hand attentively, getting him with a half-cocked smile.

"We're great! We've installed the front set of blockades, we just gotta get 'em round back and we're done." The foreman was proud to promote his progress. The workers had been driven like slaves, working through the night to achieve a quick turnaround. Zimmer walked up to one of the steel poles, testing its strength with a kick.

"Solid! I love it. How are we doing on overtime?" The CEO constantly worried about operating expenditures.

The foreman arched an eyebrow. "Well, Sir, we've got about six guys who've been working for fifteen hours. You want me to cut 'em?"

"Fifteen hours? Yeah, hell yes I want you to cut them! We only have 200 hours of labor for this project. Don't run us into the ground on our first job. I'm counting on you to watch for this stuff." Zimmer wasn't thrilled. The cost of doing business was dependent on proper scheduling.

"Ah, shit, sorry, Sir. I'll have them off the clock in a few minutes." The foreman was disappointed. It seemed the managers were never quite satisfied. He'd worked through the night to ensure their progress was above par. As always, management found something to bitch about, regardless of the progress.

"Thanks. I'm going to take a look around." Zimmer split from the foreman, making a quiet lap around the bank. Hardhats stopped, looked, and sped up their pace as they realized that he was there to evaluate their work. He phoned the director as he completed his round. Overtime was crucial. He was ready to let loose on the director.

"Bill! Mick Zimmer. We've got a problem with our overtime allowance." Zimmer climbed into his car, avoiding the obnoxious sounds of construction equipment.

“Overtime? What’s going on down there? We allotted three hundred hours to the project; what’s the problem?” The director’s voice sounded annoyed.

“Three hundred? No, no. We only have two hundred on the books.” Zimmer felt the annoyance, rebutting with the correct numbers. The director paused, loudly sifting through paperwork.

“Ah, damn. You’re right. I’ll adjust it with the foreman.” Embarrassed, he realized his critical mistake.

“I already fixed it with the foreman. Just make sure these guys stay on track.” Zimmer hung up the phone. He knew they only had a small window of margin for the labor. He set the phone down on the seat next to him.

“Don’t speak. Just drive the car.” Decklin leaned up from the backseat, pressing the revolver into Zimmer’s neck.

He jumped at the sound of Decklin’s voice, turning rapidly. “What the hell are you doing?” Surprise riddled his expression.

“Stop talking! Just drive!” Decklin jammed the barrel into his skin. Zimmer fumbled with the keys, starting the car without hesitation. He pulled from the parking spot, driving timidly from the lot.

“I have a few hundred bucks in my wallet. You can have the car! I don’t care, just don’t hurt me,” Zimmer pleaded with Decklin.

“I don’t want your money, Mick. I know who you are. I know what you’ve done.” Decklin was a wreck. He fought the urge to pull the trigger. His mind raced with anger and horror as he faced the man he thought had a part in killing his wife and stepson.

"What? What have I done? What did I do to you?" Zimmer drove down the road slowly, fearfully peeking into the mirror at his assailant.

"You killed her. You killed my family! What, you don't remember that? Is that something you do without remorse?" Decklin pulled a picture of Angela and Pete from his pocket. His hand shook the photo in front of Zimmer's face. "Look at them! Look! You killed them, didn't you?" Zimmer glanced back and forth from the image.

"No, God, no! I am in business! I don't kill people! Why would you think I did that? I'm sorry you lost your family, but please, hear me out." Decklin stopped the speech with a cold pistol whip. He cracked the butt of the gun against Zimmer's jaw, sending the car veering into the other lane. Zimmer corrected the steering, screaming in pain as blood poured down his face.

"Shut the fuck up, Mick, I know you were there. You and Dominick Craig."

Zimmer turned his head briefly in surprise. "Mr. Craig? Oh God! No, I have nothing to do with him, or what he's done! He is just the government liaison for my company!" He pleaded, driving less than carefully.

"Bullshit, you were there! I saw you in the car! Tell me where you were on May 19! Prove it to me! *Prove it!*" Decklin lost himself, completely immersed in revenge. His finger quivered on the trigger. He knew Zimmer was part of it. He had to be.

"Ah, ummm." Zimmer's mind raced through his past schedule. He drew a blank under the pressure. "I don't know, I think...ahhhh." He finally grabbed it: "I was in Los Angeles! I was at a meeting!"

"With whom? You're full of shit! You were in Minnesota!"

"Richard Hayfield! Richard Hayfield! He was there. We can call him, I can prove it!" Zimmer stopped at a stoplight. His brow drizzled nervous sweat. He fumbled with his cell phone, going through his address book until he found the name. "I'll call him!"

"If you tell him anything about me or that you're in trouble, I swear to God I'll kill you where you sit." Decklin pulled the barrel from his neck, pressing the gun to his sweating temple. Zimmer put the phone on speaker. The line rang three times. Richard Hayfield picked up.

"This is Richard. What can I do for you, Mr. Zimmer?"

Zimmer looked at Decklin, trying desperately to shake the nerves from his voice. "Hey, ah, Richard, how are ya?"

"Good, Mick, did you have a chance to look over the portfolios? Whaddya think? Nice, ah?"

"Yeah, yeah...nice. Say, I am updating my calendar. Can you tell me the date we met last?"

The man paused, realizing the unusual vibe of the conversation. "Yeah? I mean, sure. I think it was May 18? Maybe the 19? Somewhere in there."

"Where did we meet again?" Zimmer rushed through the conversation, pushing him for answers.

"Are you feeling okay? Is something wrong?"

"Yeah, yeah! Everything is fine. Reconciling my schedule. Where did we meet, Rich, just tell me!" His tongue was rushed and nervous.

"Okay, okay, Jesus. We met at Chasers Lounge on Second. You sure everything is okay? You sound like hell!"

"What city is Chasers in?" Zimmer felt the barrel push against his head.

"Ahhh? Unless it's changed, it should still be in L.A.?"

"Great, Great. Thanks, Rich! I'll call you back." Zimmer hung up the phone, looking in the mirror at Decklin. "See, I was there, not Michigan or whatever, please, just let me go!" Decklin leaned back, sitting in the middle of the rear seat. His gun dropped to his lap. Feeling frustration and disappointment as he realized Zimmer was not his man.

"How do I find Dominick Craig?" Decklin asked. The tone of his voice was human, almost ashamed of his actions.

"Mr. Craig? He'll be in the office this afternoon." Zimmer felt a weight lift after the phone call, but his hands still trembled.

"What time? What office location?"

"I'm not sure. He comes and goes as he pleases. Maybe 5:30 or 6:00? Our office off Third Avenue."

"Okay, 5:30 or 6:00, I can handle that. Take me back to the construction site. I want you to drop me off and go straight home. If you even hint to anyone that you saw me, I'll kill you. I have your home address. I know your wife's name is Margaret and your daughter is Sicilia. Don't fuck up, Zimmer. Listen to me and just forget this ever happened." He looked apprehensively at Decklin in the mirror. Zimmer did exactly as he was instructed. He turned into the bank parking lot, adjacent to the construction area.

"That's it? Just drop you off and I'll never see you again?"

"Yep, unless you tell someone. Keep quiet and I will be a distant memory." Decklin slid the revolver into his pocket. He felt the plump wad of bills as his hand slid from his pocket. He pulled out a few hundred dollars, throwing them into the front seat. "Zimmer? Do you appreciate your family? I mean, do you treasure them?"

"With all my heart."

"Good. Take your wife and daughter to dinner, surprise them. Appreciate every second you have with them." Decklin got out of the car without another peep. He watched Zimmer drive away, spinning his tires as he fled from the parking lot.

CHAPTER 22

Patriot Barrier Corporation
San Diego, CA | 32°44'57"N 117°11'50"W

The zoom feature magnified the door to the Patriot Barrier Corporation. He'd parked in a nearby parking lot, far enough away not to draw too much attention. Decklin watched through the screen on the back of the camera, waiting for Dominick Craig to exit the building. Nerves were a roller coaster. Every time the door opened, his heart skipped a beat. He checked his wristwatch every few minutes. After two hours of impatient waiting, the time read 7:04.

Craig's indifferent expression was difficult to read. The board droned on about numbers, profits, workloads, and other business-related topics. Craig sat near the back of the room. His mind was elsewhere, planning the next mission. The business gurus he'd placed at the Patriot Barrier Corporation were more than capable of handling the business in his absence. Precisely what he needed.

The meeting concluded, spilling executives from every door in the conference room. Craig was the last to leave. He enjoyed watching their demeanor as they walked. He could tell much about a person by the way they carried themselves. He flicked off the lights in the conference room, picked up his laptop and exited the building.

He spotted his car parked near the front of the building. Even after hours of cool evening weather, the leather seats still burned his back. He pulled from the lot, eyeing the traffic. Craig drove west, heading in the opposite direction of his hotel. Military protocol taught him to take alternate routes, ensuring he would avoid roadside bombs and tailing assailants.

He made three right turns, watching the green car in his mirror. The license plate was missing, replaced with a cookie cutter rental car plate. His mind ran through a checklist. Rental Car—check. Followed for more than 6 blocks—check. Made obvious traffic infractions to ensure they didn't lose his car—check. He was onto the tail. Craig smirked, whispering under his breath, "Mexican military. Always looking for more."

He knew it was a shakedown. He hadn't paid the crooked Mexicans enough for the airline transaction. In every dealing, they always complained about the pay. This time, he knew they were after his bank account. It was standard robbery procedure. Follow someone home, break in, hold him at gunpoint and transfer money to an offshore account. He was already ten steps ahead of them. It was textbook.

Craig pulled into a downtrodden part of town. Drug dealers and pimps watched from porches as he passed down the lonesome streets. It would take local cops 30 minutes to respond to a crime in that area, a perfect place for an urban, daylight crime. The green car followed, but not too closely. "Amateur," Craig whispered. He turned right, pulling into a street with a dead-end sign. As he reached a blind spot behind a house, he gunned it, sending the car into a 180-degree spin. The hood of his car faced the entrance to the one-way street. He leapt from the car, leaving the engine running and the door open, perfect for rapid escape. The magnets broke free from his car as he pulled off the license plate. He threw the plate into the front seat and bolted behind a parked car. He waited.

Decklin sped along the drive. He was losing Craig. His body shook with anticipation. He was ready to face Angela's executioner. He looked at the passenger seat, eyeing the pistol. Revenge was finally approaching.

Craig's car took a turn down a distant street, sliding from view. Decklin gunned the engine, hoping to close the gap. He ignored the stop sign, blowing through it to catch up. Blinkers clicked as he rounded the corner. Craig's sedan came into view. Parked and open, it sat suspiciously in the middle of the road.

Thunderous gunfire ripped through Decklin's windshield. Glass sprayed wickedly throughout the car. Decklin clenched the wheel, watching the power of the bullets thrash the electronics in his dashboard. His eye caught a heart-stopping image of Craig. Time slowed for merely a second. There he was. Dominick Craig. Decklin blinked in slow motion, recognizing him from the street in Minnesota. He snapped back, smashing the accelerator to avoid the raining gunfire. Craig was relentless. His trigger stopped moving only long enough to reload.

Decklin jumped the curb, turning sharply to avoid the dead end. His hood crashed through a chain-link fence, sending metal wires through the interior of the car. His wheels spun. Helplessly, the car rocked in the dirt. Decklin yanked the transmission into reverse, setting the car free. The constant crackle of gunfire paused as Craig sprinted to a closer position. The rental car raced back, smashing into a parked car.

Craig smiled, watching the vehicle come to a solid stop. He breathed slowly, lining up the sights with Decklin's twisting silhouette. His fingertip pressed gently on the trigger. Decklin anticipated the shot, ducking beneath the seat without a moment to spare. The round clipped the headrest, leaving a tattered exit wound in the fabric. Decklin blindly pulled the transmission, crushing the pedal. His car jerked over the curb again, demolishing the fence as he passed through the rubble. Craig cocked his head, dissatisfied with his shot. His fingers pulled the trigger aggressively, popping rounds from the barrel like squished bubble wrap. The bullets tore through the trunk, leaving a trail of circular wounds in the paint.

Decklin lifted his head above the dash, watching the road as he flew from the scene. Pain ripped through his calf as the last bullet passed through the trunk, into the backseats and through his thin leg meat. The pain sent a shock wave through his body. The steering wheel jerked as he winced, sending him haphazardly over another curb. He quickly corrected, sending the car back onto the road. The burn of the shot pulsed pain up his leg. The wound didn't stop his car from gaining speed as he escaped the narrow street.

Craig smugly holstered his gun. He wouldn't take chase. He knew better. His odds of getting caught went up by 48% and his risk of injury went up 34%. He'd made his point. The Mexican military would need a few more weeks to recoup their plan. He sauntered to his car, closing the door gently. He sat in the center of the street, adjusting the radio station for a few minutes. He tuned to a gentle symphony station and nonchalantly drove from the bullet-ridden street.

San Diego Master Hotel

San Diego, CA | 32°42'33.7151"N 117°10'3.0567"W

The rental car sputtered into the parking lot. Decklin parked in a distant corner, hoping no one would notice the damage. He took off his new t-shirt, wrapping it tightly around the wound at the base of his calf. Blood oozed from the shirt. Painfully, he hobbled through the parking lot to the front entrance.

"Oh, my God, are you okay?" a young woman at the counter asked. She fixated at the dripping t-shirt.

"Yeah, fine. I was in a bike accident. Nothing to worry about." Decklin tried to walk faster, ironically attracting more attention than he intended.

"No, I mean, that looks bad. Seriously, you should go see, like, a doctor." The staff was loud, bringing a lot of eyes on his wound.

"No! I am fine, thank you. Please send up some towels, ice, and a couple of Tylenol."

"Oh, right. Okay, Sir. I'll send that right away. You sure you don't need..."

"I said I am fine!" Decklin glared as he hobbled onto the elevator. He limped to reach his room. The pain throbbed on every step. Disappointment was heavier than the pain. His master plan of getting revenge on Agent Craig was less than cinematic. Not only had he put Craig on guard, he completely lost his element of surprise. Decklin was wounded and cynical. He slid the room key into the door, flinging it open forcefully.

Blood and flesh leaked from his t-shirt as he pulled it from the wound. An inch tear ran along the far side of his left calf. He groaned as cool air seeped into the wound. Grunts erupted as he leaned on the bed. He raised his leg in the desperate hope of slowing the bleeding. He looked at the ceiling, letting out a painful tear. "What now, babe? What the hell do I do now?"

The knock on the door surprised him. "Who is it?"

"Grand Hotel housekeeping! You need towel? Ice? Bandages? Pain peels?" The Hispanic accent was thick.

"Come in."

The man entered, dropping the towels on the bed and the ice and painkillers on the dresser. "Jew look bad, Sir. Jew need an ambeelance?"

"No, I am fine. Thank you." Decklin dismissed him quickly, wrapping a new towel around his wound. The ice dug deeply into the nerves. Throbbing jolts of pain sent a line of sweat along his brow.

The cap popped off the pill bottle. Decklin didn't count tablets, he simply chugged a small handful. He lay on the bed, fixating on the articles on the wall as the ice tingled pain through his skin. He read the title of the article over and over, trying to distract himself from his leg. Genius, he thought as he read the title again: *The RC Act passes.* Hope was swiftly restored as he pondered. He'd previously admired the creativity of the bank robbers, using remote-controlled cars to do their dirty work. Why couldn't he do the same? He sat up optimistically, feeling the intense burn of the bullet wound. He groaned with annoyance and discomfort.

Nick's Hobby Shop

San Diego, CA | 32°46'6.9023"N 117°8'51.8344"W

Aisles were packed with miniature versions of racecars, trucks, and airplanes. Decklin favored his left leg, limping considerably. He looked over the different versions of radio-controlled devices. They had helicopters, jets, tanks, monster trucks, just about everything. He eyed a mammoth box containing a sports car. It was electric, boasting a long battery life.

"Help ya with something?" A clerk approached, peeking down at his tightly bandaged leg.

"Yeah, actually. I am looking for something big. Something that can carry a lot of…stuff." Decklin hesitated, realizing that he needed to choose his words wisely.

"All right, well. We've got some RC bulldozers over there. Oh, and a few pickups over there; those can carry up to fifty pounds without slowing down." The clerk pointed to brightly colored boxes along the wall.

"A pickup? That might work. Where is that one?" Decklin liked the idea of a heavy payload. He followed the clerk to the truck section. The pickup truck was huge, overshadowing its miniature counterparts. "Really? This can carry seventy pounds??"

"Yes ser-ee-bob. This one is made for pulling trailers." The clerk pointed to a box containing a trailer and a miniature boat. Decklin subtly mocked the thought of simulating a day at the lake, pulling a trailer with a radio-controlled car. But, the truck was perfect. "That will work." The clerk hefted the huge box to the counter. "Hey, also, I need a pulley system, something that can pull another car." Decklin had no idea if they offered anything like that, but thought he'd ask anyway.

The clerk rolled his eyes. "The truck has a winch on the front." He pointed to a miniature pulley system on the front bumper. "Everybody knows these things come with a winch." The clerk laughed at Decklin and his lack of knowledge. Decklin squinted at the odd, belittling comment. He wondered who these people were, spending their time pulling boats and winching fake cars. Again, it didn't matter; it would do the trick nicely.

Decklin paid the man, and asked, "Can I ask you a favor? Can you help me get this thing into my car?" The clerk rolled his eyes again but agreed to help. He eyed the bullet-ridden car with suspicion. "Special effects. I work in Hollywood." Decklin was stretching it, but the clerk believed it nonetheless.

The rental car grumbled as it started. Clearly, the bullet wounds had taken their toll on the mechanics of the engine. Decklin's next stop was unplanned, but managed to nicely work its way into the preparation. He stopped for gas, realizing the gunfire must have punctured the gas tank. The pump stopped around fifty bucks. Decklin noticed the plethora of propane tanks along the wall of the entrance. He picked one up, casually setting it on the counter. The clerk rang up the sale, but disagreed to help Decklin carry the tank to his car. Decklin gritted his teeth on every step, carrying the heavy tank to the backseat.

Throbbing pain in his calf continued to grow. He needed a few more items before he could put his leg on ice at the hotel. He drove cautiously, realizing that a thrown cigarette butt could send his car into flames because of the gas leak. His GPS led him through the city to a department store. He hobbled inside, aiming directly to the toddler section. Baby monitors were plentiful. A decorated box near the front of the aisle caught his eye. He picked it up, ensuring it was both wireless and had the ability to broadcast video. He scoffed at the price; the industry charged ridiculous amounts for such a simple system. Decklin could afford it, but he felt terrible for brand new, young parents on a tight budget.

He limped into the hardware section, picking out a few tools and adhesives. After filling his small cart, he moved slowly toward the checkout line. Every step sent a chill up his spine. After the long, arduous walk, he was greeted by a genuinely kind cashier. She even helped him carry the bags to his car. Decklin was outwardly grateful.

San Diego Master Hotel

San Diego, CA | 32°42'33.7151"N 117°10'3.0567"W

Decklin parked his car near the rear of the hotel. His pace was slow but steady as he approached the front desk. He requested a bellhop, requiring much assistance to unload his car. A man in his thirties appeared from a back room, greeting Decklin with a proper hello. Decklin tipped him well, paying for anonymity. The bellhop accepted the bribe and wheeled the RC, the propane tank, and the tools to his room. He made the hotel attendant reassure him of the confidentiality. He agreed again nonchalantly and took another set of hundred-dollar bills from Decklin. He shut the door, looking over the mountain of tools and boxes. Tears streamed across the box of the RC. He pulled the truck from its cardboard holster, plugging the unit into the wall socket to charge. The RC was huge, towering above his knees. The baby monitor was unwrapped next. Charging cradles were set gently next to the outlet while he slid the power cord into the same outlet. While they charged, Decklin picked up his cell phone, dialing the personal cell phone of Mick Zimmer.

"Hello," Mick answered after only one ring.

"Mick, I need you to do something for me." Decklin waited for the expected, confused response.

"Who is this?"

"It doesn't matter. What does matter is what I am about to tell you. Remember me from your car earlier this afternoon?"

Zimmer hesitated nervously. "I thought I was done. What do you need me for?"

"I need Dominick Craig. Can you set up a meeting with him tomorrow morning?" Decklin tried his best to sound dominating and scary, like something from a movie.

"What? Wait, I thought you said you would never contact me again!" Nervousness clouded his voice.

"I ran into a little trouble today with him. I need you to call him and set up an appointment at your office for 9:00 a.m."

"If I do this, will you promise to leave me alone?"

"Absolutely."

"Okay, I'll do it. Can I call you back at this number?"

"Yes. But I'll have you know that this is a prepaid phone. There is nothing tying me to this number. If I even think you're trying to find me, or if you call the police, I'll kill you. Remember that." Decklin knew he couldn't back up his threats. Regardless, he did his best to sound convincing.

"I understand. I'll let you know what I find out." Zimmer hung up quickly. Edginess bled into his voice throughout the conversation.

Decklin tossed his cell phone on the bed, focusing on the radio-controlled truck. Handyman he wasn't, but he knew he could rig something good enough to do the job. The propane tank was lifted onto the bed of the truck, secured with glue and half a roll of duct tape. After a quick wiggle test, the unit proved solid. Mounting the pistol was a more intricate task. He needed the winch to pull the trigger, sending the bullet into the propane tank. He wrapped the grip in tape, sticking it haphazardly onto the rear of the unit. Once the angle was right, he secured the pistol with another pillowed layer of glue and tape. He stood back, eyeing his masterpiece. It looked terrible. Globs of glue dripped from every inch. He wiped the glue carefully, ensuring he didn't disturb the angle of the gun. He added the baby monitor camera to the front of the truck. It too was taped solidly into place. The truck had been transformed into a ball of grey plastic.

The controls were easier than expected. He tested its driving, pushing on the joysticks to move the unit. The truck bumped forward and back, left and right. It worked flawlessly. His finger grazed over the red button on the top of the controls. The miniature winch pushed out the metal line. He emptied the pistol, testing the winch's ability to pull the trigger. It snapped back, sending the hammer into the empty wheel. "Perfect," he whispered.

The phone rang, surprising Decklin. "Yes?" He recognized the number.

"He can't do it tomorrow. He's flying out in the morning to the Middle East. The only time he is free is in an hour. Is that going to work?" Zimmer was apprehensive. He knew Decklin was up to something, but didn't dare ask or object.

"One hour? Really? That's too soon!" The stress in Decklin's voice was shrill.

"Sorry, that's all I can do. He will be out of the country for a while. That's really all I can do for you! Truly, I'm sorry."

"Okay...it'll work. You're safe again, Mick. I won't call you again."

"Thank you." Zimmer hung up the phone.

Decklin set the phone down gently, realizing the impact of their conversation. Dominick Craig was finally within his grasp. He knelt at the foot of the bed. "Forgive me for what I am about to do. I'm not sure if it's wrong, right, or somewhere in between...But, I am going to make him pay for what he did."

CHAPTER 23

Patriot Barrier Corporation

San Diego, CA | 32°44'57"N 117°11'50"W

The sun dipped behind the horizon. Crisp evening air brushed his cheek through the open window. Craig pulled into the empty parking lot, not surprised by Zimmer's tardiness. He killed the engine, sitting in silence as he waited. The building looked serene in the dim light of dusk. Windows were glossy, hinting the subtle reflection of the setting sun. The thunderous noise of the traffic had dulled. Craig enjoyed the peacefulness of dusk.

He checked his watch, tallying the minutes like a scoreboard. Slowly, he turned the knob on his radio, faintly increasing the volume. He tilted his head back, lying snugly against the headrest. An earthy musk floated from the fine tobacco as he pulled a cigar from his pocket. He snipped the tip, placing the freshly cut end into his mouth. Smoke wandered from his lips as he puffed happily on the stogie.

Metal scratched the passenger side of Craig's car. He perked, checking his mirrors. Nothing was visible in the small reflection. A high-pitched whine from the RC's electric motors became slightly audible. Craig flipped the radio off, listening intently to the unusual noise. He flinched as the propane tank scraped against his door again. In a skilled, hasty movement, he drew his gun and kicked open his car door. A palm-sized flashlight slid from his coat pocket, illuminating the end of his pistol. With calculated angles, he rounded the car. He crept toward the passenger side. The flashlight captured something, an unusual object. He couldn't decipher the shape until he moved closer. His flashlight hovered over the truck, focusing the beam on the picture taped to the front of the unit. He stepped closer. The image was too familiar. "Angela Marks," he whispered.

Decklin's fingers trembled violently. Tears flowed wickedly along his cheek. He watched on the small screen of the baby monitor as Dominick Craig approached the unit. Decklin's heart beat deeply, sending flashes of red into his vision. Sweeping memories consumed him, transporting him to their wedding day. His drenched eyelids closed.

Flowing lace dragged along the grass as she approached the altar. Blessed weather pelted his back with warm sunshine. The wind died, just for her. Radiance bloomed along every pore of her beautiful skin. She smiled as she warily paced down the aisle, sending a shiver down his neck. Angela was a supernatural, resonating a splendor only known by goddesses and Aphrodite. Her father hid his glossed eyes with a wipe. Her hand slid tenderly into Decklin's grasp. He was nervous. Not nervous to be married, or to commit, but the kind of nervousness that a composer felt before his greatest symphony. Tranquility calmed him as she winked. A simple wink. She settled his thumping heart with an effortless gesture, a power she alone possessed. Vows were articulated genuinely. Fairy tale tears dribbled along her cheek as she spoke the final declaration. "To have and to hold, from this day forward, for better, for worse, for richer, for poorer, in sickness or in health..."

Decklin's fingers trembled on the remote control to the RC, wavering lightly on the red button. The final words reverberated: "...to love and to cherish. Till death do us part."

His heavy finger pressed the button on the top of the remote control. The gunshot was loud, but swiftly overshadowed by the aftershock. The propane tank ignited. Brilliant balls of blue flame erupted from the RC. Craig's body shattered, blowing fragments of metal and bone into the atmosphere. Decklin dropped the remote control, weeping uncontrollably. Blurry eyes met the sight of Craig's fragmented car. Unrecognizable parts filled the interior of the mangled car. The engine compartment was a warped inferno. Agent Dominick Craig was finally gone.

Decklin buried his face in the steering wheel. Deep cries filled his lungs, drenching his cheeks with salty tears. She was really gone.

EPILOGUE

Charles Unit Investigations

Rochester, MN | 44°4'4.8282"N 92°30'13.7157"W

Who is he? Who was the second man in the car? How the hell will I ever find him now? Decklin's thoughts growled. Blurred memories were frustrating as he sat in the dim office.

Three weeks passed since Agent Craig met his demise. Decklin stared at the picture of Angela and Pete. His leg hurt frequently. Scars formed around the gaping hole in his leg. He drank often, numbing his pain with a single swig.

Knock, knock.

Decklin fluttered. Food fell from his growing beard as he wiped his face, trying quickly to look presentable. He'd failed. His skin was rough and dry. His clothes were dirty, reeking of depression. He limped to the door, unlocking it slowly. Slivers of sunlight beamed in as he cracked open the door.

She peered through a thin slice of the opening. His face was gruff and unkind. "Oh, hello. Are you Charles?"

Decklin hadn't uttered a word in weeks. The outside world was foreign. His voice echoed in loneliness: "Ahhh, yeah? I am. What do you want?" He hadn't grown accustomed to his new identity yet. Hearing the name caught him by surprise.

She pictured him much differently. Tall, dark, and handsome he wasn't. She envisioned a sharp detective, teaming with confidence. "You're Charles? Okay." She paused, contemplating. "I've driven a long way to meet you! I have a case you might be interested in. Are you taking new clients?"

Decklin panicked. *SLAM!* The slap of the door nearly hit her in the nose. He leaned against the wall, whipping through his limited options. Who was he now? Could he really investigate? He wasn't the great Charles Unit, he was Decklin Marks: a nobody. "What now, honey? What do I do?" he muttered under his breath.

Her voice echoed in his thoughts: "Do your best."

He opened the door, waving to the woman. She'd walked away, nearly reaching her car. "Wait! Wait! Yes. I *am* taking new clients. Would you like to come in?"

THE RC ACT

THE SHATTER ACT

COMING SEPTEMBER 2013

PROLOGUE

Hayes, Louisiana | 44°4'4.8282"N 92°30'13.7157"W

Highway 14 held numerous treasures. First prize went to the toothless man on the porch. Eerie smiles erupted from the weathered, porch-bound southerner as he passed. The second trophy went to the local street sign creator. Not one was legible. Letters were painted drunkenly on slabs of oak, nailed to the sides of wilting willow trees.

Decklin flinched as branches slapped his windshield. *Rustic* was an understatement. *Why would he come here? What the hell is he doing in Louisiana?*

GPS systems and cell phones were useless. Even satellites ignored the Deep South. He checked the map. Surely, the house couldn't be too far off the beaten path.

Both feet mashed the brake pedal as a pair of hillbillies sprung from the ditch. They seemed unmoved by the city-boy's attempt to spare their lives as they crossed the road. His aching leg spun a shrill spike of pain up his nerves as he pulled his feet from the brake pedal. The taller one, wearing an orange hunting jacket and a ripped-bill baseball cap approached his window.

"Whayya headed bo-ah?" His accent was unmistakable, his words clouded with chewing tobacco and the pungent aroma of whiskey.

"What?" Decklin rubbed his aching leg.

"What now? I say whayya headed?" He shifted his weight, flashing a rusted belt buckle as his shirt moved.

"Where, what? Ohhhh, where am I headed?" The southern light bulb clicked on. "I'm looking for Jacob Nelson. Does he live down this road?" Decklin talked slowly, hoping his words would seep past the sideburns and intoxication.

"Yep now, Jake Nuhsuh. He live just down theyah." He pointed down the gravel road.

Decklin thanked him politely, slowly pulling away from the odd duo. Branches scratched his paint as he slowly paced down the gravel. Eventually, the road curved into Jacob Nelson's driveway. Decklin checked the address against the one he crudely jotted on the edge of the map.

He parked next to a trailerless fishing boat. Wind chimes met his ears as he closed the car door. Jacob's home was fairly well kept, an oddity for the region. It was small, but held the clean blue paint with dignity. Wicker furniture dotted the porch while an American flag blew in the wind above the front steps.

The doorbell was broken, replaced with a handwritten sign that read: "No bell. Knock loud." Decklin did as instructed, knocking with knuckle-crunching vigor. He waited, and knocked again. Creaking floorboards echoed through the door, followed by the growing sound of footsteps. Decklin stepped a few paces back, giving the doorway a respectable privacy bubble. Locks turned. The door opened.

"Yeah? What can I do for ya?" Jacob stood in the doorway. He held his figure well for a man in his forties. His profile sported a thinning hairline and a jutting jawbone. His jeans were clean, t-shirt white. He presented himself casually for a priest.

Decklin extended a hand. "You are a hard man to find, Mr. Nelson. Your mother has been trying to find you for quite some time now."

Jacob arched a brow, flipping his inquisitive, welcoming expression to disdain. "My mother sent you? Why? Why the fuck would she need to find me? Oh God... Do you know what you've done?" His hand shook as he nervously ran his fingers through his sparse hair. Decklin's surprise was evident. He'd never encountered the F-word from a man of the cloth.

"Mr. Nelson, I'm sorry. I don't quite understand. You've been missing for years! Your mother has been worried sick. She didn't know if you were alive..."

"...Or dead? That was the point! I wasn't supposed to be found. There is a damn good reason I'm difficult to find! Oh, Jesus... You opened a big ol' can of worms. I hope you have an army packed up in that mid-sized sedan of yours." Jacob peeked over Decklin's shoulder, angrily pointing to Decklin's rental car.

"Army? ...Nope, just a few bags and a useless GPS. Why would I need an army? What do you mean?" Decklin surprised himself. Words twisted into questions, realizing his role as an investigator.

"You really don't know, do you?" Jacob's frustration anxiously showed in his wringing hands. Angling his body, he pushed himself past Decklin onto the porch. Boards creaked as he walked, stopped, and examined the landscape. Watchful eyes scanned the trees. Decklin studied him, sensing a growing paranoia. Jacob muttered as he glared into the trees. "They know."

"I'm sorry, who are *they*?" Decklin lowered his tone, quietly interrupting his mumbled stupor. Jacob didn't respond. His body turned sharply, grabbing Decklin's arm, leading him into the quiet home. Decklin hesitated. "What have I gotten myself into here? You're making me a little nervous." He was.

"My mother didn't send you." Jacob flipped open a Bible that lay innocently on the table beside the door. Gleaming steel slid from the pages, announcing a secret cutout within its binding that contained a pistol of ridiculous proportion. Decklin glared at the size of the barrel. He didn't know what type of gun it was, nor if it was a large caliber, he only knew that Jacob meant business. "If my mother didn't send you, who did? Let me guess... Dante? Arianna? Of course, it was Arianna, that bitch. Only she would use someone else to do her heavy work." Decklin froze in the shadow of the barrel. His eyes fixed on the deep hole containing what appeared to be the most sinister bullets ever created.

"Mr. Nelson, I was hired to come here, by a woman who claimed to be your mom."

"Ha. Of course. No ties. Convenient. Let me see your wallet." Jacob motioned with the pistol as he talked. Decklin's hands were shaky. He pulled the thick wallet from his pocket. Bills bulged from the seams. His Minnesota driver's license and social security card blossomed from the creases as Jacob reviewed the contents. "Charles? I had you pegged for an Italian. Maybe, Gino or Salvatore. Charles, huh?" Rummaging fingers tore through the wallet. An investigator's license, a few receipts, and a pack of matches fell from its tight pockets. "Appears ya're who you say you are, Mr. Unit. Why, you're not Italian at all. You a Catholic?" he asked, repositioning the gun toward Decklin's belly.

Decklin thought about his question. He knew Jacob was a priest, or still is a priest for the Catholic Church, however, Decklin feared that his answer in either direction would prompt a poor reaction. Truth, he decided, might set him free.

"No, sir, I am afraid I am a nondenominational kinda guy." Decklin squinted, waiting for the bullet to rip through his chest. Instead, Jacob casually slid the pistol into his pocket.

"Nondenominational kinda guy... Heh, well... You definitely aren't one of them. They'd consider that blasphemy, and that, sir, is something they take very seriously. Sit for a spell. I have something for you." Decklin's legs were a bit mushy. Softness met his rump as he parked in the closest chair, feeling the anxiety leave his body. Pain struck once more in his leg. Adrenaline masked the dull roar that constantly nipped at his nerves, until of course, he relaxed.

Jacob disappeared, creaking his way to the back of the house. Decklin's shaking stare was interrupted by a plethora of southern, country décor: sunflowers, wicker furniture, and bland pictures puked from every pore of the home. The golden cross tacked to the dining room wall caught Decklin's attention. Photos of Jacob surrounded it, reflecting years of service to the Church: weddings, services, counseling, smiling children, and a peculiar picture of the Vatican itself. Decklin approached the picture with polite curiosity. The image showed a row of priests, holding the Holy Book and a rifle.

Decklin made an audible "hmmm," as he became enamored in the curious image. "...Guns?"

"S'me in Italy. I spent many years there, ironically, you don't know anything about that." Decklin's heart fluttered as Jacob surprised him from another entrance into the kitchen.

"Yes, interesting picture. Can you..." The interruption was blunt.

"Listen, you're an investigator, you know what to do. Take this..." James tossed a small leather bag to Decklin, and continued, "...follow the creed. This is the only way I know my family will be safe." He peered out the window, as if he were expecting a militia to barge into his home at any moment. "...They know now. They know where I am. This is the only way."

Decklin, utterly overwhelmed with the new confusion of his case, asked, "What? What is the only way?"

Jacob shrugged, asking a simple, eventually devastating question, "Will you follow the creed?"

"Yes, of course, but wha..."

Jacob's hand slid into his trouser pocket, revealing the menacing glow of the pistol. As if planned for years, he motioned across his chest in a cross pattern, slid the barrel into his mouth and pulled the trigger.

Decklin dropped the bag, launching himself back into the chair as the red spatter danced along his cheek. He wiped his face quickly, eyeing Jacob's lifeless body as it cascaded to the floor. "Jesus, fuck! What the hell!" Mangled arms met a zigzagged chest and crossed legs. The slump drooled a neon flow of blood from the spot that, moments ago, held a man's face.

THE SHATTER ACT

COMING SEPTEMBER 2013

THE RC ACT

A NOVEL

VINCE TAPLIN

THE ACT SERIES

HEROINE PRESS

ADDICTING BOOKS. PERIOD.

www.HeroinePress.com

www.TheRcAct.com

www.TheShatterAct.com

www.TheVelvetAct.com

"GRIPPING, INTENSE—TAPLIN'S THRILLER HITS A HOME RUN."

~ SUSAN WINGATE (AWARD-WINNING AUTHOR & #1 AMAZON BEST SELLER)

"THE RC ACT, A NOVEL BY VINCE TAPLIN, IS A CRIME DRAMA/THRILLER THAT WILL UNDOUBTEDLY RISE TO THE TOP OF READING LISTS."

~ EDITING, TLC HIGHLY RECOMMENDS THE RC ACT BY VINCE TAPLIN

"PHENOMENAL! SEXY! I COULDN'T PUT IT DOWN! THE SHOCKING STORYLINE KEPT ME WONDERING - WHAT'S GOING TO HAPPEN NEXT!?"

~ SAMM ADAMS (MORNING SHOW RADIO HOST – KROC)

About the Author

Vince Taplin was born in Rochester, Minnesota. He grew up in the rural area of south Rochester, where he spent his childhood riding bikes and selling homemade lemonade to passersby. He is the son of Lee Taplin and Sally Schultz. He has one older sister, Monica Yoon, and two nephews; Rocco and Declan.

Following his graduation from High School, Vince Taplin moved to San Diego, marking the beginning to an extensive career in security, public safety / law enforcement, and investigations. Over the years, he acquired numerous commendations, certificates, and diplomas relating to his field. In college, he studied administration of justice/criminal law, receiving a specialization in law enforcement. Aside from his on and off bout with the good side of the law, he successfully created a side career in general business management, payroll, IT support, risk management, graphic design, and sales/business development.

In 2010, he moved back to Minnesota. He works as the sales manager for an inc500, e-commerce company. In his spare time, he dedicates himself to his writing. Of course, he occasionally slips in a walk by the river or an evening filled with barbecues, good cigars, and Bloody Marys.

www.ingramcontent.com/pod-product-compliance
Lightning Source LLC
Chambersburg PA
CBHW030237200626
46816CB00002BA/396

* 9 7 8 1 7 3 4 8 1 3 8 7 6 *